THE NEVERSEEN

A Young Adult Dystopian Novel

B.B. BRIGHTON

THE NEVERSEEN

CHAPTER ONE

Kana

September 17, 2049
Kana

If this is the real world, I'm doomed. A swarm of older teens, about my age, buzz around the Zipline Adventures area chewing gum and throwing their wrappers on the floor. My skin crawls at the sarcasm and negative tones of their voices. I take deep breaths to calm myself, hiding behind the cash-out counter in the middle of the room.

A buff guy with a glowing beer shirt toggles the new clothing's built-in lights and A/C on and off. The shirts blow cold air and light up like Christmas trees. "Stellar," he mumbles but uses profanity when he jerks up the price tag to read. "In your dreams," he says with an air of pretense, like a bird landing on a new car, pooping on the windshield.

"What are you looking at, dude?" He asks, gunmetal-gray eyes shooting daggers. "You got nothing."

My gut jolts, causing me to knock the clipboard with the zip-line list off the counter. After picking it up, I raise my hands in surrender. What does he mean by "nothing?"

He throws around profanity like my brothers and I would use colored water in our squirt guns to see who could plaster the most color on the others. Dad warned me that America has become an entitled people who don't care how they act. I nod and feel an icy chill running down my back. *How am I ever going to fit in and make friends? I'm so different.*

I pretend to smile at the crowd as I stand behind the counter on this, my first morning ever volunteering to work, but my throat tightens. *I'm glad they don't know that I've never talked to girls in my life. That I don't have a chip in my wrist with its social security number and identity like they do. That I'm a cloistered nobody-Neverborn.* My fists clench. I shake my hands to relax them, and I glance at my left wrist, wondering if anyone can tell that there's no chip scar.

A short blonde walks to the counter and gazes up at me. Her eyes graze on my name tag. Though I divert my eyes, she says, "Hey Kana, is this where we sign up? We didn't like, call ahead, or anything, but you have room, don't you?" She tilts her head to one side as her eyes hound me. And she moves as close to the checkout stand as possible, like she's trying to read the fine print on my soul. A pungent perfume draws me to her and yet assaults my senses. Maybe because it seems like a call for attention.

I back up and bump against the counter. *Be calm.* I swallow and glance down. "Let me look at our roster," I mutter, my voice not sounding like me. My fingers fumble with the clipboard, but my supervisor, Jason, snatches it away before I can focus. He's the guy who never gets nervous.

Jason strides up to face the girl. Charm oozes from his lips as he says, "Sure, you and everyone who wants to zipline today, I'll scan you." With the flourish of a magician, he swooshes up a hand-held scanner to swipe over everyone's wrist, which inputs the newcomers into the database. On the computer next to him, I see a customer charged eighty-five dollars. "Okay, everyone, move into the back alcove, and we'll get you hooked up with gear." He pushes "print" on the computer and a new roster spits out from the printer under the counter. Jason leans in and whispers to me, "Dude, show some backbone." His grin is as sly as it is encouraging.

I blink and look down. My face feels on fire.

The crowd moves into the small alcove opposite the entrance with cubbies for gear, but the blonde doesn't move. I see her playing with a carved turtle magnet stuck on the countertop stand. Her eyes find mine again, and my heart skips a beat. Other tourists file through the front door and filter back to the equipment alcove—they must have paid already.

"Would you like to join your party?" I keep swallowing.

"Sure, Cowboy," she says, locking her eyes on mine again.

I wish she would stop staring into my eyes. My nerves rise and fall like waves in a storm. I turn to look at the alcove where I want her to go and leave me alone.

The buff guy who turned on the A/C clothes scrutinizes her from the equipment room with eyes painted with superiority. "Come on, Doll." He glares at me. Dominance, with a twinge of contempt. *What makes someone believe they're more valuable than others? Is it a projection to hide their fear like the geckos who push their forearms up tall and puff out their necks to look intimidating when they're afraid?*

She turns to glance up at me again. *Dang.* I look down. *Jason had drilled the procedures all morning. Now I can't remember a thing.* Sweat drips down my forehead, and I wipe it away with my arm, hoping that I don't stink.

Everyone gets their gear, and we go through the back door of the alcove and pour into a waiting passenger van. The A/C air cleaner scent reminds me of cucumbers. An older guy named Buzz will drive the twelve-passenger van through the strip mall of tourist dress shops and restaurants and up the highway toward the intersection with the mountain road. With the sun's spell on the earth already, it's warm. I sit in the row behind the driver with Jason and Tennessee, another employee. Tennessee introduces himself and shoots out a callused hand for me to shake. He's my height—six feet—but his broad frame takes up more of the seat than my skinny one. Once the bus starts, Jason calls back in his television commercial voice, "Okay, Kana is going to give you the Kauai low down. Listen up."

Is he messing with me? My eyebrows jack up as my stomach dives to my toes with this news. With a deep breath, I turn around and stare at the rear window, imagining my mother standing there smiling at me. "Kauai is the oldest of the Hawaiian Islands, therefore it has the most erosion, and ergo, the most vegetation. That's why it's called The Garden Isle, because the land has had the most time to develop." I pause and direct my gaze to Jason.

He smiles at me. "Keep going." There's surprise on his face. *Does he think I'm a complete idiot? I am.*

I explain Kauai's history, but some guys look bored, so I transition to talking about the helicar track in Waimea and the unofficial one-man mini-helicopter races that take place at night.

"How can a guy get into one of those races?" A twenty-something guy with narrow slanted eyes like mine asks.

"When you find that out, let me know," I say, and the people chuckle. *Are they laughing at me?*

A woman raises her hand. "What's the plant with the brown pods hanging down?"

"*Hale Koa.* Captain George Vancouver probably brought it from Mexico. The name, '*Hale Koa*,' means 'house of the brave.' Perhaps we get brave cattle when they eat the beans. Its wood burns well in a fire—useful to know if you get lost."

Laughter ripples from the group. I smooth back my stubborn hair and continue by talking about Captain Cook's adventures in Hawaii.

We roll up to a lookout point where we'll start our first zipline, and everyone gets off. The van wobbles down the uneven primitive road back to the storefront.

"You sure know your plants," the blond girl with the boyfriend says.

If only I could just disappear. I smell my armpits to make sure I don't stink. My sweat outweighs the minty scent of my deodorant. My temple blazes.

The boyfriend puts his arm around her and looks down his hook nose at me, cackling at my expense. I stare at my hands. *I'm no genius. I wish I could tell her that I've learned everything I know from my skilled and knowledgeable two aunts, two uncles, and my folks. That our secluded complex on a back canyon in Kauai kept us from mixing with outsiders.* Still, her buff boyfriend's way of speaking to her grates against the respect I believe everyone deserves.

We arrive at the drop-off site. The fresh smell of the breeze coming off the ocean refreshes me. Jason sidles up. "Kana, watch as I buckle the customers in. You're doing the second half."

I nod. "Okay." My stomach tightens like a too-small belt.

We hike along the ridge on a path to the first zipline takeoff ramp. A warm breeze tousles my hair as I marvel at the teal ocean spreading out far below. The sun casts shimmering reflections on the vast water's surface, and ocean waves are distant whispers of white.

I climb the five steps up the sun-bleached fir ramp. The zipline cable they're about to ride on attaches to their harness. Jason clips Tennessee in first, so he can help people stop at the other end. The cable clicks into place, and Tennessee runs off the ramp like it's just another step on the sidewalk. The lock lies between people's legs. A queasy sensation creeps into my brain. *Will I need to push a cable into the lock between a girl's legs?* Like thunder in a storm, my heart pounds.

The first customer, a guy with a Southern accent, struts up and peers out over the vast sky. Then he turns to look up at the muscled mountain above.

"Hot damn!" he says. His blond hair reminds me of my brother, Canyon, back at home. Canyon has a way with girls I don't begin to understand.

The customer shuts his eyes and steps off the ramp. The cable drops several feet under his weight before becoming taut.

"Whoa, Nellie!" he yells, as he flies down across the canyon. Hau and kukui trees grow below, their tops too far to touch. "Go Cowboys!" He laughs all the rest of the way. Tennessee eases his descent, steadies him on the other side, and assists him in unhooking.

Jason continues with the next person, but it's just a visual noise outside of the panic rolling around in my stomach. My chest feels tight. I visualize trying to hook a girl to the cable and messing it up.

He sends three more people down the zipline, two guys and a girl, leaving another girl and a guy.

"Okay, Kana. Your turn." He steps back. "Katrina, you're next." He tells her, then looks at me.

Oh no. It's her. My lungs seem to stop giving me air. I stumble forward feeling the breeze blow the across my panicked face.

Katrina steps forward, fixes her gold and bronze hair into a claw clip and pulls the harness between her legs. She grabs the cable hanging down and waits for me to hook it. Her eyes find mine.

I blink and study the cable. *How can I do this?*

Glancing at my feet, I pause. My heart slaps against my ribs. *I can't just quit and walk away. Dad talked his friend into letting me work here just for tips. The owner, Walter, could turn us all in, sending Mom and Dad to prison and me into the military.*

"I don't bite, you know," she says, flipping her hair over her shoulder.

Taking a ragged breath, I stumble forward. My hands shake as I reach out. I close my eyes and push the lock into its holder. I open my eyes and push it farther in. It's in but doesn't click. Hesitating, I step back. Why didn't it click? Did I do something wrong?

I bend down to look at it, wishing I could take the two pieces and try again, but not wanting my hands anywhere near her body. "Okay," I say, confused.

"You're good. Stop staring at her legs, Kana," Jason says, with his hands on his hips. "and get out of the way."

My brain turns to ice.

"Wahoo! I'm good!" Katrina hoots, leaning back while I step aside, puzzled. *Was a leaf blocking the locking mechanism? Will it hold her weight?* I want to throw up. My hands are lead. I can't think.

Jason steps forward to push her off. In my mind, I hear Dad's voice telling me, "Wait, boys, before you go ziplining, remember, always pull on the cable before you launch to make sure the connection is solid."

There's a twig on the ground, under the cable. A piece of a twig. *What about the twig?*

Time freezes. The cable hangs before me like the mechanism that holds the helicopter blades to the fuselage. Break that connection and the helicopter falls from the sky. Like Katrina falling from the ramp. My heart pounds in my ears. I want to stop time. *I need to stop time. I need to stop her now!*

Twig. Cable. Connection. The twig. In the cable. Blocking the connection. My voice forms the word—

"Stop!"—but nothing comes out. My chest seizes, starved for air. Frozen. Fractured.

Katrina grasps the cable. Jason pushes her. She squeals in delight, and winks at me, gaining speed from the push, her mouth open wide. But the cable drops under her weight. Drops. Ripping sound as she claws at the cable. Screaming. Too late. Too fast. Too far. Down. Headlong down the cliff. The cable swings empty. Her scream echoes through the ravine. Her body cartwheels out of sight, leaving only a swirling cloud of dust. Thud—she crashes onto the rocks below.

No! No! No! This can't be real! I stumble backward. *I can't have done this!* The chaos falls away, swallowed by a suffocating silence.

CHAPTER TWO

Kana

Panic bolts through me as Katrina's scream slices the air from below. She plummets down the mountainside, disappearing behind the shrubs. I'm dumbstruck with panic.

Jason curses.

I freeze, staring in disbelief.

Katrina's boyfriend turns on me, his face morphs into hatred. His nostrils flare as he turns to stare down the slope, his hands tightening into fists. He shoves me, cursing, his face twisted with fury, veins bulging in his neck. His fist slams into my jaw. Pain explodes as I fly off the ramp into a *haole koa* shrub. My jaw screams with stabs of pain.

"You idiotic imbecile!" he spits. "You didn't buckle her in! What if she dies?"

Jason stands, phone in hand, staring at us, eyes wide, as if he can't believe what just happened. Then he snaps out of it and calls 911.

Katrina's boyfriend paces the cliff's edge, swearing and calling to her. "Katrina! Kat! Where are you?"

The whole side of my face and tongue throb. I wipe the blood off my chin from biting my tongue. Broken branches knife the skin on my back where I landed. I roll out of the shrub to make my way down toward Katrina. My brain stutters.

It's like a nightmare that I can't wake from. Then, her scream snaps me out of it, and I scramble down, muscles screaming as I fight to keep from slipping. Sweat stings my eyes and the cut on my lip. My feet turn at a 45 degree angle for traction navigating the steep decline. The soil crumbles under my feet, gritty and loose. I slide but catch my balance, tasting the dust that's kicked up around me in the breeze. The sun beats down, oblivious. Even the tall grass doesn't grow here. How could I have let this happen? A vise seems to squeeze my chest, remembering the terror in her voice. *It's my fault she's crashed, broken, horror-struck.*

She's lying close to a young ironwood tree on a small ledge. Her boyfriend won't be able to see her. A steep drop-off below her threatens. Katrina's lower leg twists unnaturally back.

"My… my leg," she gasps between sobs. Her erratic breathing shows her shock. Blood on her hands and arms are multiple but not deep. "It's broken, I know it is." Her voice trembles. She tries to sit up and moans. "I don't want to die! Please, do something!" Her voice screeches. Tears stream down her cheeks.

Her sobs shatter me. *This is my fault* "Stay still, you'll be okay," I say. "Lay back down; you're in shock." By clearing the sharp pebbles from under her head, I can cradle her head as she lays it down comfortably. Our weight could create a landslide, causing us both to crash far below.

"I'm so scared. How will they get me out of here?" Her voice quivers as she speaks.

"They will, by helicopter," I say. "You're going to be fine." I take off my belt and secure it around the young ironwood tree trunk next to her. I loop my arm through it and use it to keep my weight from putting pressure on the precarious ledge we're perched on.

"Oli. Where's Oliver? I don't think he can get down here." She glances up at the bluff above. "It hurts! Please—make it stop." Katrina says through her tears, mascara running down her face.

"You'll see him soon, I promise," I say, but even I hear the shake in my voice. I can't help it; the thought of what I might have done to her knots my stomach. "Just hang in there." Her body doesn't show any signs of heavy bleeding.

Jason arrives to our left and stops near the sapling. He bends branches to see. "I called 911."

"Did you bring any water?" I ask.

One side of his mouth droops. "Dude, all you think of is yourself. She's here, lying with a broken leg, and you ask for water?"

"Not for me, but for her," I say.

"Hey, can you throw down a bottle of water for Katrina?" I call to those peering over the edge above us and see Oliver starting down. Jason inches toward us. "Jason, don't come any closer. The ledge may not be stable."

"What are you talking about?" he says.

"The ledge we're on may not be stable. It could slide. Don't come any closer."

Jason steps around the tree toward us, ignoring my warning. "You're full of it. I'll take care of . . . "

"I've got a bottle. How do I get it to you?" A guy with a fiery red beard says from above.

"Roll it down, I'll catch it," I say.

He tosses it down the embankment, and I reach over and grab it as it rolls by. After pouring some over Katrina's head, I say, "Can you drink some?"

She nods, and I lift her head and shoulders enough for her to drink.

Jason pokes at her knee, and Katrina screams.

"No, Jason! Stop! Leave it for the medic!"

"Sorry!" He says and pats her leg.

She screeches in pain again.

I hear Oliver working his way down the cliff, stumbling, and catching himself getting close to us. "Get your grubby hands off my girl!" he yells.

I'm sure he'll punch me again, and there's a good fifty-foot drop from here.

Jason's gaze flits between Oliver and me. It's like he's debating whose side he's on, but he just stares, mouth open, until Oliver's threats snap him into action.

Oliver approaches with a flushed face and fists clenched, formed into weapons. He stands next to Jason. "I'll sue your pants off! There won't be any blood left in you when I'm done." Oli says, using his hands on the ground to steady himself. "And I'm going to sue the company, too. You won't have a dime left to do business by the time I'm done." Oliver says to Jason.

"Kana, get out of here. You're fired. I never want to see you again. Now," Jason says with granite eyes, standing with his arms crossed.

Jason stands and faces him. "Kana's a volunteer. We never hired him. He was just helping. A Neverborn who . . . "

At the word "Neverborn," Oliver snarls, "You stinking Neverborn, you're not supposed to be alive. Even your mother didn't want you. I've heard how you Neverborns steal. Well, I'll fix you and do everyone a favor." He starts toward me. The weight of Jason and Oli on the ledge worries me. But I can't just leave her.

The owner told Jason that I'm a Neverborn! The very word clangs in my ear, a curse, the proof that I'll never belong. *Even when I try to help, I only bring more pain. Oliver won't be the only one who wishes I was never born. The guillotine is set.*

A crackle erupts from under us, sounding like bones cracking. Shivers rip through me as I pull Katrina toward me with my left arm. The ledge shifts. Below the tree that my belt hangs from, the whole ledge breaks away and slides down the mountain. A deafening scream echoes from Katrina's small mouth as her legs drop. My heart leaps to my throat as we swing in the air. I hang onto her with one arm. My other arm clings to the belt. Dust swirls like smoke around us, blurring the cliff's edge in the sun's glare. Every dry leaf and crumb of soil feels ready to betray us.

Jason and Oliver tumble down, cursing. Katrina screams in my ear.

We swing.

"Katrina, reach your arms up and feel for the trunk of the tree."

She keeps screaming.

"Katrina! Stop!" I yell.

She stops and takes a quivering breath.

"Reach your arm up. You can feel the trunk of the tree."

Her hand slaps along the ground above. A few pieces of dirt drop down the hill. "I can't feel it!"

"It's okay, keep moving your hands around. It's there."

Her body weight shifts, and she reaches her other hand up to find the trunk. "Got it." She hangs onto the trunk with both hands. "Hurry!"

"All right, hang tight. I need to move out from under you and get us to a better position."

"I'm scared! We're going to die," she says, her voice shredded with panic.

"You'll be fine."

My feet work along the cliff for a foothold. I work my way up to the trunk and pull myself up. Then I reach down and pull on the back of Kat's pants to hoist her up to behind the tree trunk. My arms ache. Every muscle strains as the cliff's grit digs into my skin.

Her broken leg still dangles. The impact might have reset her femur, but the pain in her eyes tells another story. She cries and hugs me, and I put my arm around her. My hands tremble as I try to hold Katrina steady, her warm tears soaking my knuckles. Each ragged breath feels like a knife through me.

"We did it. Thank you, God. You'll be fine," I say, hoping it's true.

Her hair is silk in my hands. From behind the tree trunk, I can't see them but hear Oliver and Jason calling to each other. At least no one can see us hugging.

Katrina takes a deep breath. "Will we be okay now?"

"Yes." Although I won't be okay if Oliver sees me holding his girl. "I'm going to move. Tell me the moment it hurts more."

"Okay." She sounds disappointed.

I slide away from her but keep a hand on her arm. "I'm going to splint you, so your thigh bone, the femur, doesn't move. Keep your leg straight and tell me if anything hurts."

Lying with my head at her feet, I ease her hanging leg up and, keeping her knee from bending, set it on the ground. She groans but doesn't scream. It seems to hurt less when it's stable on the ground rather than hanging down. The emergency helicopter should be here soon. I break off two limbs from the tree, put one on either side of her thigh, and tie it with strips I tear from my t-shirt. It will save the medics time, perhaps preventing another landslide.

The sound of Oliver's grunting comes closer. He creeps below our ledge.

"I'm going to kill you! This is all your fault!" His gruff words come out like flying foam from a rabid pig's mouth.

"You're fine now," I say to Katrina. "I have to leave." Before she can respond, I turn and scramble down diagonally, traversing from side to side, always looking one step ahead. I glance up toward Katrina, then leap off a cliff's edge and fly toward the top of an Albizia tree just below me. Panic jolts through me like electricity. Wind sweeps back my hair. Crashing onto the top canopy, I grab a central branch with both arms and hold on with all my strength. The branch crackles and swings down, up, down, and up again. It takes a few moments before the rocking stops. *Thank God I didn't fall to the forest floor.*

Oliver yells down strings of profanity toward me, but I deserve it. Katrina broke her leg and crashed onto the rocks because of me.

"Katrina, I'm sorry," I shout up at her as my voice echoes through the lush green canopy. A helicopter buzzes closer, drowning out my heartfelt apology. *I've ruined everything.*

Jason had asked me to wear tennis shoes as part of the uniform. Climbing down the smooth tree trunk with shoes is like peeling potatoes with gloves on, but I'll need them. I shimmy down the tree trunk, the bark sliding under my feet. Years of jumping into Albizia canopies with my brothers come flooding back.

Once my feet touch the ground, I bend over with my hands on my knees, trembling and breathless. How long will it take to hike back to the storefront where my cycle sits? My hopes for tips, a job reference, a chance to learn how to relate to people—are all gone.

The helicopter arrives. Its powerful blades churn the air as it hovers over Katrina to whisk her away to the emergency room. *"Lord, I pray the medics can help her." I shake my head. "I just ruined my entire life." I don't know how you can give me any kind of future now, especially since I'm such a loser for not ensuring I buckled her in.* Cupping my head in my hands, I mumble, *"Amen."*

If I follow the canyon, I'll end up farther south than I want to be. It makes more sense to climb the rugged ridge, then follow the road. Jason will take the rest of the group that still wants to zipline on eleven more zip trips back and forth across the ravine. He won't let me ride back with them.

The canopy closes around me, shadows swallowing up every sound from above. Every step crunches, the guilt heavy, dragging me like the forest itself doesn't want to let me go.

I turn to the ridge and blaze a path upward. Sweat pours down my face. Ten-foot-tall guinea grass blades cut and irritate my skin, so I follow the path left by the van's tire tracks. Joyous sounds of screams reverberate from up the mountain where Jason's group is likely flying down their last zipline for the day. I hide behind the large, waxy leaves of a noni tree until the van meanders down the path toward the storefront with everyone except Katrina, and perhaps her boyfriend, if the helicopter allowed him to accompany her. The van rumbles by. I conceal myself and nibble on a large, transparent white noni fruit for its moisture. It tastes like soap.

"Kana, wherever you are, I will kill you for this," Oliver screams out of the van window, his voice hoarse and desperate. The sound bounces off the mountain faces and resonates within the confines of my soul's crumbled walls.

Another person, besides my birth mother, wants me dead. Loser that I am.

The tropical sun leaves few clouds to mitigate the heat, and I rub noni fruit on my cuts for its healing and antiseptic properties. It reeks.

Descending the mountain gives me too much time to think. I've ruined everything and put Mom and Dad in danger of being exposed as having "co-kidnapped" me by raising me, knowing I was scheduled for an abortion. And what if they get marched off to prison? And what if the owner gets sued because of me? And what about Katrina? Is her leg permanently damaged? How much pain and rehabilitation will she have to endure? Ocean breezes blow through me as if I'm empty.

Why didn't I say something? Why didn't I stop Jason from pushing her off? I gaze out over the endless ocean and unending regrets and doubts crash over me. *God, I've destroyed everything. How can you possibly meet me here? How can you do anything with my life now?*

CHAPTER THREE

Kana

With each mile closer to home, my gut tightens, and my breath grows shallow. *I've flunked everything. If anyone's safe, it won't be because of me. Katrina must* hate me. My boss fired me. *Who could blame him? And now Oliver knows—I'm a Neverborn. He'll stop at nothing to hurt me or anyone I love. My parents, who gave up everything for me, are at risk of being arrested for kidnapping because of me.* They took me in despite the danger, and now I've put them in this position. Nausea hits me. *Please, God, don't let Dad and Mom go to jail because of me.*

My motorcycle hits an unexpected rut and rocks back and forth. I struggle to keep my balance. My stomach lurches, and I pull over to the grassy shoulder. The invasive banana poka vines above me choke the ironwood tree, like my fears strangling my only wisps of hope. *If the tree could sing its sorrow, we could do a duet.* I plant my feet on the ground, and my trembling hands clutch the handlebars.

"Pay attention, Kana," I scold myself. I could've been thrown into the oncoming traffic, causing a pileup and endangering others.

God, I've utterly failed.

The weight of my failure snuffs out any flicker of hope for the future. After some deep breaths, I start my metal steed and jump into traffic again. *No thinking, just focus on getting home.* My eyes strain to stay alert, but my heart feels like it's one big coconut that has fallen off the tree, cracking wide open. Only my ribs keep it from spilling all over the road.

By the time I see the familiar row of Cook pines lining our driveway, my hands tremble and my arms and shoulders are cement. I must have been squeezing the handlebars. I've made it back, and they're all waiting for me. Heaviness like a load of rocks fills me.

Kekoa's car sits out front. My dear brother, the one who's always been the golden child. They must think I've had a smashing success of a day, that I've mastered the art of talking to girls and excelled at my first day "working." He's here to congratulate me.

I ride my bike up to the house, dismount, remove my helmet, and take a moment to observe their faces. Mom, Dad, both uncles, aunties, and my brothers, Canyon and Kekoa, come out to greet me. Their faces radiate love and joy, like the suns they are.

"What's up, Kana?" Kekoa's voice says. He notices something's off.

Mom approaches and engulfs me in a long, wordless hug. *I didn't know a hug could feel so comforting, but when she finds out the truth, she'll be ashamed of me.*

"Son, come in and tell us all about it," Dad says, rubbing my back to comfort me. I struggle to recount the whole stupid story, and my family hangs on every word. Dad keeps his hand on my shoulder, knowing how hard this is for me.

Mom prays, "Lord, we don't know why you have allowed this girl to tumble down and break her leg, but we trust you will use it for good. Give us protection now and guidance as we try to figure out what to do and how to be safe. Amen."

The collective "Amen" is heavy, like a shovel full of dirt hitting the lid of a coffin.

"Dad, did you tell Walter that I was your adopted son?" I ask.

He rubs his white beard between his thumb and fingers. "No. I think I told him I know a wonderful young man, a Neverborn, who needs a chance at life. But if he's pushed or angry, he'll probably send the authorities here first to look for you. We need to disappear, so the feds don't find us all together and realize we raised you."

"No," I say, determination in my voice. I pause, the load of my decision weighing me down like the world itself. *This is my life—dropping to the bottom of the ocean.* I swallow hard, steeling myself. "I'm going to join the military. That way, there's no reason the police will have to trace me to you. No one comes here and finds me. You hide your photos and burn my stuff." *I would die if they went to prison because they raised me—the kidnapped baby that was supposed to be aborted.*

Mom gasps, her eyes flood with tears. Her voice stifles to a whisper, and cracks as she says, "Son, please don't. We'll find another way. The war—" her voice cracks. "We can hide you."

I turn to look into her teary eyes. "It's the only way." Rising, I head to my room to pack. *It's only a matter of time before the police come for me and everyone else gets caught up in it.*

Kekoa follows me, his eyebrows furrowed, his eyes betraying more sadness than he's ever shown. "Bro, you sure about this? Can't you find another way? You can still . . . "   His eyes plead.

"Yep. Go. Now. You found your birth mother, who allowed a chip for you. Stay with her. Don't come home. Lawyers from Zipline Adventures may come here investigating, or the police." I stop, turn, and give him a heartfelt hug. Kekoa, my bro. *I'll miss him terribly.* I force myself not to cry.

Canyon comes up behind me, and I give him a bear hug. "This is the worst! You can't leave, bro!" He says, and he squeezes me tight.

Our foreheads meet, and we grasp each other's shoulders. I bolt to pack. I stuff clothes into a pillowcase when Dad brings me a duffle bag. His hand trembles on my shoulder. I turn and see the love and sorrow in his eyes. "If you have to go, take our love with you," his voice breaks. "I'm very proud of you."

I clutch at him, and he bear-hugs me. Dad pats my back and rushes out of the room.

With my Bible, my clothes, and a favorite medical book packed in the duffel bag, I give everyone a quick round of hugs and get into the truck. The ironwood tree by the stream stands tall, free of parasitic vines. But because of my failures, my life has succumbed to the dangerous entanglement of joining the military.

Dad and Mom drive me to Kukui Mall where the recruiting headquarters are located to receive the one identity Neverborns are allowed—that of a soldier. As long as we're laying down our lives, we're allowed the privilege of calling ourselves American citizens. Neverborns are the first to be put on the front lines in our war with China. I don't think I'll ever see Mom and Dad again. But Oliver will put them in prison in a moment if he makes the connection.

He parks in a remote corner, so no one will recognize us, and we get out to say goodbye. I'm several inches taller than Dad, but I lean down to put my cheek next to his and then hug him again.

"Thank you, Dad, for giving all these years to me. I love you very much." I cling to Dad a little longer, memorizing his earthy smell, his wrinkled arms grasping every ounce of me. *This might be the last moment I'm safe and loved.*

He can't find the words but manages, "I love you, too. My son." His body trembles in my arms.

Mom's tears pour down her face. "Be strong, Son. Remember whose you are. We're so proud of you."

I hug her, grab my duffel bag, and run into the mall. Every step toward the recruiting office hammers another nail in my coffin. I see the glass door ahead. It's not the door to a hospital or research lab where I'd imagined walking in with my first job offer in hand. Instead, here I am, lining up to throw away the life I've wanted. *This is not only the death of this life I've loved. It's the death of the one I dream of. How can I shoot people and play soldier in a farce just because some Chinese emperor decides he wants to rule the world?*

I pull open the Navy enlistment door and stop to glance back one more time, trying to say goodbye to the future I dreamed of and to all those I love. I hesitate, but a soldier comes up behind me, and I go in. There's no turning back now. The air conditioning can't cool down my throbbing heart. I don't believe the massive poster on the wall that says, "This is what you were made for."

My folks raised me to love. To protect. To sacrifice for those I love. And now, this is my sacrifice. It's all I have to give to those I love.

CHAPTER FOUR

Kana

The stinging in my wrist intensifies as the anesthetic shoots through me. A machine slices into my skin, implanting a chip with sterile efficiency, leaving my wrist numb and aching. Blood seeps through the bandage like it's trying to escape. *Doesn't matter,* I tell myself, trying to ignore the turmoil twisting my stomach. I chose this. A way out, a fresh start.

In the cramped exam room, I pull on my uniform, feeling the weight of my decision to cut off my old life. It's heavier than a million chips.

I step into the unadorned waiting area of the RTC, Recruit Training Camp in Great Lakes, Illinois, bracing against the biting cold. It's only September, but the chill jars my bones, shattering any illusion I'll ever be warm here. Not like home. The fog hangs heavy, and the sun struggles to break through, casting an eerie gray over everything. *Chicken skin,* I think, glancing at the goosebumps on my arms. Mom's term for it.

"Private Munson!" I look up. Private First Class Baumann is calling my name. I salute and reply through chattering teeth.

"Get your gear and follow Petty Officer Schmidt to your barracks."

The six concrete U-shaped housing units loom before me, creating a makeshift city of new recruits, each building packed with potential sailors. My camouflage uniform offers little protection from the cold, and frosty breaths escape me as I follow Schmidt. My mind buzzes with questions, one breaking through the rest.

"What do you think this war is about, sir?" I blurt out.

He stops, his gaze assessing. "Politics," he says with a grim smile. "Millions die, so America doesn't have to pay its debt to China. China's emperor, Xi Jinping, is aiming for world domination, and they've got the manpower to back it up. Cut us off from tech, and now we're struggling to keep up." He glances at me. "And you, soldier, are here to stop them." He chuckles and turns back toward the barracks.

Inside, starkness hits me—a couple of bunk beds, a mirrored closet door, a single poster on the wall, *Integrity Conquers All.* I unpack the few things I brought—my Bible and a Sarah Young devotional Mom tucked into my bag. I run a finger over the worn cover. *I chose this.*

The door opens, and a short, stocky guy throws his duffel on the floor. "Hey, sailor, roommate, buddy," he says, extending a hand. "Name's Bumble. Private McFee to the Navy, from Austin, Texas."

"Kana," I say, shaking his hand. "Private Munson."

"A sardine can, huh?" He looks around. "Whoa, I can grow to not like this." He flops onto the bottom bunk like he's testing its durability.

"I guess I'll take the top," I mutter, already missing any sense of privacy.

"Good, you weigh less than me," he says, smirking. "I'd probably break my neck falling from up there."

I can't help but laugh. Bumble's deadpan humor is a relief, a reminder it's okay to feel out of place.

"Want to see my girl?" he asks, pulling out a photo of a redhead with a bright smile. "She laughs at my jokes—rare gift, I tell you."

I smile. "She sounds awesome."

"Yeah. Takes a real talent." He grins. "So why'd you join the Navy?"

"To keep my parents from getting arrested," I admit. "I ran away."

Bumble nods, glancing at my Bible. "You're a Neverborn too. Bummer."

At dinner, we load up on hamburgers, salad, fries, and yellow cake. Bumble's eyes dart around as he digs in.

"When can we get seconds?" he asks a recruit nearby.

Private Abel, his accent thick and Southern, chuckles. "Enjoy that cake, brother. Might be the last piece you get."

Bumble grins, dipping his finger in the frosting. "But don't you want me to be happy?"

"Happy? This ain't about happy, bro," Abel replies.

As we head to orientation, the gym-like room fills with recruits, and officers shout their expectations. *Stay strong, stay focused.* I'm relieved by the structure, the rules. Here, no politics, no drama, no lying. *Integrity Conquers All.* I could use some of that.

As one officer scans the room, his gaze sharpens on me. He'd tested me earlier, impressed by my ASVAB scores. I wonder if they're enough to qualify for MANA, the elite division. If I have the discipline, maybe I can make it.

And maybe, here, I'll learn what it means to stand for something real.

CHAPTER FIVE

Kana

At dawn, we gather for PT—physical training. I shiver in my navy and gold shorts, hopping in place to keep warm. Around me, hundreds of bodies move in sync, their breath barely fogging the air, but the cold gnaws at me alone, like even the weather knows I don't belong.

"Kana, quit jumping around. You'll get enough exercise," Bumble mutters beside me, glancing around as if he's embarrassed.

We start with agility drills, sixty push-ups, sixty sit-ups, and then a mile run. My new tennis shoes blend into the steady beat of feet pounding the gym floor in circles. I'm tired, but at home, Canyon, Kekoa, and I ran up the ridge to watch sunsets often enough that I'm not too winded, finishing near the front. Bumble huffs to a stop after the first hundred yards, his face flushed. The drill sergeant's shouts fade behind me as I jog ahead, glancing back once. I could slow down, but I don't. Not yet.

Afterward, we shower, change, and march around the training center. Lake Michigan stretches on one side; the massive brick administration building looms on the other. We march endlessly, singing mindless cadences like "Old MacDonald Had a Farm" with new words.

Days blur into weeks, hammering my body into something stronger, harder, even as my mind feels stretched thin. I make friends with the guys, but never with the girls—they seem like a different species, too much distance between us.

Eight weeks later, Bumble has lost twenty pounds. I've gotten used to the gas he passes all night and his corny jokes, and I'll miss him if we're separated. I don't worry as much about what people think of me anymore. The military has a lot of Neverborns—some worthy, some not. Bumble only talks about being a Neverborn late at night, when past pain surfaces in his words like wounds that never heal.

Just before graduation, Chief Blick buzzes the intercom in our room. "Privates McFee and Munson, report to Leeward Bullet Compound, room 103, at 0800."

A couple dozen men and women are already there, talking quietly, the air thick with anticipation and nerves.

"Sailors, today marks a milestone," Commander Dreswell announces. "Your exceptional ASVAB scores, along with unanimous approval from our officers, have earned you a place in a newly established branch of the military. Congratulations. You are among the most capable and intelligent, and together, you will join MANA—an acronym representing the Marines, Army, Navy, and Air Force. You could serve in Thailand or other locations worldwide, applying your unique talents for our country."

We're handed letters of endorsement and travel instructions. Later, at the graduation ceremony, Bumble and I, along with other MANA recruits, step forward to receive certificates of honor.

I chose the Navy, hoping I wouldn't have to kill anyone with my own hands. My stomach turns at the thought of the uncertainty ahead.

"Where am I going?" I ask Petty Officer O'Ryan during morning PT.

A ghost of a smile flickers on his face. "You'll find out when you get there."

Boot camp ends. We pack, hug, and say our goodbyes. Now, we're new men—fit, disciplined, obedient—and ready to serve the U.S. Navy, ultimately fitting the country's mold. I wonder if obedience makes us any better fit for God. Maybe life is just a boot camp for something bigger.

The door swings open, and Bumble steps in, looking forlorn.

"Man, I'm gonna miss these guys," he says, pulling me into a hug with a fake sob. "I hope you're not ditching me." Beneath the joke, there's real worry in his voice.

I hug him back. I'm hoping we'll stick together too.

At dinner, there's only a handful of us at the corner of one table among hundreds. We raid the cooler and eat all the leftovers we want—ravioli, pork chops, green beans, salad. Bumble sighs as he plops down, but he just eats quietly, like it's the last supper. We still haven't gotten our orders. I pace, wondering what's waiting for us out there.

As we're packing, an intercom message crackles to life. "Privates Munson and McFee. Report to Port Lee, room 101, at 1830."

"Sir, yes sir," we respond in unison. Bumble slaps his hands over his face and mutters, "What's going to happen?"

It's like fear is our third roommate.

We have an hour before the meeting, so we wander around the complex, reliving memories of endless marches, drills, lectures, and nights trading half-serious questions. Back in Hawaii, I thought my mind was the best part of me. Now my body has earned its place too.

Room 101 is lined with portraits of former generals, decked with medals and ribbons. In the center, a table holds long white envelopes waiting for us. The informal tone of the room throws me off. Petty Officer Stanley calls each name and hands us an envelope. Mine feels like it weighs a ton. I dread deploying somewhere foreign and unknown, but at least it might be warmer than Michigan.

I tear open my envelope. I'm assigned to a post on Kauai's western coast, near Kōkeʻe. It makes sense—similar to Thailand's terrain, ideal for war prep. I didn't even know MANA had a training base on Kauai. I'll be close to home, but I won't be able to see my family or even tell them where I am. My hands go slack. Every part of me aches to see them, to laugh and pretend nothing has changed.

"Dismissed," someone says in the background.

Bumble snatches my letter, sneaking a peek. "Yee-ha, brother! We're going together."

I return the high five he insists on, clapping high, then low behind our backs. In the envelope are plane tickets with seats together. We're set to meet Private Perry at Parking Lot Eisenhower, space 325, for a 0700 ride to O'Hare.

That night, sleep escapes me as I think about Kauai. It'll be a brief stay before MANA ships us to Thailand, where we'll probably die. At boot camp, it's an open secret—and a grim joke—that Neverborns get sent on the most dangerous missions. We're considered disposable. Thailand's climate is like Kauai's—tropical, lush. I wonder if they have centipedes too.

From below, Bumble sighs. He's awake too.

"Bumble, what's the worst that could happen to us?" My voice barely rises above a whisper.

He rolls over, groggy. "We die…or worse, we're tortured until we beg for it."

"What do you think happens when we die?" My shoulders are cold; I pull the blanket tighter.

"I don't know. Think I'll turn into an ant?" He tries for humor but sounds bleak.

"Do you believe in reincarnation?" I chuckle softly.

"Nah. Religion is just something people cling to when they can't make sense of things they don't understand.

"Or because they don't want an authority over them?" I venture.

"Man, do you ever stop thinking?" He halfheartedly swats at my bunk.

I turn to face him. "Would you rather live in fear, not knowing what's out there?"

He groans. "How does anyone know for sure that Jesus is who they say he is?"

"Think about it—prayers answered, peace you can't explain, my family's love that I don't see in people here. And the disciples didn't die for a lie. Most of them saw the miracles," I say, gathering steam. "If we're just evolved bodies, where do things like beauty and morality even come from?"

"What if you're wrong?" He sounds irritated.

"Then I die having loved more, forgiven, lived for what I believe pleases God."

"You're never afraid?" His tone is mocking.

"I'm afraid right now. Praying helps. It's like talking to someone who understands."

He's silent for a moment. "But why would a good God let mothers kill their kids?"

His voice drips bitterness. I know why he doesn't believe—he can't forgive his mom.

"This isn't heaven yet, Bumble. People have choices, good or evil. We had to suffer from their choices, but that doesn't mean God doesn't care. He loves you."

Bumble grumbles and sighs. "Maybe. You ever pray about getting a girlfriend? It's weird you haven't had one. I haven't seen you talk to one girl here." He trails off, turning away.

I breathe out. "Girls terrify me."

The next morning, we sleep through the alarm. The intercom crackles. "Privates, where are you?"

I scramble upright. "Whoa—Private Perry, we'll be down in ten!" My legs barely hold me as I jump down, muscles half-asleep. "Bumble, get up!" Panic twists in my gut. What happens if we screw this up?

CHAPTER SIX

Kana

Bumble swears the moment I wake him up. Missing dinner is one thing, but being late for a flight? This won't impress the Navy. We grab our bags and bolt, racing for the parking lot to catch our ride to the airport.

O'Hare Airport sprawls out, with gates for what looks like two hundred planes. I'm grateful Bumble and I are traveling together, even if he talks all the time. We take the tram and run to find our gate. A voice echoes, calling the final boarding announcement like it's summoning lost souls to the mothership. After having a breath test for illness, a pretty flight attendant takes my ticket, ignoring my blush. Once we're seated, I take the window, and a teen girl hoists her carry-on into the overhead compartment. I move to help but freeze. Talking to a girl—especially one I don't know—feels like stepping into a minefield.

Her mahogany hair falls in her face as she struggles to lift the bag. The soft, flowy blouse she's wearing catches and lifts slightly, revealing a bit of her tan stomach. She notices me staring.

My face burns, and I turn away. *She must think I'm a creep.* I want to apologize, but my throat locks up. She straightens her blouse, closes the compartment, and sits down beside me, sighing as she checks her ticket again, as if she can't believe where she's sitting.

Bumble steps in behind her, grinning like it's his birthday.

"Well, well, who do I have the pleasure of sitting next to?" he says, practically filling up the whole row.

The girl leans away from him, but when she sees me, she shifts back to the center of her seat—trapped.

"Hi, I'm Mia," she says quietly, like she's not sure if she should be talking to us. She pulls a can of tart cherry juice out of her bag and opens it.

"My name's Bumble," he says. "And next to you is Kana. He doesn't like girls," Bumble laughs.

My heart sinks to my toes. "I—Bumble!" *Why don't you just broadcast it in stereo?*

"Just kidding!" Bumble glances at me and realizes he's said too much. He tries to laugh it off. "He probably likes girls. Who knows?"

I lift my hand to protest, and say, "Bumble!" as my hand jerks forward. Suddenly, her can of juice tips—right onto her lap. *Just perfect.*

Mia yelps, grabbing the can, but it's too late—her pants are soaked purplish-red. The tiny napkins we scramble to get don't help much. Bumble calls for a flight attendant, but by the time he gets back, Mia's light blue pants have already absorbed most of the liquid.

"Now everyone's going to think I peed my pants," she mutters, "or worse." Mia digs through her purse for more tissues. "I hate guys who try to impress you."

I nod. Guilt stabs me, and I turn to stare out the window. She sighs, resigned to sitting between Bumble and me for the whole flight. Bumble grumbles under his breath and buckles his seatbelt.

He monopolizes the conversation, going on about boot camp and his childhood—stories he's never told me before. I watch Mia slump deeper into her seat.

"Bumble, Mia brought a book. Maybe you should let her read," I say.

He grumbles.

Mia glances at me like I'm an alien. "Yes, I do want to read," she says, opening her spy novel and nibbling on a granola bar while Bumble stares at her. Poor girl.

I pretend to sleep, sneaking peeks at her.

Eventually, she asks to go to the restroom.

"Man, why'd you have to embarrass me in front of the lady?" Bumble hisses as soon as she's out of earshot. There's a bitterness in his voice.

"Bumble, when you talk about yourself more than you listen, it's just robbing her. Did you notice she didn't ask you any questions? If you want someone to like you, you've got to discover them, not over-talk."

"Like you know anything about girls."

I laugh. "Not that I'm an expert—but Mom always says to look at someone's body language. Mia shrinks when you go on and on. Ask her about herself."

"You do it, *Dog Breath.*"

I smirk. "Nah, I'm good." I blow my breath in his direction.

"Cut it out! Why don't you mind your own business?" He pouts, his lower lip sticking out.

Mia returns, and I get up to use the restroom. When I come back, the tension between her and Bumble is obvious.

I sit down and decide to broker a truce. "Bumble, didn't you want to ask Mia what she likes to do to relax?"

He stammers, "Y-yeah, Mia?" He glares at me.

She glances at me with a hint of a smile and tucks her hair behind her ear. Her golden skin glows under the plane's lights, and a small mole near her eyebrow peeks out from under her hair like it's saying, *I'm real, not some doll covered in makeup.*

"Thanks, Bumble. I like to read, write poetry, and come up with healthy recipes," she says, her dark brown eyes flicking around the cabin.

Bumble almost jumps out of his seat. "What? You cook? I love food."

For the next hour, Bumble pumps her for recipes, and they talk about food. He shares stories about his mom's cooking. There's much I want to add to the conversation, but I just sit there like a doofus. Eventually, Mia says she's ready to read, and the three of us fall silent until we land at SeaTac.

The plane skids down the runway, and Mia pulls her ticket from her teal, hand-crocheted purse. I see we're on the same connecting flight.

"Umm," escapes my mouth before I can stop it.

Mia looks at me, her dark brown eyes puzzled. I pull out my ticket and place it next to hers. Bumble blows a raspberry and pulls out his ticket to compare. We're all sitting together on the next flight. Could she be a MANA recruit too? I can't ask without breaking regulations.

"Well," Bumble says with a grin that practically splits his face, "I guess we'll be seeing more of each other."

"I guess so," Mia says, tying her sweater around her waist to hide the cherry stains.

As we walk through SeaTac's massive airport, I'm grateful to stretch my legs. Bumble takes charge, finding our gate. Mia writes in her diary while I google Thai money. Going to Thailand feels like stepping off a cliff—killing, being killed, getting wounded, talking to girls. Still, the idea of seeing an exotic country, one with a climate like Kauai's, sends a thrill through me.

For the next flight, Mia asks to switch seats, so she can sit by the window. I end up squished in the middle, wedged between her and Bumble. He gives me the stink eye for switching. I close my eyes to avoid looking like I want to talk.

"Hey, Mia, want to hear the funniest prank I've ever pulled?" Bumble asks, leaning forward.

She doesn't even look up from her book. "We'll have plenty of time to get to know each other later."

I'm pretty sure that's her way of saying, "not now."

My hands cover my face. *I've blown my chance to get to know her.*

CHAPTER SEVEN

Kana

Kauai's warm air blows back through my hair as I step off the Lihue Airport ramp. My body can't relax, as if there's a centipede in my gut stinging me. I guide Bumble and Mia to baggage claim, struggling to slow my pace enough for Mia's short legs. We pass through the hall and see the gallery of vibrant history—displays of antique muumuus and posters showcasing Kauai's lush landscape and ancient cultures. If I tried to escape and run home now, I'd risk the police showing up at my door. I should be excited about this opportunity to serve with MANA, but I'm not. My free hand keeps opening and closing into a fist. I want to do the right thing, but how?

A military bus waits at the curb, with the breeze carrying its moist, gentle air. Rainbow Shower trees sway just behind it. The distant ocean sparkles with its unspoken invitation to surf and forget my troubles. My stomach churns back to reality as a guy in a camouflage uniform holds up a sign with about twenty names on it. The list has Mia's name, too. She stands on the fringes, looking around.

We exchange glances as we gather around the driver, like children peering at Christmas presents, unsure if we're about to get our favorite toy or a pair of socks.

After a two-hour bus ride, we arrive at the base—a small compound, all cement, with solar panels on the roof. We gather with another fifty recruits from the Air Force, Army, Navy, and Marines. The room is air-conditioned but lacks windows, pictures, or decor. It has just chairs, a whiteboard, a computer, and a standard microphone on a table in the front.

"Welcome, cadets." His raspy voice carries a drawl. "Congratulations. You've earned the right to train to become MANA warriors," says Lieutenant Pearson. He's about my height—six feet—but built like a tank, standing with his legs spread, hands at his sides. His gold and brown camouflage blends into the drab room. "Once you leave here, you'll be on exclusive missions, requiring the best, the brightest, and the bravest the U.S. has. You may give your lives for our country. You may save lives. When our country needs spectacular skills, they'll look to you. But if you're full of yourselves, you won't succeed. If you think you're all that, we don't want you. Leave now, and we'll give you a dishonorable discharge. If you're not teachable, you're not worth having."

His narrowed eyes sweep the room, but no one moves or makes a sound.

Bumble leans toward me and mutters, "Like that's a choice?"

"Cadet, how many push-ups can your chubby body do?" Lieutenant Pearson strides over to us, glaring at Bumble.

"Oh, about sixty, sir."

"That's *Lieutenant* Pearson, sir, to you." He towers over Bumble, who's sitting next to me in the back row. "Give me a hundred here and now, or you're on latrine duty until further notice."

Bumble starts doing push-ups.

The lieutenant swings a white pointer and whacks Bumble's forearms hard. "Touch your nose to the floor when you do a push-up. Didn't they teach you how to do push-ups in the Navy, cadet?"

Bumble struggles through fifty and starts shaking at the last ten. He collapses at sixty-five, blood dripping from his arm and hand, a result of the lieutenant's repeated whacks.

"You're on latrine duty, cadet. Learn how to do a push-up. If you can't hack it—leave."

My heart pounds against my chest as I watch helplessly. I want to help Bumble, to comfort him, but I can't.

For the next hour, Lieutenant Pearson lectures us on the structure and expectations of MANA. Men and women are supposed to train and serve as equals, but the disparity in the way he looks at the women turns my stomach, and his pride is palpable.

After receiving our clothing allotments, we place our hands in clay to create forms for specialized gloves. The officer takes three samples of our index fingers as if that's the only finger that matters. Something about leaving my handprint feels unsettling—like I'm giving away a piece of myself. Then we break for dinner.

"You okay, Bumble?" I ask as I find him alone at a table. No one else seems to want to sit with us. My tray of fish tacos and mixed vegetables is a letdown. The fish looks like it was frozen and shipped from New York, far from the fresh ahi or opakapaka I'd expect on the island.

Bumble looks as wilted as the vegetables. "I'm good," he says, though he glances at his wounds, disbelief in his eyes.

"Keep your head down. We don't know what we're up against," I advise.

Holding up his wounded arm, he says, "I have an inkling." He shakes his head, his eyes filled with pain.

About fifty cadets sit at a dozen tables in the cafeteria. The women gather at a couple of tables, whispering among themselves. All except Mia have cut their hair short. She sits on the outskirts, not part of the conversation. The men are loud, and their laughter fills the room.

Some go back for seconds, but when I try, the server says, "Move on, cadet. No seconds for you." *Does he know I'm a Neverborn? Has someone told him?*

My shoulders sag. *I'll never be good enough for them.*

I glance at my name on my uniform. Unlike the others, the first letter in mine isn't capitalized. It could be a mistake, or maybe a deliberate slight. I scan the other Neverborns' uniforms. Each one of us has only lowercase letters for their names. The message couldn't be clearer, we're marked as less, in every way they can think to show it. "Why are they segregating us?"

Bumble just shakes his head.

A white wall between the entrance and the windows lights up with projected lists. It's a screen. Bumble and I finish eating in silence and check it out. We're both on latrine duty, along with Mia and five others. She comes up behind me, so I step aside. Her name is lowercase, too. I want to ask her about it, to hear her story, but I don't. I don't have the heart to tell her—we're all outsiders in our own country. Unwanted, branded like the Star of David, with lowercase letters on our chests. catch my name on my shirt—*kana,* lowercase like it's a mistake, or maybe a deliberate slight. I scan the other Neverborns' uniforms. The message couldn't be clearer, we're marked as less, in every way they can think to show it.

"Oh great, we get to clean toilets," she whispers. "Nice promotion from the Navy." Her eyes meet mine, filled with worry, though she offers a fleeting smile.

Bumble starts to say something, but he just shakes his head. We head to our barracks.

Our stark room has two bunk beds, a small bathroom, and a closet that smells of stale beer. It reminds me of a jail cell. All our clothes have our names printed inside. "Mana Power" is engraved on my three gold camouflage shirts and shorts, my three green camouflage sets, and one white dress uniform with gold trim—perhaps a symbol of power. My underwear, dress shoes, casual shoes, and other items are standard issue.

At 0500, an alarm jolts us awake. A wall-mounted reader board displays the day's schedule: PT at 0530, breakfast at 0630, training at 0700 in the Stargazer Conference Room, lunch at 1200, latrine duty from 1400 to 1600, weapon training from 1600 to 1800, Thai language school from 1800 to 2000, strategy from 2000 to 2100, and lights out at 2200.

At training, we go through cycles of running and exercises. Various instructors tally our push-ups, snap-ups, rope climbs, and mile runs. I glance at a tablet and notice a star next to my name. *Why?*

At lunch, I sit at a mixed table. Some are from the Navy, others from various service branches. A few brags about their scores, but mine top them all. No one talks to me, though. Their laughter is loud, their banter filled with insults. I stay quiet, sensing their need to dominate. In the Navy, our commanding officer emphasized brotherhood, but here, a sense of oppression hangs over us.

The next day at PT, Lieutenant Black starts out setting up a competition. He tallies the scores. "The former Airforce cadets rank highest in fitness, followed by former Marines. Next is the Army, and last is the Navy. Disturbingly, our Neverborns seem to drag each of the groups down. None of the Neverborns scored acceptably."

I suck in my gasp. *That's not true. Why would he single out Neverborns?*

We join our former servicemen to spur each other on. On our tally sheet, the scores posted are much lower than I think were true.

Copper, a surfer from Southern California, yells at me as I work through the last of my hundred push-ups, "Come on stinking Neverborn, get your sorry nose down on your pushups." Contempt bleeds from his voice.

My arms quake. Sweat drips onto the floor as I push myself to finish. I'm weak. How are the others?

The tally sheet has checkmarks next to my name, Mia's, and Bumble's, too. The Navy built a camaraderie with all their enrollees. I've never been singled out and persecuted before. At lunch, I sit with Bumble.

"Did the score sheet accurately report your scores?" I ask him between bites of fake instant mashed potatoes and fake meat mixed with mushy vegetables.

"No, my score was ten points higher. I want to tell Lieutenant Black but get this bad vibe from him. Something's going on, man." Bumble pounds his fist on the table. "They're screwing with us."

"Yeah," I say and look around, a fire growing in my belly. *These liars! Why are they out to prove the Neverborns are unworthy?*

At the girl's table, I think I see Mia, but her hair coils on top of her head like a snake. *Why does she hide her beautiful hair?* My stomach twists with concern for her. She sits at the end, not talking to anyone. When she rises, her figure has changed, like she's wearing padding to look like a man. She walks like she's lost her confidence. Another woman strolls over to her and whispers something. As they walk to the bussing area, a couple of guys come up to them looking down their noses at the women, saying something that seems to offend them. I see Mia's body shrink. She looks around like a bird watching for danger. He blocks her as she moves toward the conveyor belt that carries away the dirty dishes. I stand and move toward her. He sees me coming and our eyes lock.

He swears and says, "Neverborn scum." His shirt reads, "Cadet Naboros." The cadet next to him pushes him with his palm and says, "Come on. These animals stink anyway." They dump their trays and strut off.

I pick up a tray to throw at him, but I stop myself. Acting like them won't solve anything.

Mia turns and stops as she looks at me. The fear in her eyes pokes through my heart. I catch her eyes and nod, hoping she can read the promise there—I've got your back. But she looks away, shrinking as the cadet steps in front of her, and something in me snaps. I want to shove him aside, to tell him to leave her alone. But I don't move. I don't even know why.

I should reassure her. My mouth turns to stone. I don't smile or say anything. *What an idiot I am.*

"Thanks," tiptoes out of her mouth. She dumps her food and leaves.

I blink and say nothing, unable to express to her how special she is.

During Strategy, cadets divide us into teams, and we're given a dilemma—a problem to solve.

"The enemy is on the ridge above you. Their scanner reads your location by your body heat. They're moving in to surround you. What do you do?" Private First Class McDowell reads the question assigned to us.

"Dig a hole and bury yourself?" A muscular girl with a crew cut hairstyle says.

"Write that down," McDowell says to Mia, handing her paper and pencil.

"Use my aluminum blanket to reflect the sun as a decoy," I say, "and cake my body with cool dirt, then if there's a stream, jump in it and go downstream, or if not, work up the ravine staying behind rocks."

McDowell's eyebrows lower in a frown. "Yeah, right," McDowell scoffs. "Let's see if the enemy just lets you stroll downstream. Come on guys; you can do better than that."

I step back, erecting an invisible wall.

No other Neverborn offers ideas, but Mia writes mine down and puts a star next to it. She looks at me and half smiles. It melts the ice I've put up around me. Or is she mocking me? I'm desperate to understand.

Then Mia and Bumble's faces turn to stone as they see the edge of anger showing in McDowell's wrinkled face when he looks around at all the Neverborns. Who is establishing this social climate? He may be a pawn, following someone else's agenda, or some guilt-laden or abusive experience in the past might be triggered by those of us who represent a political party to him, or a religion, or a person. I need to know, for Mia's sake, and Bumble's, and all the rest of us. We need to stay strong and not absorb this gas lighting and lies.

After Strategy is over, I close my notebook and turn to Bumble, "We need a list of all the Neverborns. All of us are being targeted. Would you ask Mia to form a list of the women Neverborns? You and I can start a list of the men."

"Yeah, no kidding. Sure." He heads over to Mia.

She listens to him amid the men and women cadets who brush past her. One bumps into her on purpose as he passes and continues walking without apology. She takes it in stride, glances at me, and nods.

Most of the group hangs together in their original Navy, Army, Marines, or Air Force groups, eating together. Some sneak off in pairs into the trees as if no one notices. Most are rushing off, chatting. I move up behind McDowell, who talks to a female cadet with a curvy figure and dancing eyes. His roster rests next to his water glass on the table in front of him. I copy the names starred on the roster as fast as I can without being observed—me, Bumble, Pete, Alex, and Montana. McDowell turns around and bumps into me.

"Cadet, what the _____ are you doing? Dishwasher duty instead of dinner, for getting this close to me. You stink. You moron."

He doesn't notice the names written on my notebook.

"Yes, sir, Private First Class McDowell," I say. The food has no flavor anyway, and there are not enough nutrients or protein in it to sustain a child, much less a young man. His insults flow off me because it's clear now. This is the enemy camp, and its name is Prejudice.

CHAPTER EIGHT

General Edward Shipley

His ocean-blue Porsche 911 clings to the corners as it descends the mountain from MANA's new home just below NASA's Kauai Astronomical Observatory. He caresses the leather steering wheel. *Only the best can afford to drive a Porsche. Who else from his graduating class at West Point drives a 911 and has ten million in the bank? No one, for sure. And the car still smells new.*

The sea glints like shards of glass, cold and uncontrollable under the sun's glare. He shifts down, feeling the gold-plated gear knob with his calloused fingers. He's had enough of the green-gilled cadets—kids. How long before retirement, when he can forget it all and move to the Cayman Islands? Too long. One more year. But until then, he'll keep looking over his shoulder to make sure everything appears shipshape. He'll have twelve million by then. Shipley smiles. *Twelve million.* He envisions the beautiful women he'll spend it on and whistles a catcall, imagining what it would be like to change identities and live a life of luxury with no responsibilities.

"From your place in hell, Dad, take notice," he mutters. "You called me a failure. Look what I've done. I'm a world-renowned hero, trading Neverborns for POWs. Brilliant. All those boys have gotten to come home because of me." He pauses to visualize a son coming home from a POW camp. Coming from certain death to life. His eyes water as his chest swells with pride. "You didn't get a fraction of the awards or money I've gotten, Dad. And the finale is yet to come."

Shipley imagines the retirement banquet at the end of the year, sees his colleagues congratulating him, tastes the delicacies, and revels in the thought of the bankroll he's maneuvered into his account. Maybe the President will even attend. He's fooled every-one. Everyone! He smirks and wiggles his fingers on the steering wheel.

No other cars clutter the two-lane road winding down to Kekaha, leaving him free to muse. Just him, his Porsche, and the long snake of a road winding down from the canyon heights toward home.

The emptiness of his house unsettles him. A result of Mary Ellen's death from cancer two years ago. She didn't appreciate him, anyway. Still, no one will have washed his clothes, no one will have a drink waiting in the fridge, and no one will have cleaned up the mess Maverick, his St. Bernard, left in the backyard. Derek must have been about ten when he brought Mav home as a pup—twelve years ago now.

The General's heart races as he remembers Mary Ellen's fu-neral. Derek, sitting just behind him, whispered to his girlfriend, "Dad killed Mom. Living with his anger and affairs would kill any woman." The icy bitterness in Derek's voice pierced Shipley's heart. How did Derek know? And who was he to judge? But if Derek knew, the rest of the family must know, too.

Shipley grits his teeth. He'll show Derek. He'll disappear with all his money, and Derek won't inherit a dime.

The General taps his fingers against the gear knob and groans. Had Serenity told Mary Ellen about their secret rendezvous? But he *needed* his women. His mind lingers on Serenity's amazing hips. Was she worth keeping? She and the Neverborn women were a small price to pay to keep him happy. His job requires him to train tomorrow's leaders, after all. Soldiers die if incompetent officers rise from the ranks. A minor infraction against old-fashioned morality. The military owes him for decades of service. And he'll get his payday.

His car phone rings jolting him from his thoughts. With a tap, he answers the call on speaker.

"Hello." His voice is gruff, but he's entitled to some slack.

"Ed, how are you? I haven't heard from you in a while." There's something distant in her voice, setting off a warning signal. His heart begins to sprint.

Serenity. And he'd just been thinking about her. "Baby," he says warmly, and a pang of fear hits his chest. "Did you tell anyone about us?" A sharp curve looms ahead. He'd better slow down, or his career—and life—will end before he can reap the benefits of everything he's stashed away. The car shimmies and whines as he brakes. Every muscle in his body tenses.

"Honey, I haven't said a word." She takes a drag on her cigarette.

He can practically smell her perfume through the phone. But maybe he shouldn't take any chances. "It's over between us. Don't call me again."

"Now, Ed," she says in her low, sexy voice.

Was she smiling?

"You're just paranoid because you have so many secrets." There's a vengeful tone in her voice that raises his defenses. She draws on her cigarette again.

"What do you know about secrets? I don't have any secrets." If he yells, it's her fault for accusing him. *A slut with the nerve to accuse a general?* He'd thought about taking her with him to the islands, but he can't trust her now. *And after all I've done for her.* The wardrobes he financed, the wines he stocked in her pantry, the condo he paid for in Poipu! He'd spoiled her much more than his wife. And now she's turning on him. Betrayal scrapes the skin of his heart.

"You've got your secrets, Ed. But don't worry. I keep mine safe. For now."

"Safe?" His pulse quickens. What does she know? A migraine threatens.

She continues. "It's not like you've earned those millions you brag about."

"I invest well!" he yells. She could damage his reputation. His thumb taps the steering wheel as fast as his heartbeats. Serenity couldn't know how he siphoned off the Neverborns' paychecks after trading them for Chinese POWs. How could she? And no one would miss the women—they all died in the swamp.

But still . . . something scratches at the back of his mind. A ghost he can't shake. He's covered his tracks. No one will ever find out. But the unease remains. His heart starts to calm, but his acid reflux flares.

"I understand you," she says, laughing. "You're afraid you'll be exposed by a child from one of your many affairs. Or that a cadet will end up pregnant with your kid. They'll have proof—heredity tests." She pauses. "I've had you watched."

Shipley's face hardens. That accusing tone again. "You had me watched?" he bellows. His palms are sweaty. "You think you know everything," he growls and ends the call with a click.

Deep breaths. Calm down. You'll be fine. She's lying. A string of curses flies from his mouth. *First Derek, now Serenity. Everyone turns on you eventually.*

The Porsche roars around the mountain curves. A whine from the motor matches the scream in his head. Even though air blasts his face, it can't cool the rising heat in his chest. The descent drags on. He needs a drink. Home is still twenty minutes away. He should've taken his helicar. His fists pound the steering wheel.

"Doodle, call Corporal Allen," he commands.

"Calling Corporal Allen," a soft voice replies.

"General Shipley, you home yet?" Allen's bass voice says with a calm that unnerves him.

"Almost. Hey, how are the wife and kids?" He says in as upbeat of a voice as he can manage.

"Fine. We just had dinner. What's up?"

"Allen, when is the survival mission scheduled?"

"In a month, Sir. October."

"Good, I'll inform you of the exact dates closer to the time." Closer to the time when the rain is heaviest on Mt. Waialeale. The Alakai Swamp has to be flooded for this to work. "Listen, you're new. Once you take the bus of graduates to the airport, you have leave until after Thanksgiving when our next batch comes in. I don't even want you on the compound. I want you at home with your family. Got it?" Shipley rubs his sore knee. "We'll talk more later, but it's my tradition to stay and clean up all the paperwork, get the last of those coming from the Survival Mission off to Bangkok. You just have a good Thanksgiving for me."

A pause in the conversation makes the General think that Allen is genuinely touched. "Thank you, Sir," he says.

"Okay Doodle, end call." A click cements his words. He grimaces and pulls a cherry cigar from the glove box to put in his mouth. *I'm not such a bad guy. Well, maybe I am.* He shouldn't take advantage of women. The idea sucks the energy out of him. *I am who I am. The world will have to deal with it.* When he gets home, he will light his cigar and do some strategizing to mitigate any other fears that haunt him about Serenity.

The health app's voice chimes in, cold and clinical, "Your blood pressure is 200 over 120. Would you like me to play ocean waves and birds singing?" Are these the demons mocking him? He slams his fist against the steering wheel. "Shut up!"

"Your blood pressure is now 220 over 125. Would you like me to call an ambulance?"

"Noooo! Turn off the health report!" He says and turns up the A/C.

"Health report turned off," the app says.

The sun sets on the ocean, dipping like a donut into the hot oil. Serenity dunked him in hot oil with her rude opinions. He won't let her win her little game. A spurt of sadness covers him. The house sits empty, like always. No Mary Ellen, no one. Only Maverick with his mess in the yard. He is alone. Who cares? He doesn't need anyone. Never has.

Finally, he nears his gated driveway. Ten minutes later, he punches the code into the metal security fence on his palm tree-lined driveway. He carries the clay models of the Neverborns' fingers to his lab and sets them next to the plaster containers with their powdery residue dusting the countertop. Only he could devise a scheme so ingenious—a plaster fingertip to transfer millions. A clay model shatters in his hand and crumbles onto the floor. Just like those women—their bones shattering on the rocks. And his bank account will keep growing, pouring in, making up for every trace of his sins. He steps up to his bar and sees Mary Ellen's half-full tequila bottle. The smell of her hair spray comes back to him. Only a drink could drown the demons scratching at his mind. Tonight he'll need several.

CHAPTER NINE

Kana

To get ready for dinner, I scrub away the sweat and grime from the day's drills, knowing it won't matter. Within an hour, the kitchen's steam and oven heat will have me drenched again. It's better than latrine duty. The chef is a roly-poly middle-aged bald guy. When I walk in, he nods to me with curiosity in his eyes.

"Cadet Munson reporting for dish duty," I say, taking in the stainless-steel room. I brace myself for the worst.

"Grab an apron in that drawer in front of you." His defeated voice sounds like the winds of calamity have carved away most of his courage.

The stainless-steel kitchen has streaks and bits of food on the walls and floor, not cleaned well, and black mold peeks out in the corners under the giant stainless-steel countertops. I try not to let the cook see me noticing. Pots rest on tall stainless steel shelving units that have wheels. There's a workstation in the center of the kitchen. I pull on the white apron with light stains.

"Call me Bones."

I suppress a laugh. With his round belly and slow shuffle, he's the last person I'd expect to be called "Bones."

"I'm Kana. How'd you get that name?" I tie the apron around me.

"Long story. You can start by washing those pots." He points to the dishwasher alcove. There's a mammoth stainless steel dishwasher cover pulled up, ready for the next load of dishes. Next to it are several twenty-gallon pots. I see the rubber glove box and start reading the instructions on the washing machine.

Bones pulls pots of navy beans out of the cooler that have been soaking in water.

"Navy beans?" I ask.

"Yeah." His tired voice matches the frown lines on his aging face, framed by salt and pepper hair. A brown, bulbous mole sits by his nose with hairs protruding from it. "General Shipley likes gourmet food at the expense of the cadet's menu."

An uneasiness needles me. "Do you get what you need for everyone to have a balanced diet?"

He looks at me and twists his face. "Two menus. One for officers, one for cadets. A cadet delivers lunches to the officer's mess hall at 1300, dinner at 1800. Neither is worth much, but the cadets' menu," He shakes his head, "It's just calories on a plate."

"What are they having tonight?" I find a stainless-steel pad to clean the burned bottom of the pan I'm washing.

"Lobster bisque, ribeye steak, roasted red and yellow baby potatoes, salad and asparagus spears with parmesan cheese for the mucky muck, navy beans for you peons."

I chuckle. "Which menu do *you* eat?"

He swears and laughs. "I eat anything I want, but you can be sure it's not what *you* get to eat."

I stack the pots upside down on a draining rack. "Do the cadets get enough protein to build the muscles the Colonel wants?"

"Not my problem."

I see cigarette stains on his teeth as he turns to me to speak.

He smirks. "Take your complaints up to the General."

"Yeah, no," I say under my breath.

"What do you know about him?" With the pots clean, I wash my hands, put on new gloves, pick up a peeler, and start to peel carrots for the night's salad.

"Nothing you should know." His shoulders droop as he opens packages of bisque from the walk-in cooler and dumps them in a pot to heat. He stirs it with a spoon, tastes it, and stirs more with the same spoon. It reminds me of a joke my mother used to talk about—a disgruntled cook spitting in his employer's soup to get back at him.

Mom would have some magic question to ask this defeated man, that would give expression to the pent-up failure his body language shares so freely. I finish peeling and find a cleaver to cut them and start on the celery. He looks over with surprise written on his face as I hold one end of the cleaver on the cutting board and pivot the knife with quick cuts.

"You worked as a chef?" His breath smells of beer.

"Every third day, my mom and I used to cook at home for our tribe of nine. She's an excellent cook. Along the way, she taught me how to use knives." The memory of cooking with her stings.

"Seven kids?" He hands me a pile of celery. "Lettuce is in the cooler. Throw it all in one of those bowls." Bones nods toward a pile of enormous bowls on the storage rack to my left.

"No, six adults, three boys, all the same age. All different nationalities from our parents." *Dang, I've said too much.* I trust

Bones, but I don't want him giving any information about my parents to the General. The lettuce in the cooler is iceberg, offering no vitamins, enzymes, or antioxidants. Beans don't have the quality of protein the cadets need to build muscle. How long before we show nutritional deficiencies? "Can I make soup out of the throw-a-ways?" I pick up the carrot peelings and show Bones.

"Fine, just don't tell anyone. And, if anyone asks, I didn't give you permission." He pulls out a water bottle holding an amber liquid with a beer smell to it.

I open my mouth to tell him that carrots release their load of carotene better if they're cooked, but he doesn't look like he cares. Once I've cut up the onions, garlic, asparagus, and Costco's fine ribeye steak, I put the scraps and bones into my soup pot. At home, the garden would flow with rosemary, oregano, basil, and thyme to flavor foods. Here, we're on the desert side of the island. The only thing I can find outside is cactus, Hali Koa, guinea grass, and Albizia trees, and they don't taste good. I browse through the walk-in and find some parsley and basil. "Hey, Bones. Can I use the stems from these herbs?"

"Suit yourself. Just don't touch the leaves. The General likes his food with flavor."

"There are twenty-five Costco chickens in the cooler, too. After I'm done with the dishes, can I debone five and put the bones and scraps in my soup?"

"Sure, as long as you save me some of your soup." Bones almost smiles at me.

I keep up the dishwasher loads but help prepare food during the wash cycle.

"Oh, darn. I accidentally made too much for the officers. I guess we'll just have to dispose of it." Sarcasm oozes from his voice.

He loads the steamy trays of mushrooms and steak, lobster bisque, potatoes, and asparagus into serving trays but puts the salad and dressings over a bed of ice. Then Bones loads two plates and hands me one and speaks into his computer to send an oral message to his watchcom, "Cadet Smith, it's time for officer delivery."

The steak tastes under seasoned as is the asparagus. The potatoes are too salty with no extra flavors. They would have been tastier if served crispy.

"Hey, before the trays go, do you mind if I season them?"

"Suit yourself, but if the General doesn't like it, I'll tell him you snuck in and did it to pull his chain." His gray eyebrows fold in with concern.

"No problem." I salted and peppered the food and let him taste it.

"Okay. I can't really taste food much anymore."

"Oh, cigarettes," I say. "Ask him for fresh rosemary and sea salt for your next order. It's great on food."

Dirty pots pour in and keep me busy.

Bones prepares to leave. "Kana, come here."

I'm warmed by him calling me by my first name.

He taps 0704 into a pad next to the door, which locks the kitchen doors. His eyes narrow. "Fourth of July, my favorite holiday. You don't know the code. Don't let anyone see you use it. I don't know what you're going to do with the soup, but it better be gone by breakfast tomorrow morning or one of the officers will notice and bite off my butt."

I nod and smile. What have I done? Dispensing soup without anyone knowing will be impossible.

Cadets scheduled for dinner duty serve beans, overcooked peas, French bread, and salad. The noise of the dishwasher resounds, and the steam billows. I create a grocery list for Bones between loads and hope we can become friends.

Cadets file in the cafeteria and some man the serving station. It sounds like a dull roar from the kitchen. I come out to get more dirty dishes and see a Neverborn woman, Cadet Winters, according to her name tag, gathers tubs of dirty dishes from the loading area to bring back to me. Her bony shoulders curl in under the weight.

"Move it, Slut," a lanky cadet says, his buddies snickering around him as she passes him. The words hit harder than any punch, and I fight the urge to step in, to say something—anything—but my throat stays tight. She cringes but doesn't speak, neither do I.

I nod my head toward the empty stainless-steel counter in front of the dishwasher. If only I dared to call her beautiful, or at least show her how I appreciate her hard work. How unfair for her to take this abuse, but I say nothing. My stomach tightens.

After rummaging through the kitchen for something to put the soup in, I pour it into a big crockpot so I can bring it to our room and let it cook overnight.

By the time I finish cleaning, it's 2000—eight o'clock to my home less than twenty miles away, but in another dimension. *Everyone is reading, or singing together, or playing a game. It's Friday. Maybe Kekoa, my brother, came for the weekend.* "Ahhhh," slips from my throat. A pummeling hits my gut, longing to be with them.

On the way back to my room, I pass a group of cadets pouring over a list. One swears and says, "Climb the rope in one minute! Seven-minute mile! How many pushups?"

"Five sets of twenty-five between the same number of snap-ups," a guy says in a Southern accent. He echoes the swearing.

I pause to listen.

"What are you looking at, Neverborn? Get your ugly nose out of here," a guy with curly red hair blasts at me. I hurry on.

Bumble's rumble of gas hits my ears before I even open the door. I leave the door open and head to the window to open it. "Bumble, you trying to kill me with that smell? What did you eat?"

"Not my fault. If I'd had a double bacon burger, it'd be a different story." He sniffs and laughs, oblivious. "What's that?" He looks at the crockpot in my arms.

"Chicken soup. Or it will be in a day or so. Hey, Bum, did you get any new workout requirements?"

"No. Why?"

"I just ran into some Cadets griping because they were going to have to run a mile in under seven minutes and do a bunch of push-ups." I pop into the bathroom to take a shower and stew over why the Neverborns wouldn't get the same requirements as the rest of the Cadets. The brass is setting up for something, but I don't know what it is yet.

CHAPTER TEN

Kana

The next morning, the chicken-basil soup's smell fills the dorm. I throw open the window. Someone's bound to smell it and rat me out. I taste the soup and then shove it in our closet.

"Bum, keep an ear out today—do any of the other Neverborns have stricter PT?" I peek outside.

"Whatever you say, Chef," he eyes the crock pot closet.

I force a smile, but it fades as fast as the warmth of the soup. Cooking reminds me of home, and home is a world away.

That afternoon, Bones asks me to taste the entrée before he authorizes it to be taken to the officers at dinner. Together, we make a list of spices and extra supplies he'll need from Costco. Afterward, I wash dishes and clean the kitchen again.

I can't wait to return to our barracks and see how much soup is left. The room is full of Neverborns when I open our door. Each is eating my soup.

"Kana, delish!" Montana eats out of a plastic pop bottle with the top cut off. His grin tells me it was worth the effort. He slurps a gulp, and it clings to his chin. Worry loosens its grip on me for a moment.

The others grunt their approval and sing, "For He's a Foul-Footed Fellow."

I smile, getting the message despite the words of the song. The crock pot is almost empty except for the bones. I finish it. The big chunks of chicken and the savory broth warm my stomach. "So…any of you hear about tougher PT requirements?" I try to keep my tone casual, but the unease inside me is building, gnawing at my gut. *Are they really setting us up to fail?*

Everyone looks around as if it's news to them.

"I'm guessing here, but what if our beloved officers want us to fail? What if the non-Neverborns are given greater requirements because there's a test coming up? We'll look bad with lower scores, giving the staff hard-core facts that we're not as competent as non-Neverborns." The silence slices through the air. "Have you seen cadets run more than usual?"

"Yes," two guys say at once.

"Then we need to up our running, push-ups, snap-ups, rope climbing speed, everything you see them do, we do."

"Will we get more soup too?" Pete asks. His t-shirt has soup stains down the front.

I smile. "I think I can swing that. We're being set up to fail. We need more protein if we're going to stand a chance. The officers won't help us, so we'll have to look out for each other."

By the next morning, our instructors in PT and Weaponry have tallied our scores. The roster of cadets and scores lie on the table as we run laps after our workouts. The whistle blows and everyone heads for the door. I run straight to the roster. The Neverborns' names have stars next to them. Their scores look average compared to the others.

"Cadet Munson, five more laps for trying to look at the roster." The Private yells with contempt dripping from his voice.

"Yes sir, Private Stonewall," I grit out, forcing my legs to move. Five more laps. Punished for being curious. As if they're producing proof that we're less than human.

Why would the officers want the Neverborns to fail? Every officer except Bones has oozed contempt toward the Neverborns.

That afternoon, I ask, "Bones, why do the officers have it in for Neverborns?" I taste the barbeque pork chops and wait for his answer, aware I'm almost panting to hear what he will say.

"Can't say. Might come from the top. The climate usually starts with the brass." He stops stirring the pot in front of him and a pensive expression emerges. "Something about the General ain't right."

I ponder his words and dump some garlic and ginger in the pork chop sauce. "What do you mean?" I taste the sauce again.

He shakes his head. "I don't know. Probably nothing. Kana, can you make chicken pot pies for tomorrow's staff dinner?"

"Sure, I'll keep stock cooking. Whenever we need to make gravy, sauce, soup, or casseroles, we'll always have it. Can I keep taking soup back?"

Bones smiles and nods. Despite his looks, the wide pores on his nose, his blackheads, and that mole on his cheek, there's a tenderness about him that makes me see past his appearance and like him.

The next day, instead of our usual routine, junior officers time us on running a mile. They tally our scores for push-ups, snap-ups, rope climbing, and swimming. I would love to see our scores and how they compare to others.

We gather afterward in the gym, stand in rows, face forward at attention. "Cadets, we're training you for missions that protect our country and provide security for those you love. These scores, along with our survival test times to help us decide who goes to the front lines and who develops strategies and support."

That's why we're set up to fail. The brass needs stats to back up what they've already decided—Neverborns are expendable. They're setting us up to die.

"You'll leave for your survival expedition in two weeks. Your condition and the time it takes to complete it will also give evidence to your future placement."

Both women and men are in the room. Neverborn women aren't getting the extra protein of my soups. I can't look around while standing at attention, but the Neverborn women I recognize in front of me all have slumped shoulders. Defeated already. Hassled because they're women. I blow out my air, slowly visualizing how people treat them here.

During dinner, between loads of dinner dishes, I study the Neverborn women eating together at the same table. None are smiling. Few even talk. Mia's head sinks.

She turns and looks at me as if she can feel my stare.

I run back to the dishwasher and put the dishes away. Then I creep back.

She's standing at the dish drop-off station with her empty tray by the dirty dish tubs like she's waiting for me. "Kana. Can I have some soup?" Her brown eyes are wide and empty, like she's been starved of more than food. Why would she do that? The thought of her wasting away guts me. And to think, I've been keeping all the protein for the guys.

I turn and almost trip over my feet. How can I disguise a quart of soup? A gallon tin of canned corn waits to be rinsed and recycled. The other Neverborns are leaving for latrine duty, so I need to hurry. I rinse and fill it with soup and stuff a clean bar towel around the bottom, plastic wrap, and another towel on top, making it look like a cleaning can. Spoons. They won't have any. Quickly, I tuck a couple inside the bar towel and hand it to her.

She takes it with wistfulness in her expression. "Thanks." If MANA is discriminating against Neverborns, what will happen to her?

CHAPTER ELEVEN

Mia

Kana smiles at me. He's wearing an apron in the kitchen, getting food out, but I know better than to trust a friendly face. The Navy men always tried flashing smiles, but these MANA officers—they're hornets, stingers primed and entitled to strike. And the General—he's the worst. Almost like he can read my thoughts, he strolls into the cafeteria and looks around at the women.

He strolls up to me, glancing at my body, then my name tag. "Munoz, I've switched you from latrine duty to cleaning my office. Think you could make it shine for me?" His smile doesn't reach his eyes. "I like things…pristine. Follow me." He leads me to his office.

A chill spiders up my spine.

"What tasks would you specifically like me to tackle for you, sir?" I look around, not wanting to look into his eyes.

"I like when things are…perfect. Those who understand that get ahead. Here's the key." He holds it up. "Make yourself at home." His voice lilts, like he's asking for something he's not saying.

I blink, the words biting into me. Another man, another jerk. Like my father, always hunting for legs to chase, like women are prizes to be owned. Anger rises. I'm not my mother—I won't bend because some man says the right words or flashes a smile. I don't buy into the illusion of love because some man says the magic words and pays your rent. It's the same hungry look I saw in the eyes of that slimeball who seduced Jasmine. My sister had fallen for the lies, for that fake tenderness. And when the truth came out, she couldn't live with it. The smell of her perfume drifts into my mind—flowery and sweet. It was dusk when I found her—gone. Her skin—cold. Overdosed on the drug he'd given her. Gone. Rejected. Alone. Humiliated. The pain crashes back, and I choke on it. I whimper without meaning to. *God, keep me safe. Help me.*

"I'm in a position to reward those who," he pauses, "please me and make my life more beautiful."

Swallowing, I say, "Sir, yes Sir." I grab the trash, the supplies, anything to keep my hands busy, to keep them from shaking. It doesn't matter if I sound crazy. I whisper a prayer, barely audible, "God, help me! Help me! Help me!" repeatedly, like a lifeline. Once I'd given the room a lightning-speed cleaning, while the General watches me, I request to leave.

"Tuesday after dinner. Every week. I want you back here, making things spotless." He pats his knee impatiently.

My face feels hot, and I picture myself hugging our big family collie, Scruff, to calm myself. Having a panic attack in the General's office might land me back home in the same toxic atmosphere, helpless without a chip again.

Back in my room, I find the scissors. My fingers tremble, but I lift the first lock of hair. One cut. Another. With every snip, I carve away the weight—the stares, the whispers, the way the General's voice claws at me. Each piece of hair falling is another piece of myself they can't touch. I'm not their prize. I'm free.

CHAPTER TWELVE

Kana

Two weeks later, once the junior officers measure our weight and document our stats, we march out of camp. Fifty of us move like clockwork, our boots striking the dirt like a drum as we chant nonsense songs. Eucalyptus trees line the road, their scent tugging at the memories of home. We halt, and an officer dismisses us at the end of the MANA driveway. A small crowd forms around the reader board, elbowing for a spot. I join Bumble, Pete, Alex, and Montana—the other Neverborn guys. Anticipation coils in my chest.

Mia walks up, determination written on her face. "Audry Talsman, Johana Winters, and Sapphire Brown plus me make up our group. Who's with you?" She surveys the groups around.

Why did she cut her hair? And the padding around her middle masks her figure. *What's going on?* Afraid to be too personal, I answer her question and say, "Bum, Pete, Montana, Alex, and I."

I'm shocked I could talk to her so easily. Will the women be safe? What will the survival test demand of us?

An officer's voice cuts through the murmurs, amplified by a microphone to say, "Cadets, this is your final exam. Prove yourself worthy of your country. Show us your skills. Find your team and be ready for this survival trek."

Mia's eyes catch mine, her smile quick and uncertain. Her short hair spikes around her face like the rays of sunshine in a child's drawing. Bumble saunters over to her. No accident, I'm sure. The guys introduce themselves to Johana. Mia already knows her, and even Peterson knows Mia. I want to think about if the other guys want to lure Mia into a relationship, but one of the officers yells a command through his watchcom, which blares out everyone else's watch.

"Load up as a group in one of the trucks to compete for your survival test." A fleet of trucks rumbles up and stops next to us.

"Let's go," Bumble says, with an air of excitement in his voice.

"Where do you think we're going?" Mia asks me.

I turn to see her face and can tell she's lost more weight. She's depending on me. I can't fail her like I did Katrina when I let her fly off the zipline and crash below. Mia looks at me expectantly. I say, "Somewhere around Waimea Canyon, I think."

Bumble stares at me and slaps my back. "Hey, don't get any ideas."

We sit together on hard benches in the back of the tarped truck bed without speaking, unable to hear over the engine's rumble. My hands are sore from hanging on in all the jostling. It's an hour before the truck stops. I can't see out the back of the covered truck to tell where we've come from, but the truck sways as it backs up and turns around. *Did we double back? Where are we?*

Private Wilhelm pulls back the tarp to let us out. We're in a eucalyptus and Albizia forest. It's cooler—we've climbed in elevation. When we've all piled out, he says, "Congratulations, Cadets, this is the first moment of your survival journey. Your task is to get back to the pickup area on your own with no mechanical or outside help." He points on a map to a small clearing northwest of the rock face. I notice the location and see a map loaded on my watchcom. "There are no rules. We base your scores on how quickly you make it back to camp. The highest-scoring cadets are chosen for the most advantageous placements. Wait here. A helicopter will take you to your survival test start location. Any questions?"

I'm thinking about the "no rules" comment. *Will other groups steal from us? Hurt us? No rules—really?*

A cadet in another group asks, "Where will we get our supplies?"

Private Wilhelm laughs. "This is a survival test. Since when do you get supplies on a survival test?" He turns, gets in the driver's seat, and drives away.

I need to get a bearing to guess our location. "Follow me." I run into the woods. When the helicopter comes, we'll be able to hear it and return. No one except Bumble knows that this is my home island. I haven't hiked in this area before, but I know the island. I turn and see the Neverborn women and men following. Once we're out of sight, I stop at the base of a eucalyptus tree. "Stay here and be quiet. Other groups may try to steal our canteens and pocket knives, so we can't beat them back to the compound. They'll look better in comparison." The curving thick bark of the older tree makes it easy to climb to the top. Around me, ridges dip and rise. We can't see the ocean from here, and it's hard to judge direction without a bearing. I lick my finger and put it up to feel the breeze.

It seems to come from a point that must be south since that's where the air currents come from in the mornings unless there's a storm front. I'm on my way down the tree when another group comes to my friends. The smack of punches, wild yells—freeze me to the core. I glance down. Two figures scramble up the tree under me. Red hair, dark skin. My breath catches, and I push myself higher. They're gaining. My hands burn as I grip the rough bark, climbing faster, but the branches thin out, creaking under my weight. They're right behind me—pulling at my legs. I kick out. My foot connects. But then—a searing pain. My pants tear. *God, help me!*

I get chicken skin on my arms and pull my knees to my chest. There's no farther I can go. The limbs are small and weak at the top. I cling to the trunk, but the madmen are right below me. One of them pulls my foot down. *God, help me!* They're ripping my pants. "Ohh, ow!" I scream. Like a bolt of lightning hits, my right leg throbs in pain. I kick with my left foot, and they withdraw but wait. Blood pours down my calf. How long can I hang on? Something wraps around my left foot. A rope? It's pulling me loose. *I can't hang on!* Clinging to the four-inch trunk, my fingers rip away. The ground rushes up at me, branches slash my arms and face as I plummet. Branch after branch whacks me. My breath catches in my throat—then—the earth slams into me. Pain explodes in my skull, a blinding flash of white. Darkness claws at my awareness, pulling me under.

My eyes open but close in pain. I touch my temple. This is ten times worse than any migraine I've ever had. Pain pulses and throbs like a wave, throwing itself onto the rock below over and over.

Mia's hand strokes my forehead, her gentle touch almost reverent. My head throbs like it's splitting open, but I fight to focus on her face. She's been crying—there's a cut on her forehead, deep and raw. "Kana, stay with me," Mia whispers, but the pain is too much. I close my eyes, almost drowning under the weight of it.

Like high-voltage electric shocks, the bolts of pain in my head dull me to everything else. Mia is close, only inches from me. She bends over, touching my hair. She cut her eyelashes off. The short hair around her face makes her look different from the Mia I first met, but her eyes hold tenderness, admiration, and affection.

I close my eyes to the whipping pain beating inside of my head, trying to make sense of it, but a familiar laughing and crackling sound brings them open wide. The cadets! Two men approach us. They take a wrestler's stance and sidestep around us. One grabs Mia by the back of her shirt and throws her to the ground. The other reaches for my pocket and takes my Swiss Army knife and my flint. He throws the flint up in the air and catches it again.

"Flint. Huh. Nice. You won't need this anymore, loser."

A helicopter thunders in and the two strut off.

Mia! I sit up, but nausea as powerful as the water pressure of a giant waterfall slams into my gut. Everything I've eaten in the past day disgorges from my mouth and covers the ground next to me. Over and over, I puke. The smell brings on my gag reflex, but there's nothing in my stomach left to vomit. Still, my stomach lurches and contracts, taking my breath away.

A soft hand strokes my head and then my back. Mia. My stomach stops erupting like a volcano. I sit curled. Mom used to stroke my head like this.

"Lord, bring Kana healing. Get those jerks!" She pleads, "Lord, we need you. Help us." She offers me her canteen.

How can I put my stinky vomit-defiled mouth onto her canteen? I look up into her soft eyes and cup my hands. She pours water into my "cup." I rinse my mouth and spit.

"Lay down," she says.

I scoot away from the puke in the dirt and lay flat face down with my head to the side. Mia's hands massage my neck and head. She rubs my temples and forehead. The pain level goes down to about a five on a scale of one to ten.

My head clears. What about the others? I sit up. "Mia, thank you!" I'm afraid to look into her eyes. "How's Bumble?"

Bumble's hobble toward me crunches the small sticks under his feet. Blood runs down his pants where a gash in his pants bubbles red. "We didn't run far enough."

"You okay?" I ask.

He collapses next to me, clutching his stomach, a purple bruise rising around his eye. Blood trickles down his leg. "Karate training, anyone?"

I shake my head, and with the levity, some of my fear seems to go. But I can't break away from the harsh reality—MANA is out to get us, even the cadets. Bumble, Mia, Montana, and I are all shaking. I can't see the others huddled in a group fifty feet away. Pete's on the ground curled up.

"They took all our knives, canteens, and the candy bars I stashed in my pockets. I took a stab in my calf, trying to kick one guy away." Bumble's voice emanates defeat, laced with panic.

I look at his wound. "We need a noni tree to disinfect that wound."

Bumble does a double take. "No. We need a hospital."

"No rules. Remember? Have you noticed their attitudes toward Neverborns? What does that tell you?"

He swears, stands moaning, and walks away.

"Bumble, sit down and put pressure on your cut. I need to check out the others," I say. Mia and Johana lumber over to each other and hug. They're standing, and I don't see any blood.

Peterson moans twenty feet away under a small eucalyptus tree. Alex stands looking dazed, with a black eye, but otherwise unscathed.

"Pete, what hurts? What did they do?" I kneel beside him and put a hand on his shoulder.

He rolls to his side and throws up. Then lies on his back, hands on his abdomen. "Gut punch," he says in breathy agony.

The punch could have perforated his bowels, causing internal bleeding, or damage to his intestines. He needs to go to a hospital even more than Bumble. There's a hospital in Waimea, but to get him there, we need to find someone with a car.

"Kana," he says and moans. "I think" he stops to take erratic breaths, "they broke one of my ribs." His swollen face looks white except for the bruising from a punch on his left eye.

"Dang," I say. "Can you walk?" His red hair clings to his sweat-covered forehead.

He struggles to his feet and staggers to the side, still holding his stomach, moaning, and falls back down again.

"We're not going back to base. We're going to get you to a doctor," I say, walking to him.

"But . . . " He says, his face looking chalky.

"I don't care about the survival test. You might die of internal bleeding if you don't get help," I say.

A helicopter lands on the road and the assigned group loads.

I run up to the pilot and yell, "We have a seriously injured man—that needs a hospital. Now."

He looks at me and calls the base. Then he turns to me and says, "No can do. Base isn't authorizing any medical help. They say it's a survival test."

Survival test? Where they set us up to die. I sway as I walk away from the helicopter. My head spins, and the thunder of the helicopter amps up the pain in my brain until I can't stand it. I drop to a sit, but Bumble shows up and half lifts me, half pulls me to the shade of a tree. I bury my face in my hands. *Too much. This is all too much. Katrina falls off the zipline ramp and now this. Why would MANA set Neverborns up to die? Who can I trust if the people who feed me and direct my every move want me dead? Who?* I want to throw up.

Deep within, I hear a voice, "Me. I have called you, and I will complete my work in you." Philippians 1:6 sticks in my mind, "He who began a good work in you will carry it on to completion." I shake my head. How can this be? I've never felt like such a failure or been this afraid. If our whole command wants us dead or incapacitated, how can we create a decent life?

The helicopter returns after a half hour, gathers the next batch, lifts, swings around, and disappears through the trees. I watch the direction it flies—north. At least, from the sky, I can get my bearings.

Three groups leave before us. The clusters of non-Neverborns point to us and laugh as they see us huddle together. A few of the men call out obscenities to us. None of them appear injured. For a timed test, this isn't fair, some leaving earlier than others.

I touch the earth with my fingers and focus on how it smells. *Ground me, God.*

Bumble disappears to talk to other groups of Neverborn cadets. When he returns, he says, "The cadets assaulted and robbed the Neverborns, but everyone else appears fine."

A private helicopter lands, the kind that takes tourists around the island on tours. The pilot gets out and yells the names of the Neverborn guys from a list. Mia's face looks as white as Mom's bleached tablecloth as I walk away from her to climb into the copter. It's only the men going on this drop-off. Where will they drop the women off? We get in and I ask, "Where are we being dropped off?"

"You want the specific coordinates?" He looks too young to fly a helicopter. His shirt bears the name Bilby.

"No. Where are the rest of the MANA cadets being dropped off?" I ask.

"On the north side of the rim. I only know because I was watching on my way to you. I thought that's where I'd be dropping you, but the coordinates showed in the swamp itself. Sorry for you," his voice sounds concerned.

I peer out the window at the huddled girls unprotected, but all the non-Neverborns are gone. The noise of the helicopter blares all the sense out of my brain. I cover my ears as we swoop up in our metal bird, flying over Waimea Canyon. The ocean calls to me in the distance, gray under the clouds. The pilot takes us north, into the Alakai Swamp. Great. I see the overflowing banks of the swollen swamp with a river of water flowing in from the peak encompassed by clouds. I'll be buried in a bog with two people who need hospitalization. Maybe three if you count me. *Lord, help us. This is impossible.*

The pilot's voice crackles amid the blades' blare. "Out you go." We stand and hang onto the chopper, looking down, about ten feet from the swamp. My stomach twists at the sight. *Great. A death trap.*

CHAPTER THIRTEEN

Kana

As the helicopter hovers, its blades churn the water below into ripples. I leap out first, plunging through the surface into the thick mud beneath, followed by Alex. Pete's screams tears through the air as Bum shoves him out the door. He hits the water with a sickening smack, flailing next to me. Bum jumps last. Alex has pulled his head above the water. I reach for Pete and then Bum's hand to make sure they can get air in this watery graveyard. The roaring beast lifts away, leaving only the swamp's eerie silence behind.

I help Pete to a little island of Ohia trees and the others follow. Clusters of Ohia trees stand like sentinels over the swamp, their roots tangled with ferns that spread like grass wherever there's soil. My view won't let me see the middle, but from the helicopter, I noticed the center of the bog was mostly water from the flooding with a few trees poking above the water. No other humans are in sight.

Others must have seen where the helicopter dropped us off. They may try to attack us unless they don't want to get into the bog. If they come for us, we'll see them—but they might wait for nightfall. I think we can make it to the rim, but what about the women?

I study the direction the helicopter flies back. Other than the east side where Mount Waialeale crests, the land slopes down in enormous canyons, draining the swamp in long waterfalls on two sides. "We have to stay out of the currents that might pull us down a waterfall. And the mud below can keep us stuck, so we can't pull our legs out."

A low cloud drifts toward us. We may lose visibility. If we get fogged in, figuring out which way to go will be impossible. The brown muck and water surround us like grass on a golf course.

My group struggles to stand in the muck. Bum swears while Pete just moans, lying over ferns. We're all sinking—in so many ways. I close my eyes for a silent prayer of desperation—*God, help us.*

Bumble swears again, wipes mud off his arms, and says, "Where to now?"

"We have to get you and Pete to the Kalalau Trail where someone can drive you both to the hospital in Waimea," I kneel, my hands shaking as I weave branches into a rough sled for Pete.

Their eyes fix on me, wide with anticipation. My skin prickles under the pressure—it's up to me to get us out. The weight of their lives presses on me—my heart pounds like a blacksmith's anvil in my chest. *I must give them some assurance, but I'm clueless.*

I glance at Bumble, who looks at me expectantly.

"We'll make it," I say, though my voice sounds hollow even to me. "I know this island. I can get us out." But my heart races—what if I can't?

Alex turns to Bumble and says, "See, I told you, he's not a geek."

"No, I am a geek," I say. "Stay here. I'm going to get more branches from the Ohia tree and make you snowshoes."

"Ow-wee," Bumble calls out. "Have you lost your mind? There's no snow here."

I suck my foot out of the mud and take a step back, shaking my head. "Think about it, Bumble."

It takes a while to get to an Ohia tree where I weave the first set of snowshoes. They're two feet long and five inches across. My tribe, tired of standing, slogs their way to me. Mud covers their clothes, hands, and arms. All of them breathe hard from the effort each step takes to pull each foot away from the hungry earth, sucking it back.

Bumble grabs my first pair. "How do I get them to stick to my shoes?"

I lace the more flexible outer stems back and forth, weaving them between the outside shell of bigger branches. It seems obvious. *How can I say it without making Bumble feel dumb?* "Get some of the smaller twigs from the tree and wrap them around your foot and tie them to the snowshoe, or bogshoe, if you please." Another group of cadets stands above the swamp on a rock plateau, dropped off on dry ground. No rules. Maybe our bog is our salvation. They'll be waiting to take us down if they think we're a threat.

I put my arms out toward my small tribe. "Come on, help me." My voice expresses the urgency my gut demands. This could get ugly. Breaking off branches, I guide them to create their own bogshoes by weaving and bending smooth gray smaller branches.

"Bumble, look above the mushy islands of ferns where the trees grow in the distance?" I point.

"Yeah, but that's like, miles away."

"Yup," I answer. "That's where we need to go, but we'll go to the rim first. It's farther but faster."

Alex takes a step with his shoes and tips over. "Yuck!" He bats his arms at the water as if he's drowning in the muck.

I pull him up, and he says, "Help!" Alex screams, grabs me, and we freefall down into the water. My hands stroke down to push me above the water, but Alex's weight pushes me deeper.

It takes a minute to get traction and push Alex up.

"That was stellar!" Bumble says when I manage my head above the mud, "I want a slow-mo picture of that."

Bumble lifts Alex out of the water onto the island.

The sound of the helicopter buzzes through the swamp. I strain my eyes through the fog drifting in. A commercial helicopter crawls across the sky. To see, I scramble up the Ohia as far as I can; only our women wait for the drop-off. It's a green copter. Four people fly out into the middle of the bog, closer to the waterfalls. I hear a woman's scream over the swamp. "Oh no!" My hand slaps against the tree trunk. The women—are being dropped into the current. That water current will pull them right toward the falls. If they go over… I don't want to think about it.

"What should we do? I can't make any headway as it is, much less muck my way out to the middle." Bum says.

"No," I study how far from where we are to the rim. "I'll get you guys to the rim and go after them."

"Oh, the knight in slimy armor, huh?" Alex slaps my back and mud flies.

"Yeah," I say in a cold sweat, thinking about it.

There are more islands of shrubs and less water closer to the edge. My heart races out of control thinking about the girls.

Using our bogshoes, we try to step as close to an island as we can and, though we fall half the time, we make it to the rim, dragging Pete in my makeshift sled with ropes made from our ripped shirts. "Okay, do you see the red dirt landslide 110 degrees from here?"

Bumble says, "Yeah, there's a Cook Pine to the left of it."

"Yes," I say. "There should be a road around there leading to Waimea Canyon. Hikers travel that road. Take Pete and beg someone to get him to Waimea Hospital."

"Dude, you're going to the middle? That's suicide," Alex says.

"I'm the knight in slimy armor, remember?" I check Pete one more time.

"Just leave me," he says. His face is burning when I touch his feverish forehead with my muddy hand.

"No one gets left," I say. "Bum and Alex are going to take you to a public road where someone can get you to the hospital."

We strip off the bogshoes. Our muscles ache, but we can't slow down. Not yet. "Hey, be sure you disinfect your cuts when you get back. You can get an infection and even sepsis from the bacteria in this mud." We all have cuts. I don't want to think about mine.

My breath comes in ragged gasps as I turn toward the girls, every step sinking deeper into the muck. The mud clings to me, heavy like the weight of their lives in my hands. If I don't reach them soon… I can't let them die. Not like this. Bending my knees low, I push through the muck faster than I did with the guys. It must be taking me hours to get to them. I can't go directly. That would immerse me in the current flowing over the edge. The cloud cover is too thick to determine the time by the sun. I only hope I've gotten north enough to find them. Fire shoots through my leg when I walk, and my throat feels like sandpaper. My tongue sticks to the roof of my parched mouth. It's a battle just to stay upright. But I push on—the girls are close. They have to be.

My gut churns. *Have Neverborns died here, lost in this swamp? How many more will MANA dump into this graveyard?* Stepping on a little island of ferns, it sinks two feet under my weight. I fall backward and throw my arms out. As I tread the muddy water, my hand grasps something. My fingers pull it to the surface, the mud slops away—revealing a human hand bone. Cold shock surges through me. I rinse it, breathless. "Whoa," I say. Others have been dropped off here, and at least one died. That makes the Major a murderer. The girls are within sight, in the distance. I fold the finger bones in my pants pocket. They can't know.

The four women are trying to crawl through the exhausting swamp. It doesn't seem to work well; they're making little progress.

"Mia," I call out.

"Who is it?" She sounds frightened. "Don't come any closer."

I'm covered in mud. She can't tell by looking, "It's me, Kana."

"Kana?" Her voice holds hope.

"Yeah. Bumble says I'm your knight in slimy armor," I say, wiping off the mud from my face using the cleaner water on the surface.

"Kana!" Audry's voice trembles with desperation.

"I'm coming. Don't be afraid. We'll all get out together," I say. No more pushing women off cliffs. I need to save them as much as they need help. Someone is flailing in the water. Mia calls, "Audry! Audry!" as though they're drowning.

I push through the muck, but Audry's hands clamp around my neck. She drags me under, her weight crushing me. I thrash, shoving her up, but the mud swallows me faster. I'm sinking deeper with every struggle. This is not how I want to die. *God, help! I'm trapped, stuck in the mud.* She loosens her grip as I go lower, but then stands on my shoulders, shoving me into the mud further. I twist, kicking to get free, but my legs are stuck. My lungs burn.

A foot thrusts down close to me. I can't pull myself up by pulling someone else down. Lungs on fire! I reach for the leg and pull. It doesn't sink. Someone is trying to help me. I pull out one leg at a time and stroke up to the air surface. Mia still hangs onto a branch that Sapphire holds onto. Sapphire stands on an island using a big rock as her anchor.

"Mia! You saved my life," I say between gasps of breath.

"We all did," she says, hanging onto the branch as Sapphire pulls her to the island.

"Thank you!" I manage to say.

The three girls are arm-in-arm on the tiny island, like three birds perched on a branch.

After I've caught my breath, I say, "We need to get out of the current." I don't want to scare them by telling them where the current leads. "Lay in the water. Pretend it's a pool, not a giant mud pie. Do a breaststroke on the top few inches of the water." I show them.

The sky darkens—it must be around six. We need to get to the rim before dark. All four women are trying to do the stroke with varied success. It's too wet in this part of the swamp for bogshoes, more like a stream with a few islands.

Audry falls behind. I find and break off the longest limb I can to pull her. "Okay, hang onto the limb and let your legs trail behind you. Do a flutter kick," I demonstrate. "Don't bend your knees much. I'll pull the limb." *Will I be able to pull her fast enough to stay out of the current?* I try holding the stick with my left hand and side stroking using my right hand and legs. Progress is slow, but we move. We swim out of the swiftest part of the current and rest on an island, exhausted.

"This is never going to work! We're going to die! I know it. We're going to die!" Sapphire cries out.

I remember when Canyon, my brother, panicked because he thought Kekoa was going to die. Kekoa got stung by so many centipedes that his throat closed. I had to cut open his trachea for him to breathe. "Sapphire, stop and take a deep breath."

"All of us! We're going to die here." Sapphire's voice shrieks. "I'm never going to see my family ever again!"

"Sapphire. Stop," I yell. My voice cuts through her sobs. She collapses into my arms, shaking. I'm trapped, unsure of what to do. They all need me. The other girls might want to comfort her. "Come over, let's have a group hug," I say. Mia, Johana, and Audrey swish over and I open my arms to them. Mia tucks under my arm to stand close…mud to mud close. She wraps her arms tight around me. One by one, the others lean in too, heads resting against me. It feels like something I should capture in a photo—but this bond—it's built on fear, not something real or lasting.

Rain pelts us, the drops leave tiny craters on the water's surface. Like lives—they touch others, sending ripples that spread outward. Every death leaves a mark, a ripple that never fully goes away. What ripple will my death send through the people I care about? My family, for sure. Bumble, maybe. No one else.

This downpour will change the swamp. After five minutes, I can tell the water has risen in the swamp. Already, fewer islands connect. Our heads are down as we inch our way forward. We've lost vision of the rim. My arms shake from the drop in temperature. The altitude makes the air colder than at home.

"We're going to need to swim harder," I say. "Stay in line, always following the person in front of you. I'm going to swim last, so I can help anyone in trouble. This area of the swamp has more of a pull than where we were. If someone gets caught in the current, they'll be in danger."

We swim into a wider stream and the water pushes us toward the waterfall. The roar of the water crashing on the rocks far below pumps adrenaline through me. Even the color of the water has changed from green to brackish brown. "Is everyone okay? It's getting swifter, do not let it take you downstream," I call out, struggling to stroke to keep my mouth above the water. "Swim hard!"

After a few seconds, Mia says, "Okay."

We get to the other side of the current that swoops down toward the waterfall. The pressure is less. I pull up to an island. "Okay, let's rest," I say, panting.

Everyone huffs and puffs. The rain dissipates to a light sprinkle. I climb an Ohia tree on an island and can see the rim through the fog in the distance. We're making substantial progress. The rain will help us, if we stay out of the main current, but the temperature has dropped. Mia's whole body shakes when she sits on a rock.

"Come here. Let's hug and get warmer," I say. We're an octopus of arms stuck together with mud, but after a while, our teeth stop chattering. "Okay, we're on the home stretch. We're all going to make it and remember this amazing feat," I say.

After another hour of swimming, I see the tree line. Grass and ferns grow next to the edge. At last, we crawl up onto the rocky shelf, exhausted. My body wants to rest, while my stomach screams for food, and my mouth is cardboard. I wish I didn't have to lead. Everyone looks to me—they need me. Maybe it's just my lack of confidence that keeps me down.

"How far are we from the pickup area?" Mia asks. Her movements are slow. She's beat.

"Less than a mile. We walk along the ridge." I study the map on my watchcom.

The girls and I sprawl out on the crumbly rock to catch our breath. They're too tired to walk farther than necessary. "Stay here. I'm going to scout around and find the best way to the pickup point," I say.

"Take your time," Audrey says, curled on the ground.

The ridge inclines. Though the soil is crumbly, I scramble to the top. The view infuses me with a longing to be home. Though darkness threatens, the ocean spreads out in the distance beyond the riveting deep canyons. Ahead and to my left, a helicopter buzzes down to a clearing that must be our pickup area. Who else is already there? We can follow the edge of the swamp until it's time to cut west to the clearing. Trekking diagonally through the brush will encumber us.

Clouds hide the stars. I shiver. Why does Mia try to look like a man, but she seems soft and feminine when she looks at me and hugs me? My heart pounds onto my chest like the giant waterfall falling hundreds of feet to pound onto the canyon floor in Waimea Canyon, just below the swamp.

Darkness leaves only shadows where color was. By the time I return, the four girls are gone! I look around in the dark. *Is this the right place? Where are they?* My breath quickens. *Did someone take them? Did they leave without me? I don't think Mia would . . . She wouldn't leave me behind. Would she?*

CHAPTER FOURTEEN

Kana

I scan the area, desperate to find the girls. A splintered branch lies on the ground. Did one of them fight back?

If the rogue cadets wanted to kill the three women, they might throw them off one of the Waimea Canyon cliffs hundreds of feet to die upon impact. *Is murder really in their hearts?* A scream cuts through the air, and I sprint toward it off the path and through the brush and trees. Dry hale koa bean pods slap against my face as I run. *"Lord, protect them!"*

"Help!" I think it's Mia's voice.

"Shut up, you stinking Neverborn."

I peek behind a shrub.

Five men circle the four women, who are standing shoulder to shoulder. The girls' hands are bound. One cadet cuts at Mia's clothing with his knife, like a wolf plays with his prey. Others have their knives out too. The canyon cliff lies at the girls' backs.

"No one will ever know why the Neverborn women never came back." He laughs. "Guess they couldn't cut it."

Mia talks, but her voice is unintelligible. She takes a breath. "You don't have . . . "

"Shut up, all you lying thieves. We've heard what you've been up to," a cadet says with his jaw set.

The women say nothing, eyes wide with terror.

Who's been gas-lighting these guys? Panic shoots lightning into my veins. A small push over the ravine and the girls are dead. The pigs in the ravines would eat their bones before a helicopter would even find the remains, not that anyone would send one. I'm outnumbered—fighting them is suicide. One push, and we're over the edge.

I gather some stones. It's a long shot. They might laugh it off or worse. *Please, Lord, let this work.* If only I had my crossbow. I throw one stone, so it rustles limbs to the group's left. They turn. Then I pelt the guy closest to Mia with the roundest rock and duck behind a tree trunk.

"Ow!" He swears. "Who hit me?" An angry voice calls out and swears. "I'm gonna kill whoever or whatever it is." He tears around, looking behind shrubs.

What do I do? I scrutinize the rocks at my feet. A large moss-covered stone lies to my left. Maybe in this steam pot ecosystem, centipedes might hide under one. *God, please!* Two centipedes scatter as I overturn the rock. One is a foot long, thick as my thumb. Perfect. I step on its stinging head. I scoop up a pile of mud where the rock had been and roll the centipede into it, coating its writhing body in muck, and finish by wrapping it with a fern. The throw hits the guy in the shoulder, and I duck. The guy I hit yells, "Ow!" He swears.

"It's a ball of centipedes! Run!" says the guy. "Ow! Ow!" He screams as he runs, his swearing growing fainter.

They scramble away, feet slapping, twigs snapping, and laughter bursts out of me, catching me by surprise. It's like being back home, flinging ripe mangoes with Kekoa and Canyon. For a split second, I'm not in this nightmare—I'm back in the jungle.

Holding my breath, I wait. The sound of footsteps fades into the distance, the rustling of leaves quiet, and only the wind remains. I let out a sharp breath, the tension draining from my body. Then I see Mia, crumpled, trembling in the ferns. With her hands bound behind her, she struggles to roll over. The moon reflects on the tears streaking her face.

My laughter dies, replaced by a knot of sorrow. I pick her up off the ground, away from the centipedes. She shakes as I pull her up, but the shaking stops when I support her with my arm behind her back. Her head tucks into my neck.

"Kana."

She raises her head and looks around.

"They're gone," I whisper.

"How?"

I can't meet her gaze but carry her to a three-foot rock protruding from the ferns. Setting her down, I pull out the knife I keep hidden in my boot, to cut her free. Sapphire comes close, holding her wrists up. I cut her free, and she takes my knife to free the other two.

Mia takes my hands. Pulling herself with my hands to stand in front of me, she throws her arms around my neck, lays her head on my shoulder, and cries.

My heart pounds in my chest, loud enough for her to hear.

"How did you scare the guys away?" She asks.

I smile and hold her close. "I hit one with a centipede mixed in a ball of mud. They were terrified."

The moon is rising over the ocean below. I'll wait to show her.

"Kana. I prayed you'd come. Then I prayed you wouldn't. They were going to throw us all over the edge." Her body still shakes, but less.

My arms pull her tight. "God didn't let them."

"How can they be this murderous? How can they hate so much and treat people with such contempt?"

"Your enemy the devil prowls around like a roaring lion looking for someone to devour," I say.

"1 Peter 5:8. And they're the ones being devoured," she says.

I laugh. "Yep, they are. Devoured by hate and competition. Afraid someone else will get to base before them. Afraid they won't win. But someone's been feeding a bunch of lies to them about us." *Let this moment last forever.* Mia's heart beats next to mine.

I know the other women might be watching us, but I don't care. "Look at the moon over the ocean," I say. Light rims the clouds, with the moon playing hide and seek. Moonlight twinkling like fireflies spreads over the ocean, too.

"Wow," Mia says, turning to the ocean with her arm around my waist.

Sapphire, Audrey, and Johana join us, arms around each other's shoulders and ours. Our eyes feast on the sunset over the ocean, a few steps away from the cliff we might have all been thrown over.

"What a view from up here," Sapphire says in an ominous voice.

"Yeah," Johana says, "But I'm still shaking. I want a hug, too."

I laugh and open my arms for all four women.

We stand and find the path again. If they need to hug me to express their appreciation, I'm fine with that. We're family now. Will we all be scathed back at the base?

"Why would our officers say 'no rules'?" Mia asks. An air of desperation lines her voice. We walk on the road, but all of us keep looking around as if we're in the Vietnam War.

"Someone has an agenda," I say. I want to tell them about the hand bone I've hidden, but it would only scare them more.

We find the pickup location and get dropped by a copter back to base. As we enter the gym, General Shipley himself perches in an office chair behind a table, watching the check-in of cadets as they arrive. His eyes meet mine the moment we enter. We're still caked in swamp mud, smelling like the bog, and I can tell by the sneer on his face that he's not pleased to see me. He scans all the Neverborn women with an air of contempt. I see the last of the non-Neverborn cadets pulling themselves onto trucks with their duffel bags ready to go to the airport.

Shipley is waiting, but I turn and go to our barracks to shower and hide the bone. When I get to our room, Bumble sits on his bunk, his head hanging, shoulders rounded.

"Pete?" I ask, but know the answer already. My body tenses, ready for battle. Forget the Major or MANA. Red-hot anger pulses through my every vein. I almost hope someone will pick a fight with me. Murder times how many? A General who sets up an attitude of superiority staging discrimination. No rules. But I want to know about Pete.

Bumble tears up. He looks at me, saying more with one look than his lips could express in ten minutes. He's angry too, indignant. And grieving for Pete. He shakes his head a bit.

"Pete . . . " Bum blinks back tears. "Didn't make it." Bumble's head drops. "MANA wouldn't authorize care. Pete took his last breath right in front of me in the ER, waiting for approval for treatment." He clears his throat and looks around like we're in the enemy camp.

I sit and put my arm around him. *Lord, use this terrible death for good. Nail the General for not saving Pete.* I can't wrap my mind around this level of evil. Grabbing the first-aid kit, I tend to Bumble's cuts and then my own leg.

Still in a fog, I make my way down to the General for intake.

"Munson, how's it feel to be dead last?" Shipley's eyes glint with satisfaction, feeding off my supposed failure. "Your time is nine hours, thirty-three minutes, sixteen seconds. A record for taking the longest."

His contempt doesn't find a place in my self-worth to make me feel bad. I saved the lives of four women, including Mia. In God's eyes, I'm a hero.

"The other cadets and staff have gone. I'll have to drive you myself in the morning at 1000," Shipley says. His voice raises the hair on the back of my head. He leans back in his chair, a smirk twisting his lips, but his fingers drum on the table. The General doesn't like that I survived—that we all did—except Pete.

Once I get back to our room, Bum fills me in on the details of finding a ride to E.R. and then tells me again about having MANA called and them refusing treatment. He needs to talk about it. When he's done, I take a deep breath. "We have work to do, buddy. We're going to expose them."

Bumble's nod tells me he's on board. Before we leave, we need to check in any supplies we're not allowed to keep.

When we get to the checkout table behind the women in our group, Shipley stands behind the table with his arms folded, contention pulling on his face. We all check in the supplies in silence.

I sneak into the kitchen to talk to Bones. He's cleaning up the dinner mess. The aroma from the oven tells me Bones cooked up a beef roast for the General. He served beans to the cadets as their final meal, now left in dirty bowls by the dishwasher in heaps.

"Bones, the copter dumped the female Neverborns off in the middle of Alakai Swamp. Close to a waterfall," I say. "We guys got dropped close to the rim. All the non-Neverborns launched on the rim itself."

Bones looks up, surprise on his face. "Wait, what? Who got dropped off in the swamp?"

"Only the Neverborns. Everyone else got a rock drop. The helicopter landed, and the other cadets got out on land. We jumped into the swamp—the women in the stream by the edge. And there's more. I found human hand bones in the swamp."

The pupils in his eyes widen like he just figured something out.

"Bones, when cadets came back in past groups, were there fewer female Neverborns after the survival test?"

He nods. "Yes. None. The Neverborn females that came back with you were the only females I've ever seen that made it back. But sometimes, I'd already gone before they could have returned. I'm not supposed to be here, you know?" His voice sounds soft, barely louder than a whisper. He looks away and sighs. "Son, this has to end. I want you to take out the trash. The key is hanging next to the cooler on a nail."

He looks at me with a knowing look. "Everybody's trash gets put in the dumpster. Trash collectors come tomorrow morning. Sort through it tonight. See what you can find."

All the trash. From the General's trash can too, he means without saying.

He continues, "You don't have much time. Be careful."

"Our women weren't supposed to make it out of the swamp," I say.

"How did they?" he asks.

I finger my chin, thinking about the weight of saving the lives of all the Neverborn. "I helped them. We meandered around the edges of the tiny islands and then swam where we could." Tears threaten me. "Bones, Pete…a cadet punched him in the gut before we even got on the helicopter, probably rupturing his spleen and who knows what else. Bumble got a tourist to take them to the hospital in Waimea, but MANA wouldn't authorize care. He died."

Bones' fists curl. He swears with words new to me. "You get that _______!"

CHAPTER FIFTEEN

Mia

My fingers shake as I pack, haunted by replay after replay—the insults, the bindings, the march to the cliffs' edge. The fear we might have been raped and murdered—or thrown off to die on impact—still tears apart my insides. *God, thank you for bringing Kana in time. Please protect us.* I don't know where we'll go next. Bangkok? If the general wants us dead, what's stopping him from killing us and dumping us into the swamp? Psalm 91:11 pops into my mind. *"For he will command his angels concerning you to guard you in all your ways."*

I calm momentarily, but then my heart races into overdrive. *If only I could find Kana, and he would hug me again.* It's against the rules, but I find myself climbing the steps to his room. My hand hovers at the door. *What will he think of me creeping up here for comfort?* I turn to leave, only to meet him coming up the stairs. He almost stumbles when he sees me.

"Kana," I say, trying to sound casual, though my chest aches with the need to be close.

"Mia?" His voice shows surprise. "What's up? There's no more soup left."

"I . . . have some questions. Can we talk somewhere?" I swallow, hoping it sounds normal. He pauses and nods. "Yeah, let's go where the moon's out."

Outside, the compound's motion activated lights blaze, but he leads me into the dark woods.

"I feel safer out here with just us Neverborns," he says, his voice calm, almost serene.

"Safe?" I scoff, taking his arm. "Nothing about this place feels safe to me."

We stop at a log where moonlight threads through the trees. I lower myself to sit next to him but have to pull my arm away to sit. The silence becomes thick and awkward until I ask, "How did you learn all these skills?" My arm slides around his.

He hesitates. "Three women came to the Ascendancy Women's Clinic to abort their late-term baby boys. The abortionist delivered them alive and tucked them away in a hidden drawer. My 'mom,' the woman who chose me, found out and spent her days singing to me while I was hooked to a breathing machine. After a couple of weeks, she brought me home with a portable unit. I was with two other newborns and three couples who raised us together. Mom always said, even though I couldn't smile yet, my hand would reach for hers. She didn't leave for hours because I wouldn't let go of her pinkie." He smiles but gets serious. "I never got an identity chip. My birth mother doesn't even know I exist."

"She missed out," I say softly, patting his arm.

Kana turns toward me, hesitant. "What about your birth?"

I exhale, a long sigh escaping. "I was born in New Mexico, in a hot tub. A doula helped deliver me—someone my grandma knew. My birthmother wanted nothing to do with me. Gammy, my grandmother, bribed her with a car to keep me from being aborted. My father didn't want me either. He said I should go to Mexico and live without a chip. So, my grandparents raised me. Mom wouldn't even look at me."

"You had a grandfather?" Kana asks, his gaze dropping to the thin gold band on my finger.

"Yes, but he died of a heart attack five years ago. Diabetes." I stare at the band, remembering. "I miss him. He'd always put his arm around me and say, 'Little Peanut, we only have today. Make the most of it.' He always called me his little peanut." Sitting close to Kana, I remember Gampa's presence again, the safety of his arm around me. "Grandpa bought me this ring."

"You couldn't go to public school. Did your grandparents teach you?" Kana asks.

Kana's eyes flick up, but he avoids meeting mine. "In my community," he says, "there were three Neverborns. We were all raised by grandparents. They'd take turns teaching us, and on Thursdays, we'd play by the river. Fridays were cleaning days—we'd go from house to house, and end with a potluck and movie night at the Smiths. They had the biggest living room." I smile at the memory, the smell of popcorn in the air.

"Did you have friends your age?" His tone is wistful, like he didn't.

"Not really. The girls my age dropped out of school to work in the sex industry. Even older men would try to buy us. It was . . . horrible." I shudder, my hand tightening on his arm.

A gust of wind tousles my short hair. Bumble's voice cuts through the trees, "Mia, where'd you go?"

He pushes through the shrubs, his eyes landing on Kana beside me. "Hey, I worked up a sweat looking for you guys. Why'd you leave me out?" His tone holds a sharp edge. *Jealousy?*

"Mia had some questions. It's quieter out here," Kana says, shifting away from me.

Bumble snorts. "Quieter? The compound's a ghost town."

"I hate being inside when I can be outside," Kana replies, edging further away from me.

"Mia, got all your questions answered?" Bumble smirks, cleaning his teeth with his tongue. "Because I found some candy." He pulls out three chocolate bars, handing one to each of us.

I shake my head, giving it back. "No thanks, Bum. Sugar leads to diabetes." I stand, brushing off my pants. "See you tomorrow." I touch Kana's shoulder as I turn to go.

CHAPTER SIXTEEN

Kana

Embarrassment washes over me. Bumble caught Mia and me talking in the woods as if I could ever pull off a romantic date. *Maybe it's best that he came. I've got other things to deal with—like a date with the trash.*

Sneaking through trash reminds me of sneaking out with my brothers to zipline in the dark when we were fifteen. **It was** exciting doing something forbidden. Trees blurred past, shadowed in moonlight, faster than I could track them. After landing on the far side of the ravine, I'd stand, disoriented, struggling to find my footing. I never relaxed until we made it back home. But this? This feels worse. People want us dead, but I can't even figure out who, or why. My heart slaps against my ribs, my head screaming at me to make sense of everything.

I sneak out to the trash bin and pull out one trash bag after another, the stink curling in my nose. It takes three trips to load all the garbage bags into the kitchen cooler. My brain won't stop thinking about the General.

Why would he want us dead? *God, how can I find out?*

In the morning, I'm still looking through the trash. Something catches my eye—an envelope, large enough to hold the bones I found and some of the papers I want to include in my package to Dad. I sure hope he can make sense of it. I can't call Dad, but I write down everything I know and tuck the note into the envelope. Sorting through the remaining papers, I find a list of guardians for cadets under eighteen. Pete's father—Jed Peterson, 2331 Geneva Street, Washington D.C. My stomach drops. Jed deserves to know the truth about his son, so I memorize the address.

Bones stumbles in at 0600, his skin pale beneath purple eyes. He eyes my stash of informative papers and the envelope.

"Bones, you don't look very good."

"I'll live," he groans, his eyebrows wild and splayed like a bird's wings. "Should've been gone yesterday." He slumps into a chair, pulling out his tablet to complete the end-of-campaign report. I've never seen him look this defeated.

I think about my folks and how I'm leaving for Thailand soon—maybe for good. Dad's eyes used to light up when I figured out how to rebuild an engine or was able to help him with a computer problem, and Mom never stopped smothering me with love. I miss them so much it hurts. Sorrow sweeps through me like a stifling wind.

A door slams in the dining room. My heart jumps. I shove the garbage bag with the records into the crumbly oven, scrubbing the appliances like I belong here.It's just Bumble, though, looking for breakfast. He pulls a pizza box out of the cooler. Some cadets must have left it behind. While he microwaves it, the smells of cheese and pepperoni fill the air.

I sit on the floor, sorting through papers from one bag after another. Nothing stands out—just lists and schedules—until I find a printout of all the cadets, including the Neverborns. My pulse quickens. I stuff it into the large manilla envelope I'd found, scrawling Dad's name and address on the front. He'll know what to do.

After tossing the last bag into the dumpster, I keep an eye out for the General's Porsche. Only the roosters crow in the dawn air. I slip into our room to hide the package.

Bumble's strumming my guitar.

"What are you trying to play?" I yawn.

"That song you sang to us, 'You Make All Things Beautiful in Your Time,'" he says, plucking a wrong chord as he sings.

I show him the right chord and sing a few lines. He hands the guitar over, his eyes disappointed. "Aw, forget it," he mumbles. His shoulders slump. "How do you hold on to hope?" His voice cracks. "Pete died in my arms yesterday. How can a good God let that happen?"

I rub his shoulder, sensing he needs the comfort. "Pete's out of pain now." *God—don't let this be for nothing.* I sit on Bumble's bunk hoping Pete had given his life to Christ and now is in the presence of the Almighty.

"Bumble, you did your best. You got him to safety."

Bum shakes his head. "Safety?" His voice wavers. "MANA killed him the moment they denied him medical care."

I rub my face with my hands. *Pete's death claws at my heart, too. It's wrong. He didn't deserve to die like that.*

"What's MANA planning for us?" Bumble's voice vibrates with grief.

I stare at the wall, my chest tight. "When we got back last night, General Shipley looked at me—like he hated me. Then he turned and walked away. I think . . . I think he meant for all of us to die."

Bum stays, but I go to the cafeteria for breakfast. I turn my attention to Bones, organizing his spices, and making notes on a scratchpad.

"Bones, can you take a big envelope to the post office for me?"

He glares at me with his bloodshot eyes and red nose.

"No way, kid. Don't drag me into this. I'm supposed to be gone before you Neverborns get back from your survival trek. The Neverborns always come back last. Now I know why. I hid my car, so the General wouldn't know I'm still here." His voice is raw with exhaustion. "Just stay out of it."

"Where is everyone?" I ask. "I know the cadets, except the Neverborns, got back from the survival test earlier than we did. They all got on buses and went to the airport. But where are the staff?"

"They're all ordered to be gone by the time you return," Bone's forehead wrinkles.

"Why?"

"That's the million-dollar question." His eyes grow distant. "I'm only here to see you made it out of the swamp." He wipes his nose. "Every time I come back to a new group, the cooler's barely touched. Either they drag themselves back and aren't hungry, or . . ."

My heart races. He doesn't finish his sentence.

"I don't know what to do with the human hand I found? I'm sending it to Dad because I don't have time to figure it out."

Bones grabs my arm, eyes deadly serious.

"Whatever you do, keep it far from the General."

After he leaves, I pray. I have to stand up to this somehow. I shove the envelope and package under my shirt and jog toward the geodesic dome—like a giant golf ball by the highway—then push on to a Waimea Canyon lookout. The sun breaks through the clouds, casting the canyon in golden hues. A couple of tourists are already there, taking pictures from the rail. It takes a moment to catch my breath while I take in the vastness of the great canyon with its orange and brown hues dipping thousands of feet down to the canyon floor.

I approach the middle-aged couple. The man's gray eyebrows bush out like bamboo shoots, and his kind eyes wrinkle when he smiles.

"Hi, where are you from?" he asks gently.

"Kauai. But I'm in the military now, MANA. Name's Kana."

"I'm Brendon, and this is Natalie. We're from California," he says. "I think God wants me to talk to you. Are you okay?"

"No. I'm not." I hold out the package to Dad and letter addressed to Pete's father. "I think someone's trying to kill us—Neverborns. We're not supposed to survive." I explain my situation.

Brendon listens, his eyes widening. His wife covers her mouth, horrified.

"Can you take these to the post office?"

He takes the mail.

Fingering the letter still in his hand, I say, "Please send this one to Pete's father, a Neverborn who died because of MANA. His parents deserve to know." I touch the manilla package. "This one is to my dad."

Brendon grips my shoulder, his eyes wet with emotion. "Sure, and we'll be praying for you."

"Thanks," I murmur, turning away before my tears can fall. *Wow, God, it's like you sent them.*

CHAPTER SEVENTEEN

Kana

The compound feels sealed off from the world, its stillness unnerving, like a tomb. We file into the conference room, faces drawn, avoiding each other's eyes. Neverborns take their seats, gathering close.

General Shipley swaggers in, his stocky frame barely contained by his belt—something the Navy would've never tolerated. He doesn't call Peterson's name at roll call. He knows. Pete's watchcom would have stopped reporting his vitals.

"Cadets," Shipley begins, his bass voice rumbling, "thanks to your outstanding skills and training, you're all selected for a secret mission . . . You must tell no one, not even your mother or lover, about where you're going, nor give anyone any details about your assignment, before, during, or after the mission. Is that understood?" The crew half-heartedly says, "Sir, yes, sir." Mia's voice cuts through the reluctant chorus. She's sitting just behind me—I hadn't noticed her come in. It's hard to concentrate on Shipley's words when I'm drawn like a magnet to her.

"You're going to Thailand," the General continues. "From there, you'll infiltrate POW camps on the west side of Thailand. Bombs are sometimes implanted without the prisoner's knowledge, and then they're released. They'll blow up—along with everyone near them, usually in hospitals. Or, if they're released, it's because they've been brainwashed. So, make sure you're not one of them." He starts to smile but erases it.

Shipley looks at his feet, shuffles, and continues, "You'll be going behind enemy lines. Your first phase is to learn the language. You'll spend three weeks in Bangkok with a Thai language teacher before infiltrating inland, posing as tourists. Because being American tourists could be dangerous, you'll be Canadian tourists, but you'll still have your MANA chips."

Bumble shoots to his feet. "Sir, are you sending us to die?" His voice cracks, but his fists stay clenched, shoulders rigid.

Shipley clears his throat and takes a deep breath. "Cadet, this is how you become a hero. If you die along the way, your country will remember you as a hero." There's a salesman-like sound to his voice.

Hero. The word echoes as if in an empty cave. *Pete won't be remembered as a hero. Just another casualty—another victim in this endless cycle of injustice.*

"Hero?" Montana's quiet scoff slices through the murmurs. Bumble blows a raspberry, and the others grunt in disbelief. The women sit like statues, their faces drained of color.

The General slaps the side of his leg with his hand, anger in his eyes. "Pack up. Clean your rooms. Have the kitchen mopped and the bathrooms spotless. Be ready to roll at 1300."

"Sir, yes sir," we all chant.

He strides toward the door stiff and hurries like we're an angry beehive he wants to leave behind.

Thailand! Our suicide mission. But what if we could save these POWs? Nothing in life must be more horrific than being a POW. Starved, beaten, possibly tortured, and then blown up in a way that takes other innocent people with you. My heart sinks. Some of these POWs are Neverborns.

"Hey, let's go," Bumble says to me. "You've turned into a zombie all of a sudden."

I turn to look at him. *What if Bumble gets taken prisoner? Would I risk my life to save him? Or Mia? Absolutely.*

The group talks among themselves. I hear, "They're running us off a cliff and pretending we'll be heroes!"

"This is garbage!" Montana says. Others swear.

"MANA, or perhaps just the General, might think he's sending us to our deaths. What if we really do rescue POWs?" My chest swells with a sense of a higher calling as I ask God about it. *Do you want me to try to find the POW camp?* I feel peace about the idea. *Wow, this is crazy.*

Fear freezes the faces of my tribe. I see it in the tension taking over. All their lives, they've been victims of the lie. They're Neverborns, with no value—impotent. They leave the room talking in whispers. Mia's face, too, has defeat written all over it.

Bumble stands by me, "Come on, Kana."

We go to our barracks, and I search on my watchcom and check to see if a POW camp actually exists in Thailand. No POW camps are public knowledge. We don't even know if there are any in Thailand.

We pack and are ready before our departure time. The reader board specifies we ride in bus C down to the airport.

I check out the bus. It's the oldest in the fleet. The oil is clean and full, and the water level is adequate in the radiator. A sense of dread fills me, though. Why don't I trust this beast? I stuff my duffel bag under the seat and sit behind the driver's seat.

I sense Mia coming toward the bus before I see her. She sits just behind me in the second seat, her presence lighting up the bus. "Kana, here's extra water." She hands me a water bottle.

"Thanks!" I'm warmed by her choice to sit close to me and her gift of water. Is she afraid? Her face looks resolute.

Bumble comes and sits next to her. Darn. He chats her up.

Mia's eyes find me, disappointment covering her face.

Everyone brings their duffel bags onto the bus and stashes them next to them on their bench seat. This bus doesn't have seat belts or air bags in case of an accident. No one talks much. Most sit by themselves and glue their eyes to their phones or watchcoms.

General Shipley himself comes aboard, glances to see that we're all present, and sits in the driver's seat with a warm smile. He closes the door. "Soldiers, ready for the next adventure?" he asks warmly.

No one responds. A sense of rebellion and mistrust wells up in me. I should pray, but I don't want to right now. The bus creaks and moans down the mountain. *We're flying to Thailand—what else could go wrong?*

Shipley's warmth disappears when no one responds to his question. It feels like the war has moved to the bus.

The tuna sandwich I packed sits beside me in a bag smelling. We packed lunches since all of us would check into the airline around three, but the idea of food turns my stomach.

The sun charges overhead, thickening the heat in the air already. We rumble down the road, jostling closer to the lookout where I'd dropped the mail earlier. Without warning, Shipley slows as the road nears a break in the bushes, opening to the vast Waimea canyon with plummeting walls and only a guard rail between the canyon cliff and the road. Suddenly, he yanks the bus toward the cliff, jerks the door open, and hurls himself out, rolling across the road's edge. One second he's there—then he's gone.

The bus jostles onto the gravel, barreling toward the cliff's edge. I lunge for the wheel, wrenching it back toward the road. The bus scrapes the guardrail. *Is it too late? Will the back wheels go over the edge?* I oversteer, careening into the bushes on the opposite side and scratching along the shrubs. If I hadn't grabbed the wheel, life would be over for all of us. I slam on the brakes—nothing. The pedal goes slack. Jerking the wheel again, I drag the bus back onto the road, away from the clawing bushes. The back tires bounce, skidding until they hit the pavement.

My heart's in my throat as we pick up speed. "Oh, no," I gasp, struggling to stay steady. Swerving from side to side, I shift into second gear. A car passes in the opposite lane, forcing me to straighten out, and the bus picks up speed. Each wild veer slams us from side to side, the tires screeching, passengers screaming.

I need to find an incline.

Seeing the road go downhill ahead, I veer to the right, plowing through a thicket of shrubs and small trees. The trees scrape and crack against the undercarriage, each hit jarring my grip. I yank on the wheel to keep from flying off the seat as we lurch over rocks and ruts. Thick trees close in on both sides, their branches whipping the windows and front. I pull the emergency brake with all my strength. It squeals but only slows us slightly.

The road dips ahead, steeper than before. If I don't stop this thing now, we're finished. I jerk the wheel again, aiming for any bushes and saplings that might slow us down. With every hit, the bus bucks, and I wrestle the wheel to keep from colliding head-on with a larger tree.

Finally, the speed drops. I brace myself and steer into a sturdy tree, deciding it's the only way. Glass shatters on impact. I'm thrown forward, slammed against the dash. Cracking of limbs and the crunching sounds of metal imploding fills the air. The bus settles, silent.

Behind me, terrified screams fade into stunned shock, chilling my blood.

Everyone screams at me at once. I stand and put my hand up. "Is everyone okay?"

All the cadets look fine. I hold up my hands in a "T" for "time-out" and say, "Brakes are gone—maybe cut. But we're safe now."

"Why did Shipley bail?" Bumble asks.

One guy clutches his chest. Another pulls his hands to his head. One opens her window and retches.

"I don't know. Maybe he knew about the brakes. Maybe he cut them and planned to jump, maybe he just wanted to live," I say and sink back onto the driver's seat, spent.

Bumble's arm is slung around Mia, and she tucks into his shoulder—willingly.

Did I miss my chance?

"How do we get to the airport now?" Bum asks after the dust settles.

Pulling out my phone, I say, "I have contacts on the island. This is where I live."

"Oh, yeah," Bumble says with delight in his voice.

I dial Dad. "Dad … Kana. I'm on Kauai at a training camp by Waimea Canyon. Can you bring the pickup and give eight of us rides to the airport? We're on State Highway 550, about fifteen minutes south of the Geodesic Dome."

Dad stammers. "Kana. Son." In a moment he says, "Sure. I'll be right there."

Everyone heard my words. Their eyes follow my hand as I pocket my phone. My gut churns. *What now?*

"Okay. Dad is about forty-five minutes away. The bus will become a tinder box in this sun. We're best off to get our duffel bags and hike back to the road, where he'll pick us up."

"Aren't you going to call base?" Montana asks.

"No," I say. "No one is there."

"I think this is another attempt to kill us," Audrey says in a rushed, panicky voice.

All the Neverborns wait as I gather my thoughts and say, "You might be right."

I pull out my duffel bag from under the seat. Others are already disembarking with theirs.

Cars slow and pass, staring at the eight uniformed cadets in the middle of nowhere sitting by the side of the road in the sun without a vehicle in sight. I'm grateful for the water Mia brought me.

Dad's arms envelop me the second he steps out of the truck, holding me tighter than ever. "I missed you, Son," he says, his voice breaking.

I nod, my throat too tight to respond.

He laughs and admires my muscles.

"Mia, come sit with me in the cab," I say, hoping she will.

Dad's mouth drops lower than sea level. "Son, nicely done!"

"Yeah, well, I had to talk to girls. I couldn't just ignore them my whole life."

"Can I sit up front too? Maybe Mia could sit on my lap?" Bumble grins.

"No!" both Dad and I say in unison.

I introduce Dad to everyone, and we head down the road. Mia is in the middle with Dad and me as we catch up on what's been happening. I feel bad she's in the middle. "I just sent you a package," I say.

"A package?"

"Yeah, and I'm texting you Jed Peterson's address and phone number. Please call him. He'll catch you up on our dilemma." I punch the address and phone number into his phone from memory. If I explain the hand-bone to Dad here, Mia will be more frightened than ever.

Dad nods and says, "Son, we're leaving the compound, buying a house in Lihue or Kalaheo. There's no . . . " He blinks away his watering eyes. "I'll miss you so much, Son. You're grown, and now you're leaving." He reaches across Mia to pat my knee. "It's been an amazing ride."

We're all silent for a few moments. Much is said even with no words . . . I pat his knee, too.

Dad turns to Mia, "What passion has God given you to make the world a better place?"

Her countenance warms. "I've studied nutrition and come up with a lot of healthy recipes. I'd like to develop an online presence and offer recipes, links to get free seeds to grow vegetables, and podcasts about health—all in Spanish. The diet in Mexico leaves the country with diabetes because they're eating the all-American diet of junk. Their rate of heart disease and nutritional deficits from the lack of vegetables, fruits, and beans have soared since abandoning their traditional foods."

Dad grins and looks at her. "What a wonderful gift for these people to offer them a way to be healthy and not be in pain and die early from heart disease and the complications of diabetes."

Mia takes a quick breath, and her eyebrows raise. She opens the gate to her heart and talks about her trips to Mexico to visit her grandparents and cousins there. The poverty and disease left an enormous impact on her. I could see her determination to help and her love for people.

With one question, he learned more about Mia than I had in the whole time I've known her.

The truck pulls up to the Lihue Airport curb. Everyone gets out. I dread this moment and yet cherish it. Dad tucks something into my shirt pocket—a familiar gesture, probably money. But this time, it weighs heavy, like it's not just cash, but the weight of everything unsaid. I wrap my arms around him for one last hug, holding on longer than I should. Will I see him again? He's in his early eighties. I tell myself not to cry, especially in front of Mia. But seeing Dad makes it hard. Our foreheads touch Hawaiian style, and I breathe in his air before turning away. His truck rolls off amid the cacophony of other vehicles pulling in and out. *My dad. My world, driving away.*

We check our bags, not surprised that no one has shown up to give us our tickets. At the Hawaiian Airlines desk, the attendant looks confused. Tapping her long nails painted with flowers, she calls base. No one answers. She checks her records and calls someone else, seeing that all the other cadets have authorized tickets.

Turning around as she talks, she scans the line and announces we have authorization. She prints out tickets for us.

I set my phone and watchcom on the tray with my shoes to get through security. My nerves are on hyperalert, wondering why the General didn't have ticket authorizations set. *Did he plan on us dying before we got here? What if we'd been injured? Would he come and finish us off?*

"Ice up, Gangster," Bumble says as he play-punches my arm.

"Gangster?" I study his face.

"It's just an expression. We're going to get some refreshment." He turns to Mia. "Want an iced latte? Or a mango-pineapple-coconut smoothie? The coffee shop's right over there." He points ahead.

She glances at me with a whisper of puzzlement on her face. "Sure." Mia follows him.

"See you at the gate," I say, wishing my voice hadn't carried my disappointment. *Why hadn't I thought of getting her a drink?*

Half our tribe arrives with me at the gate empty-handed. *Why didn't I stop to get a snack?* My stomach bounces around like a ping-pong ball in play. *I'm leaving my island.*

Only my brother Canyon and his parents are at our compound now. It's safer for Dad and Mom to be in town and not have a direct link to me, but my stomach rolls. *My childhood has passed, never to return.*

Once we breathe into the infection tester and are waved through, we stand as the moving breezeway floor carries us to the plane. I rub my stomach, nauseous. Our plane is a half-hour late, but we're booked. My middle seat sits between two men with broad shoulders, wearing masks over their mouths. At least, I don't think the plane will crash. MANA wouldn't kill a bunch of civilians just to eliminate us. They'll find another way.

My introvert hole sucks me inside myself as I buckle in, trying to be small. My shoulders touch my seatmate's. Bumble's voice rises above the noise of people opening and closing the overhead compartments and those chattering with their new neighbors. *Wouldn't you know it? He's seated by Mia? How did he pull that off?*

My stomach sinks to a new low, somewhere between my feet and the ground. The engines power up like a line-up of beater cars getting ready to crash into each other at the demolition derby Dad took us to when we boys were twelve. If only I could stand and disembark. Tears threaten me. *Mom. Dad. Kekoa. I even miss Canyon. They know me. No one else gets me.*

As I buckle in, my stomach tightens. It's not just the thought of leaving home—it's this feeling, gnawing at the edges of my mind, that something's wrong. So wrong. I glance over at Bumble and Mia in the middle section, curious. Are they pretending it's all okay?

The jets roar, and my body slams against the seat. My breath catches as the plane surges forward. Every cell in me screams to disembark, to run—but I'm trapped, pinned by the weight of my fears and the pressure pushing me deeper into the seat. Just like that, we're airborne, tipping back, digging into the air to climb higher and higher. The burly guy next to me blocks my view of Kauai.

My breathing speeds up. Kauai's mighty mountains are but a memory. Tension fingers up my neck and through my head. The government is fulfilling my birth mother's wish. Death awaits me. My head dips to my chest, pretending to sleep, pretending to live, pretending I'll have a life. Not just me. Mia, Bumble, and the others. Maybe the General did Pete a favor. He killed him off early. Now Pete won't have to go through that which awaits us. Imprisonment by the enemy? Will this be where we die—on some battlefield in a foreign land? I can almost hear the whispers of death trailing after us, waiting. Germ warfare—soldiers rotting from the inside out. The images flood my mind, of bodies torn apart by sickness, drowning in their own blood and bile. Slow, painful deaths where your liver and kidneys shut down, then your bowels rot. Finally, your lungs fill with fluid, and you drown in your mucus gasping, clawing at your throat frantically until you don't. *God, what are you doing dumping me into a war?*

CHAPTER EIGHTEEN

General Edward Shipley

Shipley's fingers tap on his watchcom as his eyes scan the health reports. Eight cadets on that bus—none of them dead. Not a single fatality. Only elevated heart rates. No wounds. No fireball at the bottom of the canyon like he'd planned.

His jaw clenches, and a sharp pang in his chest hurts as his heart rate spikes—another alarm on his wrist. He dismisses it. Kana sat behind him; he'd pin it on the kid. An entry in the log— *cadet error, brake fluid not checked.* Just another rookie mistake. But how had they survived?

He trudges through the dense underbrush for twenty minutes until he reaches the hidden motorcycle beneath the Hale Koa bush. The weight of sweat soaks his shirt. The heaviness of his failure soaks up his confidence. *Cockroaches, he thinks. These Neverborns are impossible to kill.*

Back at base, he launches the drone, squinting at the screen. There it is—the bus, off the road in the trees, where it would have rolled right into the canyon if those blasted kids had left it alone. The sight twists his gut. *The bus didn't crash.* These idiot kids were cocky or lucky. Either way, they'd dodged him. Again.

"Damn them!" Shipley snarls, turning up the air conditioning.

When he gets home, he grabs the bottle of Scotch. He pours a glass, the cool burn dulling the edge of his anger.

His hand hovers over his watchcom. He has a backup plan. As always. He punches in a call to his ace—Uhane.

"A million dollars," Shipley says coolly. "Take care of eight cadets by the canyon. Drug them, push them off, and tell me where."

A pause. Shipley hears the faint clinking of glasses and background noise from wherever Uhane is. "Eight kids, only a million? No way. Five mil or no deal."

Shipley grits his teeth. *Five million.* But if those kids get to the airport without tickets, people will start asking questions. And if anyone discovers the bodies in Alaka'i swamp or reports Pete's death . . . *No,* prison isn't an option. Not for him. His life, his career—it all hangs in the balance.

"Fine. Five million," Shipley hisses, his hand tightening the grip on his drink. "But do it now, before they get a ride."

"Half up front," Uhane replies, his voice steady. "In cash. I don't lift a finger without it."

Shipley's watchcom beeps again, another health warning. His pulse pounds in his temples. "I don't have millions sitting around my house! The kids are moving now!"

"Your problem, General," Uhane says. The sound of him sipping a drink comes over the phone. "Let me know when you have the cash."

As Shipley mutters curses under his breath, the drone feed flickers. A pickup truck stops at the highway, and the cadets pile into the back, none of them bleeding. None of them even limp. His stomach twists further. They'll be halfway to the airport before Uhane can even get there.

"Forget it!" Shipley snaps, ending the call. His hand trembles as he pours another glass of Scotch.

There is nothing to do but sell them to the Chinese once they reach Thailand. *Let someone else clean up this mess.* He downs the drink, with cold fury twisting in his gut. The Neverborns outwitted him today, but their luck has run out.

Thailand awaits. He had connections in Thailand. The Neverborns won't escape again.

CHAPTER NINETEEN

Kana

A salad bowl of languages, noises, and people fills the bustling Bangkok airport. A pair of teens walk hand in hand, their top-of-the-line backpacks slung over pristine, air-conditioned shirts. Next to them, an old man in rags drags a worn canvas bag over one shoulder. Hundreds pass by every second under the domed roof, beyond which manicured palm trees and Buddha statues catch my eye.

"Move it, Kana," Bumble says behind me.

I blink, realizing I've stopped. The air clings to my skin—moist and hot. I take in the massive beams arcing up like a cathedral, the spider-leg-like protrusions reaching out into the airfield where planes unload passengers, only to be restored for their next journey.

Bumble passes me and leads the way to baggage claim, weaving through the crowd like he's done it a hundred times. I follow, but I can't keep my eyes in front of me—there's too much to take in. Storefronts, restaurants, people, statues, advertisements. It's overwhelming.

Once we reach the escalator, men approach us, their voices persistent. "I take you. Come." "I be your tour guide."

I hesitate, but Mia grabs my arm and pulls me away. "Stay with us. You don't want to get lost here," she says, her voice tight.

She's right. China uses germ warfare in high-traffic locations like this. We should have worn masks, especially with these crowds. We wait at baggage claim, side by side with the same people who were packed into the plane with us for the last eight hours.

Our luggage rolls down the belt, and a reader announces our names as each suitcase passes the scanner. Mia stands next to me, her expression unreadable, as if waiting for direction. Bumble and Montana join us.

Alex steps forward, breaking the tense silence. "Okay, no one from MANA showed. Let's find out where headquarters are."

"Sure," I say, nodding along with the others.

Mia glances at me, and Bumble places a hand on her shoulder. We follow Alex down the escalator to the chaotic buzz of honking horns and battling cars fighting for curb space.

The sticky air outside smells of fuel and something sour, like garbage left too long in the sun. I raise my hand to hail a taxi. The clouds and thick atmosphere remind me of home, but a military truck, parked fifty yards away, catches my attention. An officer jumps out, studying a device in his hand before pointing at us. He shouts at his men, all armed, waving them in our direction.

Alex stops, dropping his duffle bag. "Who's got money for a taxi?"

"Go!" I yell, the word tearing out of me. "We're being hunted!"

"What?" Alex looks at me, incredulous.

A taxi screeches up to the curb next to us. "Get in!" I shout.

Mia and Bumble scramble into the back seat of an old Camry, their duffels burying their faces. I hop in last, hugging mine.

"What's the hurry?" Alex says.

"Look!" I point toward the soldiers, who are closing in. Alex shrugs, as if there's no real threat. The others still act like we're tourists here to sightsee.

The driver hits the gas, and I barely close the door in time as we swerve into traffic. I look back through the rear window just in time to see the others raising their hands, surrendering to the soldiers. Guns are leveled at their heads. My stomach twists in a knot.

"MANA headquarters," Bumble says to the driver, his voice cracking.

The driver glances back at him, saying something in rapid Thai. When we don't respond, he tries again. "American?"

"Yes," Bumble says. "Do you speak English?"

"Lek thi," the driver replies.

We'll need to learn the language, and fast.

Bumble writes "MANA" on a notepad and shows the driver, who shakes his head like we're idiots for coming here unprepared. Then, without another word, he punches the gas, weaving through traffic like he's being chased by a swarm of angry bees.

Outside, Bangkok blurs past—mobs of colorful clothes, towering buildings, signs, and banners in a language we don't understand. I long for the stillness of a beach, the calm of gentle waves lapping at the shore, but all I have now is chaos.

I bury my face in my hands. *Did Shipley tip off the soldiers? Did he plan this, hoping we'd be caught as soon as we landed? My gut feels like I should have done something to protect the other cadets, but what?* I want to cry.

"Bumble, I don't think we should go to MANA," I stammer. "Didn't you see what just happened? Shipley's got us marked. They're tracing us."

"We've got to," Bumble says, though he sounds uncertain. "Shipley can't run the whole MANA operation. Someone here must have some sense. We need our unit."

"Bumble, no." My head pounds, fear gnawing at the edges of my thoughts. Mia's face is pale, her eyes wide, frozen in shock.

The driver pulls up in front of a stone building flying both the Thai and American flags. It's new, the structure built from recycled plastic bricks with impressive technology.

The cab driver holds out his hand, and Bumble hands him some money. The man pockets it but holds his hand out again. We're being ripped off. I hand him twenty more, and he waves us off. We climb out and line up on the steps, our duffle bags slung over our shoulders.

"This might be a trap," I say. "MANA might want to finish us off."

Bumble shakes his head. "The General's crazy, but not that crazy."

Bum steps forward to a security booth where a short Thai woman in uniform sits, her black hair tied back. She scans his wrist, her expression neutral until something on her screen catches her attention. Her eyes widen. "Chip deactivated. Which means . . ." she mutters to herself slow enough in Thai for me to understand. The woman looks around for a security guard.

"Bumble, we're about to get arrested," I whisper.

"For what?" he asks, bewildered. "The airport thing was a mistake."

I don't answer. Instead, I grab Mia's arm. "Run."

Without waiting, I take off down the busy street. Mia follows, her duffle bag bouncing on her shoulder. Behind us, the woman's scream cuts through the air like a siren.

"Wait for me!" Bumble yells, his footsteps pound the pavement behind us.

We duck into an alley, dodging trash and debris, until we find a dumpster to crouch behind. Breathless, we collapse, sitting on our duffels.

"I can't believe this," Bumble says between gasps. "The General must have set us up. That security guard—she thought I was a terrorist!"

"We have to take off our watchcoms," I say, yanking mine off my wrist.

"Take them off?" Mia sounds shocked.

"Yes! Shipley's tracking us through them. Now."

"No, just turn them off," Bumble argues, fiddling with his watchcom. "There's no tracker if the watch is off."

"I don't know." My fingers twitch with uncertainty. What if there's a hidden tracker? I throw mine into the trash bin. Bumble follows suit.

Bumble groans, puffing out his chest. "We're in Thailand now. Chips aren't required here. We'll be fine. Anyone want to check out Thailand with me?"

Mia glances at me, unsure. I think she must have thrown hers in too, but I didn't see her toss it.

I grit my teeth. Montana, Alex, Audry, Johana, Sapphire— they're POWs now. Will they survive? Will a bomb tear them apart from the inside? "We're not free until we know if our mission is legit. I'm not leaving them to die."

Mia places a hand on my arm. "I'm with you."

Bumble grumbles. "Yeah, me too."

I pull them into a tight embrace, something shifting in my chest. We're a team. We love each other.

"Hey, there's a fire escape ladder. Let's climb and see if anyone comes after our watchcoms," I say and stash my duffel in a corner. Mia and Bum do the same and follow me. It's too far up for Mia to reach, so I put her on my shoulders, and she scrambles up first. Bum pulls over a trash can.

"Hey, buddy, hold this can still," he says and uses me to stabilize himself to stand on it. He jumps up and swings on the bottom rung.

"Come on, go Bum," I say, not sure he's going to be able to climb from a hanging position, but he does.

I run and jump off the wall next to the ladder to give me the height I need to catch it. When all three of us are on the roof, a military truck stops at the end of the alley. Troops with guns storm the alley, kicking over trash cans. An officer holds a scanner in his hand. He stops at the dumpster that holds our watchcoms. Though he's speaking in Thai, it's easy to figure out what he's saying. I see soldiers opening it up and crawling in. Others laugh at their plight. Mia, Bum, and I can hardly keep our laughter quiet, but being heard would mean capture or death. Their laughter continues for a while, until the officer gives a command, and the soldiers in the trash dumpster get out. The remaining soldiers search the rest of the alley. What if they see us?

The roof has no hiding places. We lay still, listening, but none of the soldiers climb to the roof. The laughter ends and the truck drives away. We're all dripping with sweat. Our hearts can stop going a hundred miles an hour. For now, anyway. We climb down, but Bum insists on catching Mia as she drops from the ladder.

139

CHAPTER TWENTY

Kana

The city transforms as the sun dips below the horizon, neon lights splashing across the streets in a rainbow of colors. Women in high heels and seductive clothes line the sidewalks, calling out in Thai.

"Hey, big boy, come," one says in broken English as we stroll down the foreign street.

"Ignore her," Bumble mutters.

Before I can react, the woman reaches for me, her fingernails painted red and orange like flames. She stands too close, her breath brushing my neck. My skin prickles with chicken skin. What does she want?

Bumble hooks his arm in mine and pulls me away. Mia laughs beside us, her eyes sparkling with amusement.

We pass sleek, modern buildings—21st-century architecture with clean lines shimmering gold, bronze, and silver. AI-designed murals splash vibrant colors, but the structures feel cold and functional, built from high-tech plastic. A block later, a Buddha statue rests on the porch of a rundown brick building, silent amidst the chaos.

The streets are alive with lights and stumbling figures, drunk or high, weaving through the confusion. Suddenly, a convoy of armed trucks rolls by. The crowds vanish. Only the elderly remain—hunched in the shadows as the rest of the people scurry away. Why is everyone disappearing?

The trucks crawl along, soldiers in the back peering out, their faces cold and emotionless. Bumble stiffens beside me, his grip on my arm tightening. Without a word, he steers us into a nearby jewelry store. Mia slips in behind us. The other customers huddle near the windows, whispering in Thai, eyes pulled toward the street.

I approach the clerk behind a glass counter lined with wedding rings.

"Why does everyone hide when the trucks pass?"

He stares at me like I've asked the obvious. For a moment, I think he doesn't speak English, but then he says, "You don't know? Chinese soldiers—dress like tourists, Americans, or Thai—take young men and women. Brainwash them. Turn them into soldiers to kill Thai and Americans."

He pauses, his expression hardening. "Sometimes, they take children too. Parents say they fight for China to save kids. But kids never come back."

Mia's face goes pale, her eyes wide with horror.

"That means we're in more danger than we thought," Bumble says, his voice low.

"Is there anywhere safer than Bangkok?" I ask.

The clerk hesitates, glancing at the other customers before answering. "Central, maybe. Inland. But not ocean. The Chinese come in small boats, too small for radar." He waves his hand like he just remembered something. "There a hostel in Bangkok. Maybe safe, maybe not."

"Where's the hostel?" I ask, a flicker of hope stirring in my chest.

He points toward an intersection a few buildings down. "Go there. On this side." He gestures up and down. "You'll find it."

We peek out the window, waiting for the street to return to life. Once it does, we slip out, heads low. If we hadn't known where to look, we never would've found the hostel hidden behind a tangle of neon signs. The old stucco building slouches under the weight of years. Inside, the air smells of cigarettes and sweat.

Laughter and conversations in multiple languages drift from the next room.

Behind a worn desk sits a young Thai woman, her eyes dull with boredom. I check us in and pay in American dollars. The community room, doubling as a dining area, buzzes with energy. A few people gather around a movie at one end, while others chat in small groups.

"Are you tired? Want to shower and sleep, or hang out?" I ask Mia.

She touches my arm, and I melt like shave ice in the sun.

"I'm hungry," she says.

"Okay," I reply, trying to keep my voice steady. "Let's drop our stuff off and meet back here in five. We'll check out the street food."

Our room is cramped, with six sets of bunk beds lined up against the walls. Bumble claims the bottom bunk, and I throw my duffel on the top one.

Back on the street, the lights blaze like artificial suns, flickering and pulsing in every color. It feels surreal, like waking from a dream, until the scent of sizzling chicken pulls me back.

Bumble and Mia exchange a glance, and we all nod. The vendor hands us skewers of sweet, spicy chicken, and we devour them in seconds, licking our fingers clean.

We're heading back to the hostel when the rumble of a military truck cuts through the night. I freeze. Two dozen men leap from the back, rifles raised. They storm the hostel.

Screams shatter the stillness. The crack of gunfire echoes in the street. I push Mia against the wall, shielding her with my body. *"Please, God, make us invisible,"* I whisper. Her arms tighten around me, and I realize she's trembling.

The acrid smell of gunfire twists my stomach. It's too terrible to watch. And too terrible not to. I've clutched Mia's face to my chest. I let go, embarrassed, but she doesn't move away. She keeps holding me, and I rest my hand on the back of her head.

More screams. A young man stumbles out of the hostel, hands raised. A soldier shoots him. He crumples to the pavement, blood spilling from his mouth. Another body already lies dead on the sidewalk.

The soldiers round up those in the hostel—young and old—forcing them into the truck at gunpoint.

Time blurs. Blood smears the sidewalk as soldiers and captives walk around the two dead men and get in the back of the truck. Gunshots fire once more. *God, help us. Don't let Mia die. Don't let Bumble die.*

I strain to see inside the truck as it passes, but the canopy hides everything. They're gone as quickly as they came, leaving the street emptier, the world darker than before.

How can people be this evil?

145

CHAPTER TWENTY-ONE

Mia

When Kana grabs me and shoves me against the glass window of a dress shop, I freeze. My mind races to understand what's happening, but before I can ask, the sound of gunshots pierces the air, followed by screams and frantic yelling. My blood turns to ice. It all happens so fast—gunfire, chaos, the screech of tires. Kana's body is tense against mine, shielding me. Did they see us? Are we next?

The truck peels away, and the shriek of approaching sirens fills the air, growing louder by the second. Kana finally releases me, and I see it—the dead men lying in the street and sidewalk, flies already beginning to swarm over the dark pool of blood beneath them. Time seems to stop.

"Oh, no!" I gasp. My voice shakes. The man is face-down, one arm extended as if reaching for something—someone. Bumble runs toward him, but stops short, and backs away.

"He's dead," Bumble says, his voice hollow.

Kana's face is stony. "Let's go."

"Our stuff?" Bumble asks, his voice trembling.

"Leave it," Kana says, grabbing my hand and pulling me down the street.

I glance back at the growing crowd surrounding the dead man as Kana turns the corner, leading us away from the chaos. The sirens scream closer. My heart thuds painfully in my chest. We're in the middle of Bangkok with nothing—no protection, no plan. God, please. Grandma, wherever you are, pray for us.

Grandma's face flashes in my mind, her deep blue-green eyes lined with age and wisdom. Faint spots and scars adorned her hands. Her hugs were warm, like a quilt wrapped around me on a cold winter's morning. Grandma, the only person who ever truly loved me. Maybe the only one who ever will.

Kana walks faster than I can comfortably manage, his grip loosening. He drops my hand. "Sorry," he mutters, without meeting my eyes. The word hits harder than it should, reminding me of the distance he keeps between us. I want more than his protection—I want him. I want to stand by his side, not be kept at arm's length. The distance gnaws at me, growing wider with every step.

We pass through the crowded streets where prostitutes now line the sidewalks in bright colors, their jewelry glinting under the neon lights. The Thai people are beautiful, yet their women are disrespected. Kana's obliviousness worries me. He doesn't seem to recognize what's right in front of him. How will he recognize danger when it's disguised, waiting to strike? How will he know the enemy when anyone—a tourist, a local—could be a threat, ready to sell us to the Chinese?

My thoughts spin as Kana raises his hand to flag a taxi. We pile into the back, and he tells the driver, "Take us to Lop Buri."

The driver points to himself, "Pan." His slimy smile leaves me uncomfortable, and he leers at me. The car is ancient, with cigarette burns on the upholstery and cracks in the dashboard. I watch the lights from the street flicker on the worn fabric upholstery, casting strange shadows. My unease grows. Pan's eyes linger on me in the rearview mirror. I pull my shirt up toward my neck.

"You American?" Pan asks, glancing at me again.

"Yes," I say, wishing Kana would reassure me with a smile. Instead, a quizzical expression leaves me wondering what he's thinking.

Pan smiles, his teeth crooked and yellowed beside his long, graying hair. "Tourist?"

I force a smile, nodding.

The car rumbles through the streets, the noise of the engine drowning out most of the external sounds. The smell of garbage fades, replaced by the stale stink of old tobacco and sweat soaked into the seats. Bumble leans against the window, already half-asleep, his deep breathing steady. I let my head rest against his shoulder, my eyelids growing heavy.

But then, something changes. I wake up with a feeling of wrongness settling over me. Kana looks back at me, his movements tense and alert. The driver lights another cigarette, filling the car with smoke. I cough, waving my hand in front of my face.

"Can you put that out?" Kana asks calmly. "It's making her cough."

Pan chuckles, the sound grating. "You do whatever she wants, eh?"

Kana doesn't react. "She's very important to me." His eyes are scanning the horizon.

The driver's expression darkens, his voice dripping with sarcasm. "You want go Lop Buri. We go Lop Buri."

Something's wrong. I can't put my finger on it, but Kana's stiff posture tells me he feels it too. Kana scratches his back, but I catch the movement of his hand—a claw-like motion, then a finger pointing toward the driver. A silent warning. Danger. My heart goes into over-drive.

I nudge Bumble, trying to shake him awake. He stirs slowly, murmuring as his head lifts from the back of the seat. "What's going on?" he mumbles, groggy but alert now.

"Shh," I whisper, not wanting to tip off the driver.

Bumble frowns but takes my hand, tracing letters into my palm. "W-h-a-t-s g-o-i-n-g o-n?"

I respond in his palm. "D-a-n-g-e-r."

Bumble rubs his forehead, his sleepy confusion clearing away.

"I need to use the bathroom," I say, my voice steady, wondering if it's a brilliant idea or not.

Pan turns around. "Gas station soon," he says.

I lean forward, pretending to fumble with my bag. Slowly, I unbuckle my seatbelt, the quiet *click* covered by Bumble's cough. I slide down, my fingers reaching under the driver's seat. My heart pounds so hard I'm sure Pan will hear it. As I feel around the small space, my fingers touch something—cold, hard, wrapped in cloth. I pull it free, inch by inch, and sit back in my seat, tucking the object under my feet.

The car pulls into a gas station. Pan's eyes dart to me. His smile vanishes. "Toilet," he says, his voice low and suspicious.

Kana surveys the area, his body tense. Pan's hand moves toward something under his seat.

Kana moves faster. "Run," he whispers, the urgency like a shot of adrenaline.

The doors lock. Pan slams the car into drive, but Kana lunges to grab Pan's arm. I can't see what he's doing, but the sound of doors unlocking drowns out the driver's yelp.

"Run!" Kana's command is sharp, his eyes wide.

I burst from the car, sprinting toward the dim lights of the residential street. Every nerve screams for me to move faster. I don't dare look back.

✦

CHAPTER TWENTY-TWO

Kana

Once I pin Pan's arm and unlock the doors, I bolt from the car, sprinting across the highway toward the ocean, dodging oncoming traffic. Pan wasn't taking us north to Lop Buri—he drove south. A driver honks, but I don't stop. Bumble grabs the cement crash barrier just behind me, and we vault over. Large rocks fall away into a patch of forest, and we drop down, staying low. Pan's nowhere in sight.

Mia. Where is she? My stomach twists. *Did Pan take her?* I force myself to retrace my steps through the traffic, but the noise swallows my calls to her. The bathroom door at the gas station stands open, empty. Panic claws at my chest. If Pan took her . . . I can't think about that. But the thoughts won't leave. My knees hit the ground, my mind spiraling. We can't move on without her. But staying isn't safe either. What did the storekeeper say? "Chinese boats come at night. They take people." *God, not her. Please.*

"Kana, what are we going to do?" Bumble's voice trembles, betraying his forced calm. He pounds the gas station wall with his fist, out of breath from dodging traffic to follow me.

"I'm more concerned about Mia," I say, trying to control the shaking in my own voice. *God, help us find her.*

Bumble rubs the back of his neck, eyes scanning the dark road. "We can't do anything right now. She's gone, otherwise, she'd call us. Let's get out of here." He's trying to sound detached, but his constant looking around says otherwise.

I frown, surprised by his response.

"We're not leaving until we know what happened." I bite the inside of my cheek.

Six walls of fear for Mia hem me in on all sides. I shake with fear for myself, Mia, and the POWs. My breathing has become ragged.

I can't sit here, paralyzed by fear. God, guide us. "Okay," I mutter, pushing through the tightness in my chest. "We have a mission—rescue the POWs. It feels impossible, but nothing is impossible with God." My voice steadies. "We'll need the language, food, and shelter first. We'll move closer to the prison camp. We can ask around, gather information." I can't believe we're making plans without Mia.

"Yeah, and that's not dangerous?" Bumble mumbles and does his growl sounds. He slaps at the side of the back of the gas station we're standing by.

I run around the perimeter of the gas station, looking for Mia. How could she have disappeared? I sprint back to Bumble, out of breath.

"We can't stay here. It's too dangerous. Did you see the ocean? The Chinese come in on small boats and kidnap people like us. She's gone. Taken by Pan."

How can we leave the area when Mia might come back to find us? If Mia could, she'd come to us now that Pan has gone. Did she really get captured? I hate that Bumble might be right. My stomach rumbles. I'm ripped in two. *Focus, Kana!*

Bumble forages for decent water bottles among the trash thrown in the old service station's bathroom trash. I wash and fill them. The toilet area hasn't been cleaned in a long time, keeping me looking only at the water. Who knows if the water in the sink is potable? But we need to drink. The door slams as I leave with two full jugs.

"Thought we might find an American to drive us back to Bangkok," he says.

We need to eat. Dumpster diving with the local competition doesn't appeal to me. I scan the area. There's a coconut palm tree up the street in the backyard of a business. "Hey Bum, I'm going to look around. Be back in a few minutes," I say. "You stay here in case Mia comes back."

"I'm not staying here," Bumble says. "Have you noticed that anyone could pull in for gas, see me, and force me into their car to sell to the Chinese?"

He follows me across the highway again and hides out of sight by the trunk of a tree while I look for food. I cross the highway and slip over a fence and into the dark jungle, searching for whatever we can eat or might give us cover for the night. There are animals in Thailand that aren't on Kauai. Malayan tigers, venomous snakes, including the king cobra, clouded leopard, and the sun bear all could be in this rainforest. Myna birds squawk like at home, and their spotted dove looks a lot like our zebra dove. The smell even reminds me of home. If only I could sit down to enjoy Mom's cooking and Dad's jokes over the dinner table. But that isn't going to happen. It's darker the deeper I go in the jungle. I need a machete to hack away vines and protect me. Through the vines, over the downed trees, and between the undergrowth clusters, I trudge on for an hour. Little light penetrates through the canopy. I stop. Something doesn't feel right.

The jungle closes in fast, with its thick vines, earthy smells, and sprawling trees. A rustling sound—slow, deliberate—sends my skin crawling. My knife is in my hand before I know it. Then, a snake slides out of the shadows. Eight feet long. Its head rises, fangs gleaming in the faint moonlight. I find a stick and shove it into the beast's open mouth, but the snake's body coils fast, wrapping around my chest. The air rushes from my lungs as it tightens. My heart races. I cut frantically at its neck. Tighter. It's squeezing tighter. *Lord, help me!*

Finally, the head snaps off, and I stumble back, gasping for air as its body thrashes. I kick the still-hissing head into the undergrowth, my heart pounding.

It seems to take forever for the body to lie still at last. Only then do I exhale.

A mosquito bites me, and I slap my neck. Moonlight seeps in through the canopy and then slips away behind a cloud.

The jungle sounds haunt me as I slice up the snake's body. My stomach churns. Piling the snake meat into my arms, I return, the weight of everything—Mia's disappearance—pressing down.

Making my way back to Bum proves more difficult in the dark. It takes me longer than I want. When I reach Bum, snoring on the ground, I put the meat down and build a small fire. In time, the fire crackles, comforting me with memories of building fires at home. I put the meat next to the coals on a rock.

"Bum," I call out when I think it's done. "Come on, dinner is almost ready."

"What? Dinner?" Bumble sits up. "Oh, you're messing with me. We're in a Thailand rainforest with no identity, money, home, food, or safety," Bumble mutters with an air of bitterness.

"No, actually, dinner is waiting," I say.

Bumble grumbles as he walks over to the fire. "What's the chow?"

"Thailand chicken." I break off branches to sit on, the bark smooth in my hands.

We sit by the fire, gnawing on snake meat that tastes like chewy chicken. Bumble eats in silence, but I can feel the heaviness of our shared anxiety.

Exhaustion hits like a club once my stomach holds a belly full of snake meat. We stretch out by the dying embers. "What are we even doing here?" Bumble finally says, his voice low.

"I know." My voice is barely more than a whisper, but I force it out. "Tomorrow, we'll face reality. Tomorrow, we'll figure it out." *Tomorrow—we might be captured.*

The next morning, Bumble and I stop in at a coffee shop and use their bathrooms. I buy us each a donut. It tastes better than any pastry I've ever eaten, and Bum eats his in three bites.

Am I fooling myself, like I fooled Bum with the snake meat? My heart refuses to leave Mia behind, but staying endangers us. The battle between my head and heart tightens. *What do I do, God?*

I see a Caucasian guy going to his car with a bag of donuts and a cup of coffee. "Hey, do you speak English?" I ask.

He startles and almost drops his coffee. "You talking to me?"

"Yeah. Sorry. We're trying to get to Bangkok. Nearly got kidnapped. Are you going that way?"

"Where are you from?" He places his coffee on top of his Honda SUV and clicks the unlock button like he doesn't believe me.

"Kauai, and Bumble came from Austin." I pause. "Can we get a ride?"

The man hesitates, like he's not sure he should trust us. Short red hair with whispers of gray in his beard swirl around his mouth. "Max, from Orange County, California." He shakes my hand, eyeing us warily. "You're serious? You need a ride to Bangkok?"

"Yeah, nearly got kidnapped. Long story."

Max hesitates, then gestures to his car. "Get in." He opens his donut bag, takes a bite.

We pile in. I sit in front.

"What are you guys, tourists?" Max pulls out his lower lip like he's puzzled.

"We started out as cadets in the military, MANA graduates."

"Wow wee. Where are your uniforms?"

I sigh, and my shoulders drop. "We're Neverborns. I think our general didn't think much of Neverborns. He sent us on an assignment here in Thailand to rescue a POW camp, but when we got here, no one met us. We were supposed to get language training and supplies, but we just got dumped."

"I can't believe the U.S. military would do that." He pauses. "Yes, I can."

"What are you doing here?" I ask.

"I'm on assignment with U.S. News and Politics. The war, the people, the stories, the heartbeat, and the drama of Thailand. That's what I'm here to get. Mind if I record your story?" He pulls the car onto a shoulder and tells his car computer to record and send the recording to his email.

Max bites into his donut again, his eyes darting between us, skepticism clear—until I mention the General's plot. Something shifts in his expression. His eyes narrow slightly. "That's quite the story. You need proof if anyone's going to believe you."

"I have a bone," I say quietly. My fingers twitch against my knee. "Probably from a Neverborn. There are more, in a swamp, maybe at the waterfall."

Max leans back, chewing over my words. "That's… dark. Do you have any other proof or connecting information about how and why?"

"Maybe. I'm letting my dad figure it out."

"Hm. What's next for you boys?"

I tap my fingers on my thigh. It's ridiculous to even tell him about our mission. "Can I ask you a question first?" I ask.

"Go ahead," he says.

"Where do you think the POW camps are located? Do you know anything about them?"

"Nah, I suspect even intelligence doesn't know," Max says. "They move people around. There's been reports of POW prisoners released by the Chinese who then find and shoot as many Americans as they can. I think the Chinese brainwash the prisoners."

"Brainwashing. That's a whole new level of torture. You lose your sanity," I say. After a few seconds, I add, "I know it sounds ridiculous, but I . . . " I look at Bum. "I feel called to infiltrate the POW camp."

Max studies me for a moment and shakes his head. "Wow, baby. Talking about biting off a mouthful!"

I drop my head and say, "I know. I know." But the verse, *"I can do all things through Christ who strengthens me,"* flows through my head. I pause. "All right," I say, "for now, where could we go to find jobs? We need to live long enough to learn the language better."

Max ponders. "There are high-end neighborhoods in the suburbs of Bangkok. What skills do you have? You don't need identity chips in Thailand."

"Bumble, what skills do you have under your belt?" I ask.

"Me, uh, I'm built like a tank. I can lift, carry, pull, push, you know, build, tear down."

Max chuckles. "And what about you, Kana?"

"He's a Kauaian version of Tarzan. He flies on vines and makes snowshoes for water," Bumble says, chuckling.

Max's eyebrows go up. "That good?"

I pull my lips into my mouth and bite them. Is he making fun of me? I'm different. "I was raised in isolation with two brothers my age. We did everything together—survival weekends, built tree forts, learned self-defense, swam, surfed, had our own zipline, went on pig hunts."

"Pig hunts?" Max looks interested.

"Yeah, it's a thing on Kauai. There are more pigs than people. We have to keep them under control, because they're not." A flood of memories makes me nostalgic.

Max pulls into a cheap hotel and pays for Bum and me to stay three nights. "Three nights, my gift to you. But you're on your own after that. You have to figure out how to earn enough money in three days to buy yourself food and find housing." He puts his credit card away but pulls out his business card. "And in return, I want you to call me and tell me what you have learned and what you have done. All right?"

"Sure, thanks!" Bum says.

"In case you get separated or lose someone. Remember, call me first, second, and third, before you call your sweethearts or parents. And I'm buying you both a hotel stay," Max says.

Bumble hugs him, and I give him a high-five and give him my gratitude. He's not going to want a stinky hug from this weirdo. I can't wait for a hot shower and clean sheets.

Is he really a news media guy? Something nags at the back of my mind. Max is too generous, too interested in our story. Is he just a journalist—or something more? I want to trust him because it hurts so much to have no one to trust. But who is Max? And how are we going to earn money when we don't speak the language and have no leads?

CHAPTER TWENTY-THREE

Mia

I sprint away from the cab driver and down the highway, heading for a rickety wooden fence behind the gas station. Flakes of white paint crumble under my grip, and the wood groans as I swing my legs over. Terror claws at me—Pan, the taxi driver, must've been planning to sell us out, maybe into enemy hands. But as my feet hit the ground, another fear creeps in—I have no idea where I am. This land is a labyrinth of unknowns, filled with dangers I can't even name. The shadows move like sharks circling in deep waters. I remember what people say—brothers sell their sisters into slavery to pay off gambling debts. The worst kind of debt.

The stench of the alley hits me like a slap—garbage, rotting meat, and something else, something worse. I almost kick a cat that bolts across my path, yowling. *Please, God, don't let me get separated from Kana.* A new fear wells up—what if Kana and Bumble were caught? What if I'm alone now? My spine tingles cold. I glance back toward the gas station. All I see are cars lining up for fuel. No sign of the guys. My phone is dead. Panic bubbles in my chest, but I shove it down. *Focus. Safety first. Don't get caught.*

I reach the end of the alley and step onto a narrow street. Two cars glide by in the night's stillness, and the lingering smell of curry clings to the air. A motorcycle roars past, and the rider glances my way. I freeze, then force myself to move, crossing the street quickly. The houses here are ancient, their shingles curled like dead leaves, roofs patched with tarps. A dog barks somewhere behind a fence. I walk, forcing my steps to appear steady. Do I act like I belong here? Or would that make me more of a target?

Where did Kana and Bumble go? I swallow hard, hoping no one notices me, a lone girl with no protection. My hand drifts to my mouth, and I notice it trembling. From one house, the muffled sounds of a TV filter out. From another, raised voices argue. Western-style rock blares from the next. I hurry back, my heart aching for Kana, but the guys are gone. Waiting to cross the highway puts me at risk, but I wait and finally can run across toward the sea. Still, though I call out their names, only the traffic noises fill the night air. *How can this have happened, God?* I return to the residential area, my chest heavy, my brain in a fog of questions. Were they here, and I missed them by waiting so long to look? Did they get taken? Shot? I can barely breathe fast enough to keep up with my pounding heart.

A large tree sits in the front yard of a house on the corner. Kana would climb that. I jump for a branch, missing twice before finally snagging it. Grunting, I haul myself up into the tree's shadowy embrace. From this vantage, I can see only shards of light from the streetlamp below, the rest of the world swallowed by darkness.

I climb higher and straddle a thick limb, leaning my back against the trunk. If I fall asleep, I'll drop to the ground. But exhaustion pulls at me like a weight.

The night hums with distant sounds—dogs barking, leaves rustling. The breeze cools my skin, goosebumps rising on my arms. I find two close branches and rest my arms and head on one while sitting on the other. The scent of leaves fills my nose, stirring memories of climbing trees at Grandma's house. I picture her standing in the doorway, Mom at her side, arms crossed. *Did Mom ever regret not raising me? If Grandma had to bribe her with a car just to keep her from aborting me, it's hard to believe she's ever missed not having a relationship with me. And Feliz—my sperm donor? He wouldn't risk paying child support or having his name on record. When Grandma dies, I'll have no one.*

I curl tighter against the branches. The unease clings to me like damp clothes, suffocating. Everyone leaves eventually. If you give them time, they always do.

***

A rooster's crow jerks me awake. Early morning light seeps through the tree branches. A memory floods my mind—I'm five years old, watching Grandpa drive away without me. Grandma hadn't realized I'd followed her to the gas station bathroom. When she climbed back in the car, they left me. I screamed, sprinting down the street after them. "Gammy! Papa! Don't go! Don't leave me!"

The ache from that day returns, raw and familiar, twisting in my chest. Tears slip down my cheeks. My heart pounds, and without thinking, I shift backward on the limb. My knees clamp down just as I tip, hanging upside down. Panic grips me. I fling one leg off the branch, rocking until I swing myself upright again. My chest heaves as I steady myself on the limb. *Life flips you upside down without warning.*

Fear pulses through me like electricity. *I'm alone. In Thailand.* With shaky hands, I climb down from the tree. Dawn is breaking, and the streets stir with life—motorbikes, cars, people, moving with purpose. I have nowhere to go. Kana wanted to save those prisoners of war, but what can we actually do?

Where did they go? I try to think, retracing my steps. *Did I miss something?*

At least I don't stand out too much here. My dark hair blends in, and I don't look quite American. No one gives me a second glance as I walk toward the gas station. *Maybe I can find someone heading to Bangkok.* The thought of home hits me hard. My throat tightens, and hiccups bubble up from nowhere. I fumble for my water flask, but it's gone—either left in the taxi or dropped somewhere while I ran.

Children appear, watching me with big brown eyes. They wear simple cotton shirts and shorts, clothes that seem suited to the heat. The largest boy whispers something to the others, and they all continue staring. Then he speaks to me in Thai. I don't respond. I remember someone on the plane over telling a young woman, "Don't speak English. Kids tell parents, and parents tell someone who might trade you away."

I quicken my pace, ignoring the children's curious stares. If this were a different world, I'd love to sit with them, find a way to communicate with signs and smiles. But neighbors, friends—anyone—can become enemies when fear and desperation take over.

The houses shift from small homes to shanties. Scraps of wood, metal, and plastic are stacked haphazardly, forming shelters. An old woman sits on a porch, gums exposed where teeth should be. Children with blistered skin play with rag balls, oblivious to flies crawling on their faces.

The stench of manure—human or animal, I'm not sure—turns my stomach. I stumble toward a bush and retch. Acid burns my throat, and I wipe my tongue on the hem of my shirt in disgust.

A tiny child approaches, her wide eyes full of curiosity. She's wearing a torn shirt long enough to serve as a dress. I force a smile, and she beams back, her joy contagious. I mime drinking, and she scampers off. Moments later, she returns, holding out a scratched plastic bottle.

I take it, brushing her cheek gently. "Thank you," I whisper. She giggles and takes my hand.

The little girl leads me through a maze of rubbish and makeshift homes, finally stopping in front of a tiny shelter made from pallets. Bamboo poles fill the gaps between slats, but the place barely holds together. Flipping up a burlap "door," I spot a woman sprawled on a cloth on the ground. Her soiled dress clings to her bony frame, one leg bent awkwardly.

I kneel beside her, touching her arm. She's clammy and unresponsive. Fear twists in my gut. *What can I do? I can't even help myself.*

The child crawls into my lap, resting her head on my shoulder. Despite the heat, she lets me hold her, and the tenderness of the moment squeezes tears from my eyes. Memories of Grandma's arms wrap around me, the crackle of her fireplace warming the room. She'd stroke my hair, whispering, "I love you."

I stroke the girl's tangled hair and say softly, "Mia." I tap my chest. "Mia."

She smiles, her small fingers tapping her own chest. "Nan," she says, wrapping her arms around me like a gift.

I close my eyes, savoring the weight of her little body. If only I could bring her home. But I have no home. Reality crashes in, cold and unforgiving. I have nothing to give this child, but she has nothing and no one to protect her. My heart wraps around Nan with a thousand strands. *How can I leave her?*

CHAPTER TWENTY-FOUR

Kana

The next morning, I wake up after a restless sleep, dreaming of home. Max gifted us this stay at the hotel, and thankfully, we didn't get abducted in the night. But my stomach still churns, and my head spins as I remember the screams from the hostel attack. Evil here feels real—danger, kidnappings, murders right on the streets.

I splash water on my face in the tiny bathroom and drink from the paper cups above the water station.

Maybe Mom and Dad are praying for me—wherever they are. I wonder if they think of me as their son—someone worth saving—or just a ghost of the boy they lost.

"Who speaks English?" I ask at the front desk, knowing this might make me stand out more than I already do, like a target with a bullseye painted on my back.

The receptionist makes a call, and soon a security officer appears. He's smaller than most men I've met here, and he eyes me warily.

"You need something?" he says in a gruff tone.

"Thanks for coming," I say. "Where can we make some money? We don't speak much Thai yet."

The officer's expression tightens as he massages his neck. "Thailand's a powder keg," he mutters. "If I were you, I'd try the American community by the ocean. More money, but . . . " His eyes flicker, as if measuring what I might do with this information. "They're easy targets too—pirates raid from small boats." He walks off.

We catch a bus through chaotic streets, the air heavy with the stench of garbage and cigarettes, thick with exhaust and heat. It clings to my skin, pressing in—not with the soft rhythm of the Great Lakes or the whisper of trade winds I remember from home. The sheer number of people surging past makes me long for the quiet of Hawaii. The sun feels the same here, and farther south, the beaches are pristine—blue oceans, white sand, mountains soaring into the sky. Pictures of southern Thailand could easily be mistaken for Kauai. But it's not the landscape I miss. How can I? I'm alive, breathing, walking through this world while millions of babies never even had a chance to see it. And the others, the Neverborn cadets, are probably rotting in prison camps by now. Maybe it should have been me. What right do I have to live?

I swallow hard and sit tall. Is this Goliath the reason I was allowed to live when so many others weren't? Millions of babies— never born, never seen, never known. After swatting a mosquito, I notice my hand shaking.

We get off the bus, not sure if we're in the right place. The homes here are bigger, with dogs barking behind gates. I spot a plumeria tree and bend down to pick up a white flower off the ground. The scent takes me back home for a split second. Traffic isn't as congested in this part of the city, but two German shepherds' growling remind me of whose turf I'm on.

"Yeah, I get it," I murmur. "I'd pet you if I could." The dogs make me think of Mischief, bounding around the jungle back home, helping flush pigs. No one pays for shooting pigs in Thailand. Dad taught me multiple skills; there must be something I can do in this climate.

"Let's sit and think," I say, stopping under a giant monkeypod tree. My bones feel heavy, like they're weighed down with the same exhaustion that clings to my soul. *Lord, make our paths straight,* I pray. I'm tired of wandering aimlessly in this sea of despair.

Fighter jets scream overhead, a reminder that we're not in Hawaii anymore. The roar takes my breath away. How long before we're caught up in the fighting?

"What can we offer that these people need?" I stretch, my back popping as I bend. "Maybe yard maintenance. Bum, are you up for starting a yard service?"

Bum chuckles. "We don't even have a lawnmower."

"We could use theirs," I suggest. "Do the first yard for free, and maybe they'll let us use their mower."

Bum stands, clapping me on the shoulder. "I'm with you, brother. Come get me when you find something." He sits, his back against a tree.

We walk down the street, past neat houses with manicured hedges. The next house catches my eye. It's a white two-story with a broad stone lanai and a porch swing. The white plastic fence looks new, but the grass is a little long, and weeds are sprouting in the flower beds. No dogs. "Sawasdi," I call, then add, "Hello!" in English.

An older Thai woman steps out from behind a plumeria tree, scissors in hand. She's thin and short, maybe ninety pounds, with graying hair pulled back. She goes straight to her hibiscus bush and snips off stems with bright orange-red blooms to add to her plumeria bouquet.

"Sawasdi," I try again.

She snaps something in Thai and waves me off like I'm a nuisance.

"Do you need someone to mow your lawn?" I ask, undeterred.

She pauses, glancing at me with sharp eyes. "How much you charge?"

I blink, surprised at her English.

Her eyes flicker with amusement when she sees my surprise. "Not everyone speaks only one language," she says, her words clipped but playful. Still, there's an edge under her voice, like she's sizing me up for more than just yard work.

I take a breath. "I'd be happy to help. Whatever you need."

She steps closer, eyes narrowing. "Why aren't you at war with other young men?" she asks, her eyes narrowing. She's asking more than just where I've been—she's asking if I'm a coward. "And why you look Thai but can't speak a word properly?"

I smile. "I was an American soldier. My commanding officer abandoned us during deployment."

"Did you desert?" She raises an eyebrow, but there is something in her tone—like she already knows the answer, or maybe doesn't care.

"I know it sounds unbelievable, but it's the truth."

"And who is 'us'?" she asks, crossing her arms.

"I have a friend." My hand extends in Bum's direction. "We were sent on a suicide mission, but when we got to Thailand, no one met us. Soldiers marched some of our group away at gunpoint."

She studies me for a moment, then unlocks the gate. "Go get him. I want to see."

I hurry back to where Bum is, his eyes closed. Together, we walk back to the house.

The woman studies me for a moment, her sharp eyes softening for just a second. I glance at Bum, who gives a small nod. It's a risk, but what choice do we have? The gate creaks open, and we step into the unknown.

"Two of you?" she says as we step through. "What your names?"

"I'm Kana. This is Bumble."

"Bumble? Like bee? Come inside. Don't let anyone see you." She hands us each a glass of cold water.

Her house is small but well-kept, with old appliances and scratches on the tile countertops. The scent of curry and spicy sauces fills the air, and plants hang from the ceiling and sit on tables near the window.

"My name Cheriya, but in the U.S., I went by Cheri," she says. "My husband and I own a Thai restaurant in Los Angeles for twenty years. He pass, so I move back home. My son marry, have child, and then he die too."

"I'm sorry," I say softly.

Cheriya's eyes linger on me. "My son . . . he a soldier too," she says, almost too quietly. "He fought with Americans. Die like others. I see the same look in your eyes. You help me?" she asks, her voice quieter now.

"We can mow the lawn, fix anything, whatever you need," I say.

"And even break what doesn't need fixing," Bum says, no doubt trying to lighten the mood.

Cheriya slaps his arm with the fly swatter and a faint smile crosses her face. "Where you boys grow up?"

I lose myself telling her about Hawaii. Bumble jumps in and talks about his grandparents' cattle ranch, his stories of riding Maverick, his horse, and getting thrown by bulls. Cheriya's face softens.

"Yes, Kana," she says. "Grass need mowing. The mower in the garage. You do?"

"Yes. I can," I say, glancing at Bum for consensus. He nods. A sweep of trepidation sweeps through me. What are we getting ourselves into?

"You good with computers?" Her voice sounds like computer skills are important.

"Yeah," I say. "Not bad."

"Good. You measure the yard and make right programming for mower. Set to run one time a week—Friday. No other day." She massages her wrist.

"Sure," I say, impressed that she has a programmable automatic mower, and worried, because I'll have to figure out how it works.

"I need help clean. Hands not work good. Come." She leads us into the pristine living room, decorated with a cream velvet couch with a large floral picture of lilies on the wall. Stained glass tiffany lamps were paired with a Thai silk embroidered tablecloth covered in flowers on the dining room table. The dark mahogany chairs, coffee, and end tables match with bouquets carved in them.

We spend the day trimming bushes, cleaning the blinds, sucking the pipes on the air conditioner, so it doesn't blow mildew with the air. She sits down afterward, looking more tired than any of us.

"Can I cook dinner tonight for you? My two brothers and I rotated cooking with our moms," I say.

"Brothers with different mothers?"

"Well, they're not my biological brothers. But then, neither are my parents our bio parents." I clear my throat.

Her face wrinkles in confusion. Then she waves her hand like she'll never understand and says, "You from Hawaii? I been. Can you make Spam musubi?" Her eyes light up with hope.

"Do you have Spam, rice, and nori?"

"I have." She shuffles to the pantry and digs around until she pulls out the Spam, a bag of white rice, and an old unopened package of nori—dried seaweed for wrapping around the rice and Spam.

I force a smile as she hands me the nori. She looks harmless, but so did the other people who sold us out. I can't afford to trust anyone. Not here. Not when every gesture, every act of kindness, could be bait.

"Cook plenty for you both and me, and some for tomorrow," she says, settling back into her chair.

As I rinse the rice, I wonder if she's testing me to see if I really grew up in Hawaii. Maybe she just misses the taste of island food. Is she trustworthy? My stomach twists with the thought. What if she's planning to turn us in for a reward or sell us into the Chinese army? I push the idea away and focus on cooking, but the unease lingers, like the faint mildew scent from the air conditioner earlier.

CHAPTER TWENTY-FIVE

Mia

My head swims from dehydration as Nan and I walk, her small voice breaking the silence as she points to things, naming them in Thai. I try to listen, but my mind drifts. Maybe one of these rich families will want a nanny. The air cools as the sky deepens into ink-black, and streetlights flicker on. Barking dogs announce our presence as if signaling to the world that a vagrant is slipping by their gates—ripe for picking. We need to find somewhere safe to sleep.

High fences guard the houses, their stone posts and iron bars topped with spikes. I find a break where a towering tree's roots bulge under the fence, just wide enough to slip through. Balancing a sleeping Nan in my arms, I lay her down, crawl in, and pull her through, settling against the tree trunk. She stirs, but falls back to sleep on my lap, her head nestled into my chest. I curl my knees against the cold iron fence and lean back, cradling her for warmth. The ground is hard beneath me, but exhaustion claims me anyway.

Morning comes in fragments of sound—cars rumbling by, birds chirping, leaves rustling in the breeze. My body aches from the hardness of the trunk and ground. Ants crawl through my bark-laden hair. Nan's soft breathing stirs against me, and I stroke her hair, fighting the knot of dread tightening in my chest. *We need food and water.*

I remember being Nan's age when I sat in church with Gammy, bored during the sermon. My fingers pull a strand of hair from Nan's eyes and sweep back her hair from her face. *Gammy used to stroke my hair, just like this.* A faint smile creeps up as I remember that Sunday I dropped her lipstick during the pastor's prayer. It rolled to the front, with a rattle that drew every eye in the congregation. The old ladies didn't try to hide their laughter. Gammy was mortified.

I kiss Nan's head softly, vowing to never let her feel the shame I experienced. *But what will become of her? Of us? Invisible.* The word claws at my thoughts. *Will Nan become invisible too? And how can I protect her if I can't protect myself?*

The embassy in Bangkok flickers in my mind. But the embassy will deny ever giving me military citizenship without my military chip. General Shipley won't go down for what he did to the Neverborns. No, they'll throw us under the bus to save him. The whole nation will make sure of it. How can I ever be successful at anything? I stand and look around.

It's Sunday morning. People are probably still sleeping in. Going door to door, begging for work or food, wouldn't help us now. We need to wait. I take Nan's hand, and we wander through empty streets until we find a small park with a playground. Relief washes over me as I spot a water fountain. I let Nan drink first.

Then I drink and wash both of our faces and arms, scrubbing the grime away. I push her gently on the swing, watching her tiny legs pump in the air, and with each push, I whisper a prayer. But it feels like I'm throwing pennies into a bottomless well. *God, will You hear me before Shipley's men find us?*

We're alone. No money, no food, no language, in a country at war.

I sit on the swing next to Nan, letting her giggles cut through my tangled thoughts. We're two lonely souls clinging to each other's emptiness, trying to soothe something we don't understand. *God, you seem so far away.* There's no one to sing with, no one to comfort us, no one to remind me You care.

Suddenly, a coldness prickles my skin—not the cool air, but a deeper chill. I glance up, heart seizing in my chest as a helicar swoops low with a deafening beating. The wind from its blades slams through the trees, leaves slicing my cheeks as I bury Nan in my arms. My stomach drops. *Are they tracking me?* I should've thrown away my watchcom like Kana said, but I didn't.

I lunge for the nearest rock, digging the watchcom from my pocket and pushing it beneath the stone. Nan lets out a small yelp because I stopped pushing her in the swing.

"Shh, Nan," I whisper fiercely, yanking her off the swing and sprinting for cover. The helicar hovers above, its engine drowning out my heartbeat. I pull her under a thick shrub. Dirt fills my nostrils as we crawl to a space between thick shrubs. I cover Nan and myself with leaves and sticks. My heart slams against my ribs. *Please, God, don't let them see us.*

She turns around and clings to me, trusting me to keep her safe.

The helicar hovers, then moves on. My breath comes in ragged gulps as I peek out. There's a black van with men scanning the park. I hear them speaking in Thai.

"Men hunt us," Nan whispers, her tiny voice trembling.

"Shh, we're safe." I whisper, stroking her hair. The words catch in my throat, too heavy to believe.

After what feels like hours, I hear the van drive away. We're filthy, covered in dirt and sweat. I stand, wiping Nan's face.

We walk along the road until a man pulls his car out of the garage. I hope he's heading to church. In Thailand, there are many Buddhists and Hindus, few Christians. I rush forward, waving my hand. "Are you going to a Christian church?"

The older man looks confused, but Nan says something in Thai. He smiles and nods.

"Can we come too?" I ask and Nan translates.

He unlocks the gate for us to enter and invites us into his house. Inside, an elegant woman with gray hair welcomes us. She introduces herself as Dara and disappears into a closet to return with a simple green dress for me. I hesitate, my trust buried under layers of fear, but her smile softens me. I change quickly in the bathroom, washing up as best as I can. Nan gets a makeshift dress—a woman's blouse with a scarf belt—and we head out together.

At church, I try to blend in, but the stares linger. People whisper, elbowing each other, but Dara stays by my side. After the service, they set up for a meal. Nan's eyes light up at the sight of food, and my stomach growls loudly. I eat slowly, savoring every bite, each taste reminding me of what I've missed.

Then the pastor approaches. His towering frame and kind eyes give him a presence that makes me feel small. "Welcome. You speak English?"

"Yes, thank you," I say, shaking his hand.

"And who's this?" He gestures to Nan.

"I found her." My throat tightens. "Her mother . . . passed," I say softly, my heart twisting.

His brow furrows. "You've unofficially adopted her, then?"

Tears sting my eyes. "I guess I have. I pray I can keep her."

He studies me carefully. "How are you surviving?"

My throat tightens. "I was in the military . . . but . . . " The words falter, the weight of abandonment too much. I choke on them.

"What do you need?"

Everything in me cracks open. "A job. A place to stay. Food. And . . . a phone charger." My laugh is brittle, broken.

He places a hand on my shoulder and prays for me, his voice a melody of Thai words, wrapping me in fragile hope. But fear lingers. What if trusting him is a mistake?

CHAPTER TWENTY-SIX

Kana

I try programming Cheriya's old lawnmower to mow on its own every seven days, but no matter what I do, it refuses to work. Cheriya, watching me from the porch, disappears into the garage and returns with something that makes me wince.

"Kana. Come." She taps the cracked, wooden handle of a rusty hand mower under a pile of junk in the shed. I imagine how many years this thing has been through.

"You look Thai," she says, her voice dry as she moves boxes and buckets to get to it. "People think you're not American. Can you push this?" Her hand lingers on the mower like it's an old friend.

"I'll see." I yank it out and find some oil on a shelf to help loosen the wheels and rusty blades. Two hours later, I'm covered in sweat and grime, my mouth filled with the bitter taste of grass, but the lawn looks neat enough.

Cheriya calls me in with a tray of mango iced tea, condensation dripping down the tall glasses on the countertop. We sit around the kitchen table, the cold tea a brief escape from the heat. She makes a list of other house projects—replacing a cracked window in the attic, fixing a broken chair, and weeding what turns out to be an old vegetable garden in the backyard.

By dinner, exhaustion clings to my bones, but the smell of the Nara Thai delivery makes my stomach roar. Half a dozen takeout boxes cover the table, and we devour every bite.

After we eat, with the evening cool settling in, I finally ask her, "Aunty, I noticed a picture in the attic of a boy. Who is he?"

Her hand trembles next to her glass, and her eyes go distant. "My grandson. He twenty-five now." Her voice is soft, heavy with a lifetime of grief. "If still alive."

"I'm sorry." The words feel hollow, a poor match for the sorrow in the room. "Can I pray for him?"

Her eyes race to mine. "Yes, pray." Her face softens. "I pray, every day. Soldiers come back from POW camps, not the same. Some shoot officers. Some kill themselves. Some bomb schools. Shame for the family. Shame for the nation."

My throat tightens. "Where is he now?"

She drops her head. "He was here, going to school online. Then Chinese took him."

My pulse quickens. "Our mission—when we came to Thailand—was to rescue prisoners from a POW camp."

Her gaze snaps to mine, fire in her eyes. She leans forward, the chair scraping the floor. "Then you go! Bring back grandson, Arun!" Her voice cracks, pleading. "Please, Kana. Go."

I shake my head, my voice faltering. "We don't know where the camp is. We weren't given directions."

"I help. You go!" She jumps to her feet, leading us to Arun's old bedroom. The woman pulls open one drawer after another, looking for something. Bumble shifts on the bed behind me, and the springs groan under his weight. With each paper she pulls out, my heartbeat echoes in my ears.

Finally, she finds what she's searching for—an old, dust-covered box and carries it to the dining room table. Bum and I follow. "Here," she whispers, setting it on the table between us. She lifts the lid, revealing maps and documents, all in Thai. I sneeze from the dust.

Her hand trembles as she spreads out a map. "There," she says, pointing to a region in the mountains of western Thailand. "Some say the camp here." She points to a point on the border of western Thailand and Myanmar. "No one know. They can move."

"How do you pronounce the river?" I ask, squinting at the unfamiliar script.

Her face hardens. "You need to know Thai. You cannot take a POW camp and not know the language!"

I nod. "Will you teach me?"

A tremor runs through her as she sighs. "If the Chinese army find out I've helped you, they torture me." Her voice breaks with a shudder.

"We won't tell," Bumble says, his tone serious for once.

"They torture you. You will tell." She shudders again. "But I teach you." Her eyes lock on mine, both dismayed and determined. "You work hard. You must learn."

She disappears upstairs and returns with an armful of old CDs and a clunky CD player. She sets them on the table like they hold the key to hope. Her fingers flick the light switch off. "Cars and neighbors must see me." She gestures toward the windows. "Not you."

I follow her upstairs to a small front bedroom. The ceiling slopes. She points to a card table in the closet. "Set up here," she says. "If someone comes to kitchen door, you come here. No one see you." Her eyes are deadly serious.

The room smells of old leather and dust, the air heavy with memories. I find a college textbook on computer science. The spine barely cracked. Her grandson's, no doubt.

She hands me a staple gun and some cotton cloth. "Cover window—no one see."

I staple the cloth over the window. The room feels like a relic from another life, a sanctuary where the outside world can't reach.

Hours pass as we repeat Thai phrases to Cheriya, tripping over words. The heat drains us, but we press on.

"Say," she beckons.

We fumble through our phrases, her corrections sharp but patient. "No one go living room or out," she warns, shaking her finger. "You gone, and I dead."

After she leaves, Bumble mutters, "Paranoid much?"

"Maybe," I reply. "Or maybe not." I flip through the textbook, the words blurring together. "Every word we learn is a step closer to our mission—and to bringing her grandson home."

That night, I fall asleep with my face pressed against the book, drool pooling on the pages. Bumble wakes me in the morning, and after breakfast, we start all over again. The routine energizes me, and I'm surprised at how quickly Bumble and I pick up the language. He leaves behind his usual clowning to focus.

Later, Cheriya pulls out her grandson's old computer and finds his password diary. The Lenovo is ancient but functional.

"Kana, Mr. Bumble, no social media," she snaps. "No police because you talk to girl."

As if I'd talk to girls I'd never even met. Bumble catches my eye and laughs.

Cheriya picks up the picture of Arun and holds it to her chest, wrapping her arms around it.

Watching Cheriya clutch that picture, I can't help but think of my own parents—their absence pressing down on me like a weight I didn't notice until now. I miss the smell of Mom's lavender cream, Dad's quiet smile. I miss the warmth, the way their presence made life seem fuller—closer to God. Without morning devotions, without worship songs, without hugs and pats on the back, life feels cold. Empty.

CHAPTER
TWENTY-SEVEN

Mia

The palm fronds hang limp, offering no respite from the oppressive heat as Nan and I trudge toward the U.S. Embassy, our shirts clinging to our skin, soaked with sweat. Maybe someone here will know what to do. *Please, God, let them. Will you? Can you?* Hunger gnaws at my stomach, my throat parched, legs trembling with exhaustion. I rub my forehead, wiping away sweat, the fire in my belly—gone. With a deactivated chip, I have no proof of anything. But would they even care about a Neverborn like me? And Nan's Thai. *Why would they help me?* But it's the only hope I have. *Did God put this idea in my head, or is it all I could come up with?*

The glass doors whoosh open, and clean, cool air fills my lungs. I hear English and let out a small moan, like a baby bird crying for its mother—longing to be seen, to be heard, to be cared for. A picture of The Statue of Liberty towers above the vast, echoing hall. Cool granite floors, polished with silver flecks, sparkle under the harsh lights, a stark contrast to the grime clinging to us. To the left, an elevator. To the right, a bathroom. The air conditioning hums. Pristine floors make me feel even dirtier.

I drag Nan into the bathroom, where the scent of disinfectant stings my nose. We scrub down in the sink, but our clothes are beyond help. Spot-cleaning only dulls the dirt. We still look homeless.

A dozen chairs line the waiting room walls, with a chair facing a plexiglass booth at the end. Two Thai women enter and sit, giving Nan and me a quick scowl. Ignoring them, I rush to the booth.

"Can I help you?" the woman behind the glass asks.

"I grew up in the States and joined the Navy. But our mission—something went wrong. Our chips were deactivated, and we were abandoned."

She pauses, her voice flat. "That's a military issue." She glances at the clock. It's barely after 8:00 a.m., and she already sounds tired.

"I don't think they'll help me," I plead, my voice cracking.

"You probably misunderstood your orders. Next." Her voice rises, dismissing me.

The two women shoot me annoyed looks as they rise. I back away, tears stinging my eyes. Nan clings to me, her small arms gripping my waist. I stroke her hair, holding her tightly, sharing our silent despair. Nan knows we don't belong here, don't belong anywhere. Except with each other. *If only I could reach Kana. He'd know what to do. He'd see me sinking beneath the weight of hopelessness and pull me back.* But is he even alive? Nan squeezes tighter, as if she can feel me slipping away.

God, I don't feel you anymore. It's all dark. If you're there, pull me out. Please.

We walk back out, arm in arm. An American man in a sharp gray tweed suit steps out of a taxi, brushing past us. He's young, his hair slicked back in the latest U.S. style—a short top with a long braid streaked with blond. His shoes look custom, the kind with built-in air conditioning. His snakeskin bag screams wealth.

"Sir, do you have a moment?" I ask with desperation in my voice.

He doesn't respond, and the glass doors slide shut behind him.

Maybe I can find someone else who speaks English. My stomach growls. A woman in a bright turquoise jumpsuit strides toward the door, her eyelashes long enough to be implanted.

"Ma'am, could I . . . " I start, but she rushes past without a glance.

Five more people file in and out, but none stop. All head for the elevator on the right. I grip Nan's hand and push through the glass doors again. At the elevator, I press the button for the top floor. As we ascend, the sound of crashing waves fills the air, and videos of rolling oceans play on the walls. The scent of saltwater drifts in, calming my nerves for a moment. The doors open just as I smooth down Nan's hair.

The man in the gray suit stands there, glaring at me.

"Is this a joyride, or do you have an appointment with the ambassador?" His voice is sharp, like a scolding teacher.

I open my mouth, but only a squeak comes out.

"Thought so." He steps in and presses the button for the lobby, then taps something on his watch. The doors slide shut, and I start sweating again despite the cool air and ocean sounds.

"Nice bag. Do they sell those at the snake farm?"

He scowls. "You've seen a YouTube video. I don't believe you're from the States."

"You have a west-coast non-accent," I say. "I grew up in New Mexico, and wish I could go home, but I'm a Neverborn."

"Why didn't you join the military?"

"I did. Went through MANA training."

His eyebrows shoot up. "Where's your uniform?"

"We thought we were being sent on a secret mission, but no one met us. Our chips were deactivated. We've been abandoned."

The doors open, and he lets us out first.

"What's with the kid?" he asks.

"She . . . " I hesitate, then take Nan's hand. "I found her next to her dead mother. Drugs, I think."

"So, you—who have nothing, who *are* nothing, who have no future—took her in?"

"Oh, I'm someone," I say, straightening my back. "Not nothing. I love. That makes me more precious than rhodium. More precious to God, and more needed in this world than you'll ever know. Life isn't about winning. It's about love." I stomp off toward the glass doors.

Two police officers are waiting outside. They let me through the door first, then slap cuffs on my wrists.

"Get in," one of them, a stubby-nosed officer, growls, opening the back door of a silver car with a maroon stripe.

Nan scrambles onto my lap, wailing, her face buried in my chest. The larger officer pulls her away and buckles her into the seat beside me. The girl fights to get back onto my lap, but the seat belt holds her in place. Tears stream down her face. Her small body shakes with sobs like the day we found her mother. Her head droops, every cry slicing through me like a knife. *My sweet girl.* I'm cuffed, helpless. *Will they let me keep her? Will they take her away?* Maybe she's petrified they'll shoot me. Maybe they will. This is worse than when we found her mother. She'll be completely alone again. Vulnerable. Abandoned.

Lord, if you're here, rescue us.

CHAPTER TWENTY-EIGHT

Kana

My eyes scan Arun's old room, filled with bookshelves, furniture, and memories, where Cheriya, Bum, and I study Thai. Speed-reading through computer science texts feels like unwrapping a treasure chest; each page reveals a new surprise. My community college classes at home gave me the basics, but this? This is the mountain itself, complete with crampons and a pickaxe. At night, I fall asleep with code snaking through my brain, curled on the foam pad—Bumble always grabs the bed first.

"Dinner's ready!" Cheriya calls, her voice cutting through my thoughts. I sit at the table, the rich aroma of coconut Thai filling the air. "Kana, I can hardly drag you away. You like my grandson, Arun. He read like you, all night, all day." She prays to thank God for the meal and for her grandson.

"I pray I get to meet Arun someday soon." I take a bite. "Auntie, can I have the recipe for this? I think Mia would love it, too."

A familiar weight presses on my chest at the thought of Mia. No sign of her, not even a whisper in the dark.

Bumble sighs, smacking his lips. "Yeah, God bless Mia, wherever she is."

"I give you recipe," Cheriya says.

"Auntie, what happened to Arun? You said he wanted to continue his online classes," I say after the prayer.

Cheriya puts her fork down and pushes back her plate, staring at it as if searching for answers. "Arun wouldn't tell what he do. He stop taking class but still work on his computer. He hid a black notebook when I come in his room, but I saw. Worry on his face. Fear."

Bumble and I exchange worried glances.

"He stay home all the time, not go." She bites her lip, pausing. "One day, I come back from market, and he gone. No blood, no bullet holes, but no Arun, either." Her face twitches, brows wrinkling as she dips her head in silence.

I can't wait to get back to the bedroom. Searching under the mattress, through notebooks with pages in the wrong order, I find Cheriya's dried tears marking some of them. The notes on the paper call to me from their silence. Understand me. Find me. All evening, I search, pulling books off shelves, feeling along the floor for any hidden cubby or secret spot where Arun might have stashed his notebook. Deep into the dark night, sleep finally gives me peace.

"What are you doing?" Bumble asks in the morning, breaking my focus.

I'm lying on my makeshift bed, looking up while moving my hands as I talk to God, asking Him to show me what I need to see. Maybe Arun stumbled onto something. It must be online, given all the books about codes. Whoever ransacked his room must have taken his computer or wiped it clean. "If you wanted to hide something important, where would you put it?" I ask.

"I don't know." Bumble scratches his armpit and looks around. "I'd hide it where no one would think—print it out and stash it in my mom's underwear drawer or something."

Rolling to my feet, I dash out of the room to find Cheriya. She's in her garden, picking a plumeria stem for a bouquet.

"Cheriya, the computer you're letting me use, that was Arun's, right?"

"No, mine. Arun taught me email. He thought I should make Thai recipe book. After he gone, it my computer in his room, wiped clean. No recipe left."

My voice trembles. "Where is his?"

She smiles gently. "He drop it down the laundry chute. It fell in basket on top of washer. I find it week later when I wash clothes."

"Where is it now?" My heart races.

Cheriya shuffles into the house and kneels by her bed. She reaches between the box spring and mattress to pull out a black computer. Then she retrieves a bag with cords and an old-fashioned mouse.

"What do you think his password might be?" I ask, rubbing my hands together behind her.

"He never told me." She hands me the computer.

"I need his password to access it." Wiping the sweat off my brow, my voice is limp at the news. My shoulders slump. Sweat beads on my forehead despite the coolness of the morning.

She nods, concern filling her eyes. "It important?"

"Yes. Maybe Arun found something or figured something out that got him kidnapped." I need to see what Arun was working on. Maybe there's something here, some clue that will lead me to him.

Her eyes widen. "Maybe it here." She retrieves Arun's old photo album.

I take it from her like it's hand-blown crystal. The old PC requires either a password or fingerprint recognition. After probing Cheriya with questions about Arun's pets, friends, favorite foods, nicknames, old phone numbers, and birthdays—all of which fail—I set the computer aside. In the back yard, I breathe in the beauty of the garden, the sunshine, clouds billowing, and bees buzzing from flower to flower, legs heavy with pollen. *Lord, if I'm here at this house for your purpose, including finding out what happened to Arun, give me the password I need.* As I stand there, breathing in the garden's calm, the weight on my chest lifts like clouds parting after a storm.

Lunch awaits. Cheriya sets out a platter of lunch meats and cheeses. "Kana, call Mr. Bumble."

Over lunch, I ask Cheriya, "Let's brainstorm other ideas of what Arun might use for a password. Do you have any thoughts?"

"No," she says, rising to retrieve a plate of Lotus Blossom Crispy Cookies. Mia would love these. She told me about a healthy cookie recipe she developed. Leave it to Mia to make a cookie healthy. I don't even have a decent picture of her.

Cheriya stops eating mid-bite and sets her cookie down, her face dazed. She leaves and returns with her phone. "Arun said one time when we eat this kind of cookie together, 'If I go, and you need to get into my computer, try this.'" She scrolls and shows me the text.

"Here." She hands me the phone.

My fingers slip, and the phone clatters onto the table. I scoop it up again, hands like butter as I scroll through the text. The message is in English—"Momma's First Cub."

"His favorite English book," she explains. "Every day, I read it to him over and over when he was a baby. He stay with me while his mother work."

I nearly knock my chair over in my rush to try the password. My hands shake as I type it in— "Momma's First Cub." The screen blinks once, twice—and then it comes to life.

It works! A Thai waterfall picture appears as the screensaver, followed by familiar icons.

All day, I read his documents and downloads, answers unfolding to questions I hadn't even thought to ask. The day whooshes by. Cheriya's eyes question me the moment we sit down for dinner.

"I shake my head. Still searching," I mutter, frustration edging my voice.

"Arun love to learn," she nods.

Bumble discovers a Monopoly game in Arun's room and insists on playing after dinner, but I can't leave the computer alone. All evening and into the night, I read.

Arun's last email surprises me with its formality, "Sir, if I may ask, would you be interested in a meeting to discuss an agency called 'Truth Out?' They advertise on social media to 'Let your rants be revealed.' In return, they promise a gift, which turns out to be chocolate-covered fentanyl. The initiating site seems to be in Western Thailand, in Chinese-held territory."

The last email is addressed to gearyqstallack@army.com.

When I figure out what's going on, I'll get ahold of Max. But would he blow my cover and publish the story, leaving me more vulnerable than before?

I go to bed thinking about it all. Why would China want social media rants from the States? If they're using Americans' rants for propaganda, was Geary Q. Stallack a spy? In my dreams, I see my brother, Kekoa, with his throat slit. My other brother, Canyon, shouts, "Spies! They're all spies!" I wake up drenched in sweat, the weight of Arun's disappearance pressing down harder than ever. A world filled with spies, kidnappings, and murder. I'm not ready for it.

CHAPTER TWENTY-NINE

Mia

The police station looms like a white stone palace, bustling with people rushing in and out. I hear Nan through the glass and see her, my heart in my throat. Nan screams in the arms of a chubby gray-haired officer, pounding his chest with tiny fists as if she can somehow hurt him. Behind a glass wall, I spill my story to a woman—who I am, why I'm in Thailand—though the words feel too thin to capture the chaos my life has become.

After what feels like an eternity, a woman in a Navy uniform checks my background against Navy records and releases me. When a young Thai officer places Nan's limp body in my arms, her tear-streaked face shatters me. I rock and sing to her, but urgency pulses through me. Kana. If he's still alive, he's racing headlong into danger, chasing a mission where peril lurks at every turn. I lean my head against Nan's and whisper a prayer for him.

My arms ache carrying her through the busy streets of a city I can't pronounce. Sweat clings to our dresses, the sun relentless, but the gnawing question of how we'll make it feels heavier than anything.

"Mama, mama, mama, mama, mama," she murmurs in her tiny voice as she stirs.

A park appears—a patch of peace in the midst of a nicer neighborhood. I find a swing and sit with her, allowing the gentle motion to rock us both. *God, I'm lost. Worst of all, I'm lost with Nan. Find me. Find us.*

After a while, Nan stirs. "Go potty," she says, tugging at my arm.

I walk her to the primitive bathroom and wait outside. On our way back, she spots the slide and bursts into a run. "Whee!" I cheer as she flies down the long fiberglass slope.

"Oh, you speak English?" A voice breaks into the moment. A cute, redheaded mom in her twenties smiles at me as her son, who must be the same age as Nan, climbs the ladder to the slide.

"Yes," I say, smiling back. "Are you from the States?"

"Yeah. I married my husband in L.A. He's Thai, but wanted to come home and fight for his country."

"So here you are without him," I say gently. "Do you speak Thai?"

"Kusa, my husband, taught me some," she says, pointing to a large stucco house with an iron gate surrounding it. "My husband's family invited us to live with them in that house."

"Beautiful! I hope you like his family." Nan returns, hugging my legs, her face still shy from all we've been through.

"Kusa's family treats me like one of them," the woman says warmly. "I'm Andrea, by the way. This is Chai."

I look down at her son, who glances at me before scampering back up the slide.

"I'm Mia. This is Nan," I say, chuckling. We exchange a quick hug, and I already feel a connection.

"What brings you here?" she asks as Nan begins to chase Chai around the slide the moment he lands on the ground.

"Do you have all day?" I laugh weakly. "It's a long story."

Andrea glances at her watch. "Dinner's an hour away. I'd love to hear it."

I dive into the tangled mess of my military history. I expect disbelief, but instead, she listens, her eyes full of empathy as I explain how I've been abandoned. By the time I'm done, I realize she's not just someone I've met—she's someone I can trust.

"You've been totally dumped in a country at war with no identity or support?" She processes my words, disbelief transforming into concern. "That's unbelievable!"

I nod, feeling the weight of my truth.

"How did you get Nan? She's Thai, right?"

"Yes, she is. That's a long story too." I begin, but Andrea pulls out her phone, speaking rapidly in Thai. I catch a few words here and there. Nan and Chai walk around us hand in hand, chatting in a language only they understand.

"Great!" Andrea lights up after a few moments on the phone. "Hakulu," she says, whispering, "Thank you!" She hangs up and turns to me. "You and Nan have to come to dinner—Mom insists."

I pull her into a tight hug, ignoring how sweaty I am, my throat too tight to say more than a simple, "Thank you."

We walk through the iron gate into lush gardens, and I'm struck by the beauty surrounding us—hibiscus, ti leaves, magnolia trees, plumeria—all like something out of a dream.

"Let's go freshen up before dinner," Andrea says. Her bedroom features floral wallpaper and wispy white curtains, looking like a movie set.

"Wow," I say, my eyes feasting on the dark wooden, hand-carved bedstead and dressers adorned with a Thai embroidered coverlet.

"Yeah. Kusa's family wanted me to feel at home." She picks up Chai and finds clean clothes for him. "Hey, I've started a discard pile of clothes I don't want anymore. It's in the basket in the closet. Help yourself if you want any."

I hurry to the closet and find dresses, pants, tops of all kinds, even sandals—all my size. "We're the same size!" I call out, sounding happier than I've been since arriving in Thailand.

After a quick shower, Nan and I dress for dinner. She fits into Chai's jeans and wears a plain blue shirt, her eyes bright with excitement, but she only wants to talk to Chai and me. This shyness is new to me, but there's nothing shy about how she eats.

Drunken noodles, drenched in sweet soy sauce with garlic, onions, and chicken, intoxicate me with pleasure. Fruit bowls, green papaya salad, fried rice, and dishes I've never seen before delight my senses until my stomach aches from excess.

Kusa's mom, Rose, eyes me until a lull in the conversation. "Mia, I wish you would teach me American food." Her voice brims with hope. "Andrea says she's not good at cooking, and our cook, she not learn."

"I'd love to teach you what I know," I say, seeing her smile bloom with possibility.

From the window, I catch sight of a pool in the backyard. After dinner, Nan wears shorts and a tank top, and we all splash and play. Kusa's dad sits in a chair under a tree, smoking a hand-carved wooden pipe with a metal mouthpiece. It smells of cherry wood. He smiles but remains quiet, carrying an air of importance grounded in responsibility. Kusa's mom beams, watching Nan and Chai play.

The backyard turns out to be a child's wonderland, filled with water toys, a mini waterwheel, and a slide dumping into the deep end. I spend two hours in the pool, ensuring the children's safety, relishing their laughter.

As the sun sets and we all head inside to shower and change, Andrea says, "Gosh, I wish you could stay. There's an empty bedroom next to mine with twin beds. Where have you been staying?"

Her words take my breath away. I know hospitality is essential in Thai culture, but I couldn't have hoped for more. Tears well in my eyes, and I struggle to respond.

Andrea disappears to ask her parents and bursts back through the door. "You can stay for a couple of weeks! We'll have so much fun! The kids will love it!"

Like long-lost sisters, we embrace. We've found a friend in a foreign land.

The time flies. I teach Rose to cook stew and fried chicken. Rose and I share cooking duties, while their cook lets me help her prepare Thai dinners. I start to develop my own cookbook as Chai and Nan learn to share toys, playing in the sandbox, water, or at the park. Pulling a roasted turkey out on America's Thanksgiving Day fills me with pride, and the room bursts with praise for my work.

As the days pass, I catch myself holding onto moments—Nan's laughter with Chai, the smell of roast turkey filling the air—knowing each one brings us closer to something I can't quite face yet. A future that waits, full of danger, somewhere beyond this peace.

After two weeks, I fight tears as I gather our new clothes into a discarded suitcase. Andrea slumps on the bed, her fist pressed against her mouth. "I wish you could stay. Do you want me to ask Dad?"

Chai, dressed only in his blue shorts, chases Nan, swiping at her long hair. Their laughter fills the room as she squeals and turns to chase him.

"I mean, I've never seen Chai this happy," she says. "He loves having a sister. It's much easier to take care of the two of them than just him." Her voice paints her sadness.

"Funny. I have no future. It's like I have a target on my back that says, 'Stand in line to shoot me.' But I feel called to find Kana and help him. I just can't drag Nan into a battlefield."

"Then leave her here." She grips my shoulders, pulling me to face her. "Leave her here. I love her. My family loves her. If you have to go, I'll help you however I can."

"Really? You'd just take her?"

"Absolutely. But stay another couple of days. Then you can figure out what to do and where to go."

My friend. I sigh and sink down to the bed. "Andrea, you are the best friend a girl could ever have."

She pulls my hands up and hugs me. "Well, I've had a year's worth of fun these last two weeks. Not to mention a year's worth of talking."

I laugh. We stayed up late every night talking. Now I have to figure out how to join a war. How do I help Kana rescue POWs? Is he even still alive? It feels like madness, like chasing a dream too big for me to grasp. But deep down, something stirs—this is what I'm meant to do, even if it leads me into the darkest places. *This is why I'm here. Is this where I die?*

CHAPTER THIRTY

Kana

Sleep eludes me. My mind races through every possibility. Did "Truth-Out" discover Arun's email? Kidnap him? Kill him? I grit my teeth at the thought—Cheriya can't lose anyone else. Not after burying her son and husband. But I can't risk emailing Geary Stallack and finding out that way.

Around two in the morning, an idea sparks. Canyon—he's always been good with videos. Maybe there's a way in. If I contact Dad or Mom, I'll put them in danger. But Canyon? He's resourceful, off the grid, and they'll never see him coming.

I pull out my phone and type, "Can—Hope you're doing well. I need your help with something big. I'm fine, but can you put together a video of young adults speaking out against the U.S.? I haven't changed my politics, but trust me on this. Miss you all—Kana."

Satisfied, I press "send."

Morning comes sluggishly, every hour pulling at my nerves. I pace until Cheriya's rug could almost unravel beneath my feet. Bumble heads out to mow neighborhood lawns, leaving me alone with my thoughts and Arun's files.

I dive deep into his notes, trying to understand his obsession with "trained to hate America." It's all propaganda, twisted into hate. I've seen it before—in history books about the Nazis, in extremists of every kind. It's the same war fought again and again. But this time, I'm in the middle of it. I never realized it because our parents shielded us from the hate aimed at Neverborns. Once in the Navy, I first saw that most Americans see us as less than human because we weren't meant to live.

An hour later, Canyon texts back, *"Man, you wouldn't believe how many people are crying about you. Of course, I'll get whatever you need. By the way, Kekoa loves Kauai Community College. He's still living with his birth mom. I'm jealous. Keep in touch! Can.*

Two days pass, my mind churning over the data. Arun's research spins in my head, his grim determination palpable in every email.

"Kana, set table." Cheriya's voice breaks through my concentration as I sit, engrossed in Arun's files.

"What?" I rub my ear as a sting shoots through it—she must've flicked me. Cheriya stands behind me, hands on her hips.

"Set table," she repeats and walks off, wiping her hands on her apron.

We sit down to dinner. The smell of refried rice and teriyaki chicken fills the air, but the tension sits heavy at the table. Halfway through the meal, Cheriya's voice trembles, though she doesn't look at me. "When can you start paying for your room and food?"

Bumble pulls out a wad of bills, handing them to her from his mowing lawns in other neighborhoods, where he couldn't be traced back to Cheriya. "Here's what I earned today."

She takes half and pushes the rest back to him.

Then she looks at me. "You. Bring my grandson back." Her eyes stay fixed on the water glass, as if she's staring through it—maybe seeing Arun somewhere far away.

After dinner, Canyon's email arrives with three video attachments. I open them, hands shaking. Two are videos of angry young people ranting about America's evils. But it's the third one that guts me—a Neverborn girl shares her story, her voice shaking as she describes being unaccepted, unwanted by her own country. My chest tightens. I tap my knee to keep calm.

Bumble watches a movie in the corner, oblivious.

I pull apart each video, embedding code designed to corrupt the recipient's software, and redirect the videos to a different destination. If I do this right, it'll cripple the Chinese propaganda machine—at least for a while. I keep Arun's files open for guidance, tracing his steps through firewalls and encryption. By morning, I have a plan—send a video that can take down their system permanently. And for the real masterstroke? The videos will look like they're one thing to the receiver but deliver the truth to all those viewing after the first view.

All I need is a throwaway computer to send them from, something that can't be traced back to me or Cheriya.

The next day, I mow lawns with Bumble, my mind racing ahead, fueled by the thrill of progress.

That night at dinner, I ask Cheriya, "Where can I get a cheap used computer?"

She raises an eyebrow. "You have Arun's. Isn't that good enough?"

"I need a dummy computer," I explain. "Something untraceable."

She seems confused, but she pulls up the Thai equivalent of Craigslist and shows me some listings.

Twenty-four hours later, I have an old Intel PC. Perfect. I submit the three videos to "Truth-Out" using the new system, biking miles away to send it, far from Cheriya's house. If they track it, it won't lead back here.

Now, I need a safe place to stash the computer. Somewhere it can charge without anyone discovering it.

The next morning, I say, "Bum, give me a hug. I'm off to plant this computer," and hug him. I squeeze his shoulders and turn to hug Cheriya. She's surprised, but hugs me back. I hop on Arun's old bike, the computer stuffed in my backpack. As I pedal out, Cheriya calls after me, "Don't you get kidnap! You come back!"

"I will," I shout, forcing confidence into my voice. The streets blur past as I ride through the town, scanning for abandoned buildings or hidden spots. I can't stop too long anywhere—people will get suspicious. Anyone anywhere could be an enemy.

By mid-afternoon, I pass a tall, white Catholic church, standing like a beacon of peace in the chaos. I stop and wander around the building, but see no outdoor outlets. The doors are locked. Disappointed, I hop back on my bike, my stomach growling.

On the way home, I pass a stucco house, vibrant pink bougainvillea crawling up its sides. With the yard overgrown and the fence rusty, I'm hopeful. Then I push on the gate—locked. No answer when I call out.

Dusk is settling in, and I'm out of time. I scribble the address on my notepad and head home. Maybe tomorrow I'll take another look. For now, I need a better plan. Taping it under a house? Maybe. But if someone finds it . . . No, I can't risk it. Not just for me, but for anyone who gets caught in the fallout.

I pedal faster, anxiety coiling tight in my chest. The memory of the youth being dragged from the hostel haunts me. Their screams echo in my head. And if I get caught? Who's going to help a kid like me? I'm used to slipping up—but this time, it's bigger than just me.

I force the thought aside, pedaling into the night.

CHAPTER THIRTY-ONE

Mia

For days, I pray for God's guidance, but my heart tightens with urgency. I have no clear sense of where to go or what to do. I can't remember Kana's phone number. Borrowing a phone to call him won't help. Goosebumps of disgust raise on my arms at the thought of him. The rock in my gut won't go away, forcing my eyes open deep into the night.

At the kitchen table the next morning, I jot down ideas that might help me locate the POW camps and possible job opportunities. Nan wiggles into my lap, her small body warm and solid against mine. "I love you, Mommy," she whispers, her eyes wide, waiting for my reply. "I love you to the moon and back," I say, tears blurring my vision. How could she possibly understand why I'm leaving? Will I even make it back to her? Her little arms squeeze me tight, and I hold her, wishing for a moment that life didn't have to be so hard.

I add "childcare" to my list of skills as Chai comes into the room, and Nan jumps down to chase him. "Cook, clean, teach English, garden." Memories of my first job at a flower nursery flood back—watering, transplanting seedlings, and selling plants. I was fifteen, a Neverborn, and couldn't officially be on the payroll, but my father showed up every payday to take what was meant for me. Still, I reveled in the miracle of growth, captivated by how life blossomed from a tiny seed.

The Majestic Garden Nursery was where I first grasped the magic of nurturing life, planting seeds, cuttings, and grafting a branch from one plant onto one with a good root system. Online, I researched plant cloning and creating orchards. Maybe one day, I could help those starving in Mexico start a co-op orchard and grow their own food.

That's what I need now, God—Your strength. You've grafted me into Your family; help me grow into you and be worthy of your love. Show me how to help Kana and Bumble— if they're still alive.

I wish I could share this part of me with Kana. We've never talked about our pasts. On a whim, I ask Andrea, "Hey, do you mind if I use your computer? I'm trying to track down Kana's brother." "Sure, anytime," she replies with a smile. "Don't even ask next time; the password is our address."

I turn to Andrea's computer, searching different social media sites for a Canyon or Kekoa around eighteen from Hawaii. There are many Kekoas—nutmeg-skinned, handsome young men with pictures of surfing and island life. The jagged mountain ridges and endless teal waters I barely glimpsed during my time at MANA call to something deep inside me, an unexplainable pull. With renewed determination, I continue my search for his family.

None of the Kekoas match Kana's brother, but one Canyon stands out. His blond hair and buff body fit exactly what Kana described. I send him a message, "Hi Canyon, my name is Mia. I'm a friend of your brother, Kana, but I've lost contact with him. Have you heard from him? I'd really appreciate any updates. I hope to meet you someday."

The next morning, I wake before the sun. To be quiet, I tiptoe to the computer and read Canyon's reply, "I'm glad to meet you, Mia! Kana is in Thailand with the crazy idea that he can single-handedly release all the POWs from a prison camp. I guess you met Kana's dad on the truck ride to the airport. He was impressed with you. Later, Canyon."

CHAPTER THIRTY-TWO

Kana

On my way back from searching for a place to hide the computer, I see a park ahead and pull my bike up onto the sidewalk, weaving through trees and around playground equipment. A water fountain by the public restrooms catches my eye. As I fill my water bottle, I spot a guy sprawled out on a nearby bench. He's wearing ripped, dirty jeans, and his bare, sunburned chest is covered in tattoos. His wild hair, dirty clothes, and the deep purple bags under his eyes scream addict.

"What you think you're looking at?" He speaks in English, voice rough like gravel.

My eyebrows lift. Pushing my bike over, I stop beside the bench. "Where you from?"

His eyes narrow into slits, and a sneer pulls at his crooked nose, like someone who's been betrayed too many times to care anymore. "Hell. Not that you care. You're not even Thai." His eyes narrow, scanning me. "What are you doing here? Looking for innocents to murder like the rest of the U.S.?"

People baffle me. What would Mom or Kekoa say to this? I remember Canyon screaming at his dad because he didn't want to wash his own clothes. I wanted to run away from the drama, but watching my uncle speak gently to him taught me a lot about dealing with emotional people. Sucking in a breath for courage, I reply, "I care. People matter. You matter." That's what Mom would say. And I mean it.

"Yeah, right." He turns his face away.

I dig into my backpack. "Hungry? I have a mango."

"I don't want your _____ mango," he growls. But then, eyeing it, he reaches out, snatching it from my hand. "Probably poisoned." He takes a bite. Juice spills down his chin.

I pull out a wet wipe and offer it to him.

He looks at me like I'm an idiot and wipes his mouth with the back of his hand.

The smell of sweat and keto breath hits me as I sit next to him. My aunt used to have that smell when she fasted.

"What's your name?" I ask and sit on the hard bench next to him.

His eyes dart to me, and for a moment, I think he might just snap. Instead, he shrugs and sits up. "Robert, but everyone calls me Bobbers." His head has a tic and jerks slightly from time to time.

"Bobbers, how'd you end up in Thailand?"

He throws the mango seed behind him, wiping his hands on his jeans. "You first," he mutters, pointing at me.

"My name's Kana. I was in the Navy, went through Basic and MANA training. They sent us here, but when we arrived, we were abandoned."

"No _____!" The venom in his words oozes out. "That's the U.S. for you. Abandoning their own. I'd kill them all."

The hairs on my neck stand up. This guy is volatile. I take a deep breath. "What happened to you? How'd you get here?"

Bobbers leans back. His face hardens, and he hisses. "Grew up north of Seattle. Went into the Navy too. Then I was sent to fight near Chiang Mai. Got caught in a bomb blast, separated from my company. The Chinese got me. Blindfolded me, tied my hands, marched me for days—tasing me whenever I fell behind. They walked me to an opal mine, working us like slaves until the mine went dry." He pauses, staring blankly ahead. "Starved, beaten, by Americans! When you're chosen to leave, you see the movies."

"Movies?" I ask, curious but cautious.

He nods, his face tight with anger, eyes bloodshot, and skin deeply wrinkled. "Movies. They weren't just regular war films. They showed Americans—people like me—torturing families, burning villages, laughing as they did it. And they didn't stop. It was like they wanted to scrub my brain clean and replace it with pure hate." He flinches. "Even my family. My…" His head shakes from side to side like he's reliving his family being hurt. "We saw things I never thought were possible. It's one thing for them to enjoy burning us with their cigarette butts, but to cut up women and children and show us doing it…" He wipes his eyes. "I *hate* them…" His voice drips with venom, an icy malice radiating from him like a frozen shadow.

I shudder and swallow. "That's why you're here?" I smell his foul sweaty odor but ignore it.

"To kill Americans," he says, his voice hollow. "That was my mission." He belches.

"You really think that's the way?" I ask softly.

His jaw clenches. "Does it matter? After what I've seen, my life's over. What else is left but fighting for the cause?"

"What cause?"

He glares at me. "To eliminate Americans. Then China and Thailand can live in peace."

"But . . . China invaded Thailand. Killed their king. They're taking over the country, killing Thai people."

Bobbers stands abruptly, veins bulging on his neck. "Who told you that?"

Adrenaline surges through me. I've pushed him too far. "You've been through hell," I say, trying to defuse him. "I'm sorry for what you've seen. No one should have to endure that."

His hands go to his ears, as if trying to block out the memories. "The sounds . . . children crying, the bayonets, the blood . . ."

My hand hovers above his shoulder, unsure if I should comfort him. "Can I put my hand on your shoulder?"

He nods, his body deflates as I touch him. "I don't know what to think anymore."

His voice is ragged, broken. "I punched the first American I saw in Bangkok. But then I realized . . . if I kill, I'm no different. No better than the monsters I hate."

"You don't want hate to own you anymore," I say. He needs God's love, but he might attack me if I suggest it. But it's what he needs.

"No. But what else is there?" His eyes plead with me to give him something.

"Do you believe in God?" I ask. A tabby cat meows, rubbing against my leg. I stroke her.

His eyes widen. "God? After everything I've done?"

I hesitate, then say, "You have a sense of justice. It bothers you a lot when people are hurt unjustly. If there is justice, there is a justice keeper. God. The thing is, that's why God's son had to die. To conquer hate. To pay the penalty, take the hit that those who hate deserve." *God, please help him understand.*

"How does Jesus make people not hate?" He uncrosses his legs and his hands rub his thighs.

"Einstein said there is no such thing as darkness, only the absence of light. Hate is the absence of love. Jesus, by paying the death penalty when he was innocent, allows those of us who want to be filled with love to commit ourselves to Him and to love."

Bobbers stares at me, silent. His breathing has slowed.

I give him some time to think and then say, "Why don't you ask Him to bring you love and quench the hate?"

Bobbers looks at me, confused but curious. "How?"

"Ask him if, when Jesus died, that love was for you too. Ask him if he can forgive what you've done. As long as you can't forgive anyone else, you can't forgive yourself. All of us have seeds of hate, toward ourselves and others."

Bobbers face looks dumbstruck. He hesitates as if fighting an internal battle and then says, "God, if you're really there. Did you really die for me?" His voice sounds suspicious and accusing. He turns to me and shakes his head. "What?" Then tears well up in his eyes. "I think he said, 'Yes.'" He sits for a long time, his head in his hands. "Whoa," is all he says.

Every cell in my body is alive with joy. "Bobbers, he did die for you. Let God be the judge and turn your judgments over to him. Do you want to do that?"

"I want to think about this," he says in a calm voice.

"Okay. Bobbers, but know God is ready to bring you healing when you're ready. Would you tell me about the opal mine?" I squash a mosquito biting my arm.

"It's all inside the mountain. The cave . . . rooms like classrooms. But the lessons were horror. They strapped us to chairs and showed us the films. Real. Bloody. Every cut felt real."

"How many comrades? How many Chinese?" I ask, leaning closer.

"Does it matter? We're all the same," Bobbers says with a bitter laugh. "Americans toss us into the dungeon. The Chinese drag us out, ten at a time, to show us the movies. Some comrades even help the Chinese—they join the underground. I don't know what happens to the ones who don't 'orient.'"

It's dark now. I hate to leave Bobbers, but Cheriya and Bumble will be worried sick about me. I can't risk giving him my contact information, either.

"Bobbers, can I pray for you before I go?" This has been heavy for him. But God can turn his whole life around.

He nods and bows his head.

"Lord God, creator of the universe. Thank you, that you hold justice and mercy in your hands. Help Bobbers to grow into your love, your forgiveness, and your mercy. Give him an opportunity to call home and find out how his family is, to know what lies have been told to him, and what to believe. Guide him to a place where he can learn more about you and grow into the man you've designed him to be. Amen."

Bobbers pats my knee. "Thank you. No one's ever prayed for me before." His eyes look more peaceful now.

"Goodbye, my friend," I say, standing to go. "Please, reach out to your family as soon as you can. The Chinese lie and drench you in their propaganda, confirm what you saw with proof, not movies. War . . . is hell."

Bobbers looks up, his shoulders hunched in the flickering street light, and nods.

I turn and head into the night. The wet pavement carries its own smell—tar mixed with the musty rot of dead plants. Passing the slums, I catch whiffs of garbage, thick and rancid, like a decomposing heap. My heart races as I dart through the main streets, cool air clinging to my skin. My eyes flicker constantly, searching for trucks, for any place to hide. The city at night feels like a stranger, nothing like the daytime scenes I remember. Landmarks blur in the dark, hidden from me like clams buried deep in the sand.

A few cars and trucks whiz by, but I don't see any more army vehicles loaded with rifle-clad soldiers. Yet my eyes flick around constantly to examine the shadows and understand the movements, praying for Bobbers, praying for Mia, praying I get back alive.

✦

CHAPTER THIRTY-THREE

Kana

Standing on the bike pedals, I push hard, racing through the slick streets. Rain pours in thick sheets, blurring my vision and stinging my eyes, making it impossible to stop if something—or someone—gets in the way. I veer off the road, skidding to a stop in front of a floral shop. Mom would have loved the flowers in the window, but I can't afford to think about that now. My eyes dart around, scanning for Chinese or Thai agents—the ones who sell kids like me to traffickers. I shudder as cars and motorcycles buzz past, speeding faster than they should.

A deep rumble rolls up the road. Heart pounding, I yank my bike into a side street, eyes searching for cover. The sound grows louder, swelling like a tidal wave crashing down. Hurry, Kana. A tall stucco building looms ahead, wrapping around the block. There's no alley to hide. I jump back on my bike, pedaling furiously on the sidewalk. The truck—it sounds like the one that takes people.

They're close. If the driver spots me, even for a second, he'll send his guys after me.

A tree appears, and I lay my bike down, scrambling behind it. The truck roars by. From my brief glimpse, it's the same type that was at the hostel, picking up captives. Time seems to freeze. I strain to hear if the truck stops or turns around. When it doesn't return, I grab my bike and ride away from the wretched vehicle. How can I get home while riding away from my Thai family? I'll be lost on the back roads. My mind registers every dog bark, every rustle of the trees, every car coming or going. The rain has stopped, but I must return to the main road if I'm ever going to make it back to Cheriya's house.

The businesses give way to residences. If someone sees me riding around in the dark, they might call the police—or the Chinese.

I grip the wet rubber handgrips tightly, breathing heavily as I pedal back toward the main road. It takes me four hours, listening and hiding whenever I hear a truck, waiting for the danger to pass.

In the middle of the night, I unlock Cheriya's gate and walk my bike inside. The lights are on in the house.

"Kana, I thought you were dead or captured!" Bumble is the first to grab me in a bear hug, nearly crushing me.

Cheriya shoves my shoulder with more force than I expect. "Why you late?" Her dark eyes narrow, filled with concern.

"Okay, if you're not too tired, I'll explain," I say, heading for a glass of water.

I share the details about my trip, the house I found, and Bobbers.

"Whoa!" Bumble scratches his neck, processing the information.

"They brainwash the prisoners. That's why American soldiers turn their guns on their own," Cheriya says, her voice thick with fear.

"Brainwashing just like Shipley said," I echo, my stomach churning. "That's exactly what they're doing to POWs."

Bumble frowns. "If we go to a POW camp to 'rescue' prisoners, they'll shoot or brainwash us. We're now their enemies."

Taking a deep breath, I respond, "Yeah. We need to understand their process and find a way to disrupt it."

Cheriya shakes quietly in her chair, fear etched on her face.

"You okay?" I place my hand on her arm.

She meets my gaze. "Arun might be there. What if he comes back and doesn't remember me? What if he kills me? What if he forgets?"

A new kind of death looms—death of memory, death of the mind, death of the heart.

"I'll do everything I can to find and help Arun," I promise.

I toss and turn for the rest of the night. Where are they? How many POW camps exist? What is their method for sweeping the minds of prisoners?

In the morning, before anyone else is awake, I eat a mango and leftover breadfruit hash browns. I start for the door, but pause. "I love you all. I'm off to the internet café to text my brother on Kauai. Be back in an hour."

The café opens at seven. A line of grumpy, caffeine-hungry people of mixed races forms. No one is eager to talk. I chuckle to myself and find a table. Once the line dwindles, I'll grab an iced chai.

Canyon has peppered me with questions in his emails. What's happening? How am I? Who's this Mia girl? He includes news of

Kekoa's blooming romance. Kekoa's parents are staying in Lihue, so he can stay at his birthmother's home. If Canyon is found at the compound with his parents, someone could prove they've raised him, and they'll go to jail. He's made a hut upstream, where he hangs out most of the time. If any flying or ground vehicles approach, he hides and stays out of sight.

I tap my fingers on the speckled fake-granite formica table, trying to think of what to say. Those waiting in line eye me curiously as the smell of coffee fills the air. My chest warms. Mia is alive. She contacted Canyon, looking for me.

"Canyon, my brother," I type, "I miss you more than I thought I would. I ache for you all. Please give everyone big hugs for me. You all mean the world to me. Thank you for sending the gifts."

I pause, weighing my words. If national security or the Chinese monitor my texts, I need to protect myself, Canyon, and Mia—by not asking for her information. "I'll send the gifts you sent me out. Remember Makanalani, the camp on the North Shore? This camp wasn't that nice. They change people from the inside out, using movies." God, please help him understand.

"I'm going to there to figure out how best to help. Pray for me. God is able to do abundantly above all we can ask or think— Ephesians 3:20. I desperately need that now." I look up Exodus 39 describing the priest's breastplate and see that opals are listed in the third row, first one in the line. "This camp is vast, like Exodus 39:12. If you don't hear from me by next week, you'll know I'll be busy. Your brother forever, Kana." *God, help him see the reference to opals in the scripture and put it together.*

I return home and grab the spy computer. Taking it to the library, my finger shakes as I push the "send" button. After wrapping it in a roll of aluminum foil, I hide it under loose boards in Cheriya's garage, hoping to avoid detection.

I ride to the empty house. The neighbors have enough internet for me to send the videos. Mixing acrylic paints, I match the colors of the faded green house and paint the wires. Even from a short distance, no one would notice the plug in the outlet or the wire. Sweat drips from my forehead in the hot, humid air. I ride down the back roads to kill time; if I stand still, I might explode.

Out of breath and soaked in sweat, I make my way back. Cars and bikes of all sorts fight for position on the busy street. Ducking under the house means facing spiders, and there's less airflow down there, but I crawl on my hands and knees, brushing away webs to check the computer.

The video has been sent to three locations—one in China, one in Myanmar, close to the border mountain range in Thailand, and one in Washington, D.C. Wow! Washington, D.C.! A spy organization? I save the results, grab the computer, and stuff it into my pack before heading home.

What if my tracking device triggers their tracking device? Is that how they found Arun? My heart races. I wipe the computer clean, stuff it in a paper bag, and dump it in a park trash can. My hands tremble. Am I being watched? Could they already be tracking the computer? Could a helicopter be on its way? My chest tightens. I leap on my bike and race away, faster—faster—like someone's already hunting me.

CHAPTER THIRTY-FOUR

Kana

A chorus of birds chatter as I creep out early the next morning to an internet cafe, texting Canyon the camp locations. I need him to know what I know in case I don't make it. Typing Canyon the information seems more like writing a movie script than the surreal task of actually creating strategy in a war. I sip my mocha and smell the coffee in the air.

Canyon,

Three camps seem promising—our capital, (figures, right?), Beijing, and one in southern Tanintharyi, Myanmar, near Thailand. Love you, K.

I hit send before I can second-guess myself.

God, please don't let him get into trouble because of me.

I shift gears, diving into online research about the opal mines in Myanmar. It's communist-held territory, though the borders are plagued with skirmishes. Most people there still follow Buddhism, their faces painted with a paste from sandalwood tree bark—a status symbol and a shield against the intense sun.

Frustration mounts as I search for information about the opal mines. How can I pinpoint where the fighting is? Max. He paid for a few nights' lodging and wanted us to stay in touch.

I swallow my anxiety and pull out his card. My phone's useless here, but his email is listed. I start typing, then pause. How do you know who to trust? My foot bounces restlessly.

Dear Max,

Since we met, we've made a friend we're staying with, doing odd jobs. I met a former POW who told me about the camps—how they use videos to reprogram soldiers with Chinese propaganda. Artificial Intelligence can make videos look like soldiers are killing POW's families or lovers, having pulled their pictures from social media which the Chinese create and use in their camps.

I stare at the screen. Who monitors emails? Is it even safe to send this?

I delete the draft and start fresh.

Dear Max,

Can you meet me for coffee at the internet café on 112/2 Phetchaburi Road, Bangkok tomorrow at noon?

K.

His reply is almost instant. "Sure."

I take a bus to Bangkok, hiding under hairspray and powder to make myself look gray-haired. Cheriya lends me some of her late husband's clothes, but the pants are too short. She lets out the hem and adds wrinkles to my face with an eyebrow pencil, smudging them to blend with my sweat-soaked face.

The muggy air clings to me, the gunk in my hair dissolving, but I push through. I spot Max waiting under an umbrella, sipping an iced mocha. I sneeze from the powder on my face.

"Hey," he says, shaking my hand. "Can I get you something?"

"Yeah, same as what you're having," I say, eyeing the tall glass, beads of water rolling down the sides. Coffee scents wrap around me like a soft invitation. My mouth is dry, and the Thai music in the background distracts me.

He brings me my drink, and we sit close, huddled away from prying ears.

"What's going on, old man Kana?" he asks with a smirk, clicking on a recorder.

I lean in, knowing he wants to use me to get a story, not because he personally cares. "I think there's a POW camp in an old opal mine in Myanmar, just over the Thailand border. They're using deep caverns as holding cells. The reprogramming videos make the POWs see Americans murdering their loved ones and turn American prisoners into killers for the Chinese." I take a breath, my hands cooling against the drink. "I learned this from a former POW named Bobbers."

Max leans back, considering. "That tracks with what we've seen—American soldiers coming home and turning on their own. Just last month, a former POW blew up an elementary school in Kansas, killing everyone inside, including himself. The media didn't hold back on the photos." He shakes his head. "Tarzan, what are you planning to do about it? March in with a white flag?"

I rub my eyes, exhaustion pressing in. "Something like that. I'm thinking of sending in a fake video—planting a virus to crash their system. I was hoping you could help."

He lets out a low chuckle. "Help you? It's suicide, buddy."

I take a slow sip, feeling the cold against my throat. "It's suicide, I know. But if I'm going to die, it might as well mean something. Every day, people are dying for nothing. and there are POWs in that camp suffering. Some of them will end up killing innocent people—maybe kids. Who else is going to do something?"

He smirks. "Nobody I know is that reckless."

I drum my fingers against the table. "What if I send in a fake anti-American video? Something that looks like it's meant for their reprogramming. But I plant a virus in it—one that tracks where it's played and crashes their systems. Then I offer to go in as a technician to fix it."

Max raises an eyebrow, amused. "You really think they'll let you near their systems? And you think they'll just invite you in to fix it? You'll be locked up the moment you step near that camp."

"But you'd know where I am. I could disrupt their videos, stop them from morphing family members' faces into their victims. Maybe I could rally the prisoners, find a way to escape."

A woman with a pink drink glances my way. I stop talking, taking a long sip of my mocha.

Max waits until she looks away. "You're serious."

I nod. "I have to try."

"What do you want from me? If you're pulling a David and Goliath, you'll need an army to back you up."

"I need you to wiretap the camp. If I get in, you'll know where I am. If things go wrong, I'll need backup."

He raises an eyebrow. "Backup? The military wouldn't lift a finger for a Neverborn. You told me yourself the General wants you dead."

"I know. But think of the story—*A Neverborn Saves American POWs.*"

Max leans forward, eyes glinting with interest. "Now you're talking."

"I need someone in Military Intelligence who knows how the camps operate—what kind of tech they use. Someone trustworthy. Can you help with that?"

Max scratches his stubble. "Give me a day to dig into it. If I find anyone, they'll contact you. And be careful." He turns off the recorder, stands up, and strides out without looking back.

I finish my drink and catch the packed bus back to Chon Buri. The riders stare at me. They're close enough to see that my makeup is a disguise. When I get to Cheriya's house, I shower and then pull out Arun's computer and start searching—*"How does the Chinese military get tech support?"*

Cheriya comes in, her breath carrying the sweet smell of papaya. She leans over my shoulder. "What are you doing?"

"Trying to figure out how to investigate the camp without getting captured."

She shakes her head, frowning. "You either help or you not," Cheriya snaps, her voice harsh like broken glass. "Arun in there. Research not bring him back. You too scared to act?" Her voice tightens, sharp, and strands of black-and-gray hair fall loose from the bun pinned by sticks.

I swallow, hard. She's right. My fingers hover over the keyboard, but the screen blurs in front of me. Somewhere in those caverns, men like me are trapped, waiting for someone to make the first move. I have to be that someone. I close the computer. Resolve tightens in my chest like a fist.

Her eyes narrow. She shakes her head with a low groan before stomping out of the room, dialing a number on her phone. I can only translate the words, "two American soldiers for sale."

CHAPTER THIRTY-FIVE

Kana

"Bum, grab your stuff. Now. Something is off. I think . . . Cheriya might sell us."

"Dude, for real?" Bumble snaps his legs under his chair, leaning forward.

"For real. I mean it," I say, my mind racing. "Head to the South Korean embassy in Bangkok. Ask for a tourist visa, figure it out from there. Go. Now."

"What about you?" Bum pauses.

"Go! This is what I came for. Get out the back door." *God, give me courage.*

"Love you, man," he yells as he runs away.

A military truck pulls up. "Go, they're here!" I yell. My chest caves in, and my gut churns like a butter paddle. But this is me. Not Kekoa, not Dad or Mom. My choice. Whether I live or die. *Please God. Help me find Arun—if he's even in the POW camp.*

Seven men with wrestler's builds leap from the truck and run toward the house. I almost stumble, walking straight toward them. They're dressed in printed short-sleeved shirts and shorts, like regular guys heading to work in Thailand—like they aren't killers who wouldn't think twice about ending my life. One approaches me. His eyes are blue, and his heart is stone. In an instant, one of them throws a brown cloth bag over my head. I jerk back, my arms up, trying to flip it off, but he slams me to the ground. My wrists sting from catching my weight.

Someone steps on my back between my shoulder blades and pulls my hands behind me and cuffs them. With the grass scent under me, and the body odor from the guy above, I press into the grass as if I could be protected by it. One commands the others in rapid-fire Chinese, their words a blur to my ears. Footsteps stomp onto the lanai, and the door swings. God, let Bumble get away. Please!

A man yanks me up and pushes me toward what must be the truck. "Climb in," someone says. Without any hands, all I can do is try to lift my leg high enough. But someone lifts and rolls me onto the dirty wooden truck bed. After struggling to stand, I'm pushed into the back. Others around me moan, cry, and yell in the chaos of the truck. The smell of cigarette smoke and sweat fills the air. Someone shoves me down onto a hard bench. I hear the clamoring of others around me, but I can't tell if Bumble is among them. My hands are secured onto a metal loop on the truck wall close to the bench. I can feel the metal, but I can't pull free. If only I could call out Bum's name, but that would give away that I expect Bum to be captured too.

I hum the old Star Wars theme tune Bumble and I used to sing before. A blow knocks my head against the back of the truck.

My eye and eye socket stings, and the back of my head hurts from where I hit the truck. Pain snakes up my spine from the whiplash. No one hums back. My head aches. The texture of my head covering is a burlap texture, rough on my skin and itchy, but it's woven finer than burlap because I can't see through it. The truck rattles and roars for hours, barely louder than the thud of my heart. Sweat drenches my shirt, and I can't get enough air through the bag. I tip my head back to allow more air to come in at the bottom. If I can calm myself, I won't need as much air, but my heart won't stop racing. A prisoner begs for mercy and a thud and moan tell me—mercy doesn't exist here. My nerves catapult through me, hyper-aware of every sound. My muscles are ready to launch me at any time, but all I can do is rock around with every bump. *Lord, keep Bumble and Mia safe.* I never got a chance to tell Mia how much she means to me. Why am I so lame that I didn't talk with her more? Discover her more?

To calm my pole-vaulting heart, I remember home. The week before I left for boot camp, we all ate the dinner Mom and I made—Hot Chicken Salad with Sweet Potato Fry Bread and salad. My mouth begins watering thinking about the flavors. I had minced rosemary to put in the Fry Bread and extra garlic. The Hot Chicken Salad had extra dried cranberries in it, adding a sweet taste to the creamy chicken casserole topped with purple potato hash browns. My stomach growls. After dinner, we all played Dominion. I didn't win, but I miss the playful banter during the game. Since boot camp, I've realized how I took for granted my family's love and all the wonderful experiences we had every day.

A sense of claustrophobia hits me, hot bodies pushing against me on both sides. The smells of vomit and blood make me want to gag.

If I die, it's fighting for the prisoners. The truck finally stops after some hours. I realize I'm tied to it with something like zip ties, and I can't pull free. Footsteps land on the street, followed by yelling and screaming. More people pile back into the truck. Muffled sobs blend into the chaos. Diesel fumes make me cough. I hear others coughing too. My tongue sticks to the roof of my mouth. I need to pee, but there are no bathroom breaks on this trip.

The truck turns onto an unpaved road, and I constantly bump into the prisoner next to me. My arms are still bound, yanking my shoulders. The captors sound gleeful, chattering in Chinese while drinking what smells like beer while the prisoners only moan and retch. Maybe they are getting paid for capturing us.

The truck stops again. Someone pushes my head forward and snips the tie binding me to the vehicle, then pulls me to my feet and to the edge of the truck. He shoves me out onto the ground. My hands instinctively jerk against the bindings to catch myself. My breathing is ragged. Dust flies into my nostrils as my hips land hard, my shoulders hitting something solid. Panic rivets through me. Guns fire. Men scream, and someone yells in broken English, "Stand up, you dogs!" Will they shoot me here?

I scramble to my feet, and someone shoves me forward. The air smells of blood, sweat, dust, and gravel. By the small opening at the bottom of my head covering, I see a small pool of blood soaking into the ground on my left, but I have no time to dwell on it. We climb metal stairs. The clanging of our feet mingles with our whimpers, reminding me of death bells. My mind explodes with terror. What awaits me? Torture? Death? I want to hug Mom and Dad one last time. And Mia. I need them to know I love them. I'm sorry for every time I thought my brothers were idiots for thinking I was always right. I'm sorry.

We enter a room with worn dirty brown ceramic tiles. The sounds echo like it's not a big room with the smell of a rock cave and feces. Soldiers stand front and back, their grimy leather combat boots unmistakable, different from the guys who captured me. Outside, there's screaming, questions yelled in Thai, something about baht, followed by gunshots. The air is thick with the acrid scent of gunpowder. A distant thud echoes, then silence falls. I want to cry. Run, just turn and run! I scream inside myself. Make no sound! my head says. Every muscle demands I run, but I can't see and would get shot before I could escape.

"Kun Cheu a rai?"

"Kana David Munson."

The man rips the mask off my head and studies my face. "You're not Thai," he says in perfect English, replacing the dirty bag over my head. His thin, leathered face is colder than ice. He wears a clean, ordinary camo shirt and pants.

"No, I'm a tourist from America," I manage, barely able to breathe. The bag clings to my wet forehead.

"Why did you come to Thailand?" he asks.

"I came to help prisoners of war."

His laughter sends chills down my spine. "You think you can save the world? Stupid, unmanly American. You are helpless!" He yells. "Who did you come with?"

"I was in MANA, but they abandoned me."

"They abandoned you." He laughs. "Because you weren't enough of a man. You were such a bad soldier; they didn't want you." The guy howls and slaps his leg, enjoying the joke. "Where are you from?"

"Kauai, Hawaii," I stammer.

"What is the name of your father?"

"I'm, I'm an orphan. No father or mother," I say, shaking, barely able to form words.

"You are lying to me!" he screams, clicking something.

The zap knocks me to the ground, pain radiating where it touched me. I pull my feet beneath me and rise, stepping forward without the use of my hands, but I slip on something that smells like urine. Probably mine. "Take a sample of my blood. You'll find a birth father and mother somewhere, but I've never met them. They don't know I am alive. I'm a Neverborn." I talk so fast that I can hardly understand what I'm saying.

"Neverborn? Ha! Your father didn't want you. He wouldn't have you as his son." His words spit venom, each one a stab.

"My father . . . doesn't . . . know."

He growls. "Who is your girlfriend or wife?"

"No . . . none."

He sighs in irritation and yells, "You can't even get anyone to love you. Who raised you?"

I hear in my mind, "Don't give them bait." After a deep breath and a cough to buy time, I reply, "The old man who raised me was 85. He's gone now." My head hangs low.

"Who else?" he demands, tapping the floor with the Taser wand. "Tell me, or I'll tase you."

"A dog, Mischief."

"I don't care about dog! Who are friends?"

His glare penetrates the bag. "No. No friends. I wasn't allowed friends." Neverborns live in shame. People don't want to be friends with Neverborns, I want to say, but the words won't come.

He throws something down and yells something in Chinese. I'm pushed sideways and hear someone behind me. Someone turns my shoulders to face left, and I walk that way, on tile, then concrete. Sounds are muffled; men are talking in Chinese from far away. What now? God, is this when I'm shot? I calm myself. Getting to see Jesus and be in heaven invites me, but it's hard to shake the panic and pain to think of heaven. And I want to free the POWs, not die without helping anyone.

I'm taken into a room, pushed down on a bed, strapped down, and injected with something. The needle jabs hard. Yelling will do me no good; they may even enjoy hearing my agony. I clamp my lips shut. Will I ever see Mom and Dad again? Will this kill me? Mia, I love you. I'm sorry I didn't ever tell you how beautiful and sweet you are.

The shot makes me woozy. Someone starts asking me questions, and I hear myself talking, but I have no control over what comes out. The interrogator sounds frustrated. "You sorry excuse of a man, Mia found a real man. She'll never come back to you." I don't know how he knows. Then they unstrap me from the table, but my hands are still bound.

Once I'm pulled to my feet, someone pushes me out the door into a hall. As I walk forward, prodded by the taser poking my back unpowered, the floor turns to dirt and gravel. A musty, dank smell makes me sneeze. The echo makes me think I'm in a hall. Leading to where? A hand pushes me to move faster. Moments later, a voice says, "Stop." I hear a creaking sound, like a giant metal door opening. A gust of wind brings a smell that nearly knocks me backward. Rotting meat, dung, urine, death. The stench hits hard, burning my throat. I step back, but a shove sends me flying into the darkness.

CHAPTER THIRTY-SIX

Mia

I stand before the Navy headquarters in Bangkok, my heart racing as if I'm at the start of a marathon. Canyon's latest handwritten message, a lifeline to Kana, is stuffed in my back pocket. I'll keep it forever, or until Kana is safe. If Canyon can keep telling me what Kana or Bumble discover, maybe I can be the link that saves them.

No medals are waiting for me inside—only the possibility of being arrested and charged with desertion. General Shipley would have labeled my report just that. My fingers tremble, refusing to push the door open.

A pair of officers step out, holding the door for me.

"Thank you," I whisper, slipping in behind them. The rush of cool, conditioned air gives me a moment to think. *God, please let me talk to someone nice. Please don't let me be arrested.*

I freeze, staring at the no-nonsense tile floors, the tan bare walls, and the folding chairs that line the waiting room.

"May I help you? Do you have an appointment?" The receptionist behind a glass window calls out.

I force myself forward. "No . . . Could I, uh, talk to someone . . . nice?" My shaking hand presses against the wall, anchoring me like a fragile leaf caught in a storm. *How can I be this weak when people's lives are on the line? Kana's for one.*

The woman in her blue uniform offers a small smile and leans closer to the mic. "Sergeant Steputis, are you free?"

"Affirmative." A middle-aged man emerges, followed by a curly-redheaded guy I vaguely recognize from Basic.

"Mia?" The redhead's face flushes. "Mia? From Basic?"

I offer a hand, a smile breaking through my anxiety. "Red, right? That's what they called you?"

He grins sheepishly, his nervous energy matching mine. "Yeah, well, I'm Zacarias. Private First Class."

Sergeant Steputis glances at Red with a look of amusement. "Well, Private, I think you can handle this." He gives me a nod and leaves.

"Come this way, Mia. We can use the conference room." Red leads me into a small conference room with a table for ten, plain linen walls, and a smartboard. He pulls out a chair for me before taking a seat across the table.

His friendliness is comforting, but a nagging thought creeps in—Does he think I'm interested in him? I shake it off and dive into my explanation, words spilling out in a jumble as I tell him about Kana and Bumble.

Red listens, then grabs the computer to start taking notes. "Kana was that guy who had trouble talking to girls, right?" His eyes study me, almost too curiously.

"Yeah. It took him a while, but . . . he came around." Heat rises to my cheeks.

"Oh, good." Red's smile is polite, but there's something behind it—something disappointed.

He types for a moment before asking, "You're mostly concerned about the two guys? Not . . . your own situation?" His question hangs heavy in the air, and I hesitate, anxiety tightening my throat.

I pause, rubbing the tops of my thighs, a habit I can't shake when I'm nervous. "This could save lives, Red. If Kana and Bumble can locate the POW camp and we get word, maybe the Navy could launch a rescue."

Red's face shifts, puzzlement mixed with interest. "Did Kana give any clues about where the camp is?"

"It's not confirmed, but his brother, Canyon, thinks it might be an opal mine."

"An opal mine, huh?" Red pulls up a map online, zooming in on a small mountain range. He keeps scrolling until a blurry satellite image shows soldiers milling around, some guarding a large door.

"Sergeant Steputis," Red calls on his wristcom, his voice more serious now. "Could you join us in the conference room?"

Hope flickers within me, but fear gnaws at the edges—what if I'm too late?

CHAPTER THIRTY-SEVEN

Kana

Hands saw at the zip tie binding my wrists, releasing me, while a thief ransacks my pockets. Someone rips the bag off my head, and darkness swallows me whole. The stench—ammonia, urine—claws at my throat, gagging me. Though darkness envelops me, I sense figures surrounding me like demons. The stench of rotting flesh twists my stomach. A screeching band spits out a distorted anthem to China's glory. The music roars so loud it drowns my thoughts, pressing against my skull like a vise. I can't think. What is it? Who else is here? Mia? Arun? Bumble?

I turn around and the clammy, near oxygen-less air shocks me. Hands claw at my clothes, stripping me piece by piece—my shirt torn away, my belt yanked free, sandals—ripped from my feet. I can't stop them. My voice gets lost in the chaos. "Hey, stop!" I yell. "What is this? Who are you?"

No one talks, but the music blares, "China will win, China will win. If you wait long enough, you'll see it again. China will win. China will win. China will win." I'm pushed down and hands drag my pants off me. I hear grunts, but the smell of sweat, fecal material, and bad breath makes me cover my face with my hands. They leave me in only my shorts. I wriggle away and push my way through a crowd in the darkness. Bites like flea bites assault my legs and arms. The room hums with the sound of wings—flies crawl over my face, landing on my eyes, in my mouth. No matter how I swipe at them, they return, relentless, buzzing like demonic whispers.

One song ends and another starts. I cover my ears with my hands and crouch down. Others are close—I can smell them. The noise invades my mind like a thief crawling in your window holding a crowbar like a softball bat. You can't think of anything else.

My eyes adjust to the darkness. I see shapes of people lying or sitting on the ground. Far above me, a tiny hole lets in light, a pinhole of light in a giant, black cavern. The ceiling and floor are uneven. This is what Bobbers talked about. He's been here. Around the edges are lips of rock meandering into alcoves and crevices, and everywhere people sprawl or sit, slumped. Something moves next to me. I grab it. A smooth exoskeleton bug wiggles in my hand. About two inches long, I know this bug—a cockroach. I throw it in front of me and try to step on it. It crunches under my bare foot.

I turn to the guy next to me and shout, "I'm Kana. What's your name?" High above me the music wails, "You are nothing without China, nothing by yourself. You will be nothing without China's help. China believes in you. China believes in you."

The guy grunts and turns away. It's all too much, the hunger, smells, hopelessness, the invasion of your privacy. I wonder if he thinks Americans killed his family like Bobbers did.

"Did Americans really kill your family?" I ask him and brush off flies.

He turns like a wild man and screams. "Don't you get it? Americans killed all our families. Every last man here saw videos of his family being murdered!"

"It's all a lie," I say. "They drugged you and got the names of your loved ones, got their pictures off social media and attached them to videos to make you think that."

He yells louder. "You stupid kid. You know nothing. Now shut up before I eat you!"

Hope feels distant, a risk too great to consider, a concept too fragile to grasp. I shudder and wonder if prisoners really do eat each other. Fear crouches at my door like a predator, bursting in without an invitation.

This world is surreal. The cave has uneven, damp, sharp edges. I sit and lean against a rock. Why did I come here? What was I thinking? My body shakes. Rubbing my temples helps with the headache I didn't realize I had until now. The pounding music chisels away my hope.

Lord, how can anyone see the truth through this suffocating darkness?

After a while, I hear inside my heart, "You tell them. I sent you."

I don't want to risk being yelled at. My brother, Canyon, jumps out to save people. Kekoa does the right thing. I analyze. *"God, why did you do this to me?"*

With my elbows on my knees and my chin on my palm, I wait.

Philippians 4:13, a verse my parents instilled in me, drifts to the surface—*"I can do everything through him who gives me strength."* *But here? In this tomb of hopelessness? My heart feels too shredded for strength.*

I nod my head. *But I can't. What can I do in this death trap?* I thought I could. Stupid heroic me. I walked toward that truck, not away from it. I thought I could save the world here. But the demons captured me.

"*I can do all things through Christ who strengthens me.*"

"What? What can I do?"

The music rocks above me, making it take longer to think and hear from God. My hands flatten, pushing harder against my ears to quiet the chaos of noise. I try to still myself. The music seems to beat out my hope as it pounds in the lies.

"*I can do all things through Christ, who strengthens me.*"

But the weight of suffering rips open my heart. I make myself move around and touch the cave edges. The rocks are jagged and damp. Someone lies in the curl of the rock opening. I can't tell if it's a lava tube or a mine shaft in the dark, but I don't feel any wood supports, just crumbly rocks.

"Go away, or I'll smash your brains out with this rock," he says. "This is mine."

A fly crawls up my nose, and I blow air out and think about what he said.

The irony. We're in the corner of a graveyard, rocky and uneven, and he's threatening someone who might take his two feet of rock. The blast of a new song grates at my sense of self like I am a piece of cheese. No. Less. A stick, thrown away, lying there waiting to be crushed underfoot. My hand finds the wet crumbly cave's side to steady myself in the dark.

Moving like a slug, I inch my way around the edge, barely able to see. Some men growl like animals when I get close, some whimper and groan like they're ready to die. Two hundred men could fit in here. All these men breathe what little air they can get from that tiny hole above. No wonder my head feels foggy. I ask some if I can pray for them, but no one even listens to me. My voice, another noise blending with the lies coming out of the loudspeaker, has no value. My passion wilts. I only want to go home.

"Hit me in the head. Take a rock. I can't take no more. No more." A man near me says in a beggar's voice, like a homeless man on drugs. But his drug is hunger. He sounds young, too young to want to die.

"Hey, man, tell me your story." I crouch next to him.

"Will you kill me then . . . please?"

Could I even do a mercy killing? The ethics of it drives my brain crazy. I can't think about it. "Where you from?" I put my hand on what I hope is his arm. It's clammy.

"Tennessee. Grandma raised me to be a rock star." He laughs, sarcasm filling his words, but it ends sounding like a sob. "Grandma."

"You a Neverborn like me?"

"Most of us are here. Nobody wants to talk about it. Country pretends we're not people and then slams us into the front line before we can tie our shoes. The Chinese traded a bunch of us for non-Neverborn prisoners."

Traded? For non-Neverborns? I bring my thoughts back. "Your life is just beginning. I promise."

"And what is your promise worth? A Neverborn in a POW camp. Twice sentenced to death."

I smile and pat his arm. "That's true. Before I kill you, tell me what happened when you first came."

"Do I have to go through it again? I can't live with the memories the first time it happened," he yells.

"Yes." I sit beside him cross-legged. The hard, slimy rocks poke up and hurt my backside.

"Bagged me like a damn chicken, dragged me inside. They shot me up, stuck needles in me, pulled out every last secret . . . " Then they threw me in here. After two days, a Chinese soldier opened the door and called my name. I stumbled out, and he put me on this chair with a screen. Poked wires onto my body everywhere. He chokes up. "That's when they show me videos of grandma being . . . " The man groans.

"Abused, tortured, and murdered. You thought it was her because you recognized her face."

He stifles a sob and shakes.

"Stay with me," I say. "Tell me, if you isolate just her face, is it a face from a picture she posted on social media?"

He puts his hands on his face. "Matter of fact, yes, her anniversary picture. We had a big celebration in the backyard."

"That's because you were shown a video where your grandma's face was dubbed onto another woman. Your grandma probably isn't dead. It's all part of the propaganda the Chinese are using. How did you respond? With anger or sorrow?"

"Oh, I sobbed like a newborn baby," he says and puts his hand on my arm. "Grandma could really still be alive?"

"Yes. If you talk to others about the video, I bet you'll find that it's the same clip with just the face changed."

He sits up, leaning on his arm. "Oh, wow. Wow." After a minute, he says, "But my baby sister?" He pauses. "Wait. It looked like the school photo she posted. Whoa." The man cries and turns to face away from me, sobbing. I put my hand on his arm for comfort. After a few minutes, he rises and says, "So, what happens now? Do we all die believing everyone else we love is already dead, so there's no use living?"

I pat his arm. "I'm a nerd who figures things out for someone else. Other people do the hero stuff. I have figured nothing out except what the Chinese are doing with their videos, but I know God. Jesus has been my friend, and I'm going to press into believing He has more for all of us than this." The swell of faith seems to come out of nowhere. God?

"Dude, you're crazy." He lies back down and rolls over. Now his back is to me. "Don't you think the Americans could rescue us if they wanted to? We're Neverborns. No one sees us either down here or at home. Society calls us thieves. The government won't let us hold a job or buy a car. The only identity we are allowed is as a soldier, to be put on the front lines. As good as dead unless they can use us somehow. Just like they harvest and sell organs from babies . . . death awaits those not chosen. And the abortionist gets rich from the death of the infants. Our country wins battles at our expense—a casualty number, not a tragedy."

Kekoa would know what to say. My mind races with horrible thoughts. I can't concentrate. The music breaks apart my thoughts. This man needs hope. *Here's the problem—find a solution.* He needs perspective. *God, help me put it into words.* I rub my neck and start in. "The whole country can think we're worthless, but that doesn't mean we are. You know people are precious. Every person, everywhere. I think that truth comes from our creator, God. If you think you're a victim, then you've made yourself a victim. Even here. Even if we die—die the man you can be proud of, die caring about others, die having made things right with God."

"Hmm," he mumbles.

Fear has less hold of me now. Even if I die, I've been able to help at least one of these desperate men.

The song blasting from above us is, "Trust the Chinese, kill the Caucasian. Know who your friends are, and who you can be, who you can be, who you can be."

This noise—it's killing us, breaking us. It's piped in somehow. I have to find it, stop it, before it destroys what's left of us. As I stumble along the edges of the great "room," the sound echoes off the sides and distorts the timing, which makes the "music" even more irritating. There seems to be more than one speaker. First, though, I have to know who's here.

"Mia! Bumble! Arun!" I yell. Only the music blares back. My gut soaks in the sorrow all around. Maybe they got away. Or were shot. Or worse.

At the back end of the cavern, there are more rabbit trails, and more people hide and catch bugs to eat, but it's darker with no trace of light. The odor is better, though. My nose is losing its ability to smell the stench, which may be the reason, or there is more rock per body ratio in the outer regions of the cave. It has to be the opal mine Bobbers talked about.

All light disappears—the sun must have gone down. I touch the ground, looking for a place to at least sit. Jagged edges of the rock rip the skin on my finger. Getting an infection now in this filthy place is the last thing I need. I suck my finger and wipe off the rocks sticking to the back of my shorts and put pressure on my cut. In time, I work my way to a sitting position without scraping my bare skin up. At home, we'd do stupid stuff, dive into Albizia trees, go on our zipline at lightning speed, throw green mangos at each other. I'm used to bruises and cuts, but these hurts were inflicted by people who hate me. Even after my not becoming a victim speech, the weight of the oppression squishes me into a marshmallow, spineless, and helpless. I get it. Everything and everyone here is hopeless.

The music stops. God, thank you! Now, I can think. Instead, I hear groans, sighs, sounds of coughing, and vomiting, mixed with someone delirious having a living nightmare—yelling and crying. My heart falls to a level I've never experienced before. Men all around me are in pain—dying. I came to deliver these men from this. But how? It's impossible. I'm going to die here.

✦

CHAPTER THIRTY-EIGHT

Kana

In the suffocating darkness of the cave, water begins to drip down the walls, a sign of the rain above. The clatter of men pressing their tongues against the rocks fills the air. Above us, water drips steadily, and scores of men slurp or suck at the walls for the precious liquid. It takes me several agonizing minutes to get a mouthful, my parched mouth pressing desperately against the stones. After what feels like an eternity, the dripping stops. The cave falls into an uneasy quiet, punctuated by the occasional moan, cry, or scream.

I wake to nearly blackout darkness. The shadowy shapes around me are ghostly apparitions. I need to find a place to relieve myself. The sounds of urine hitting the ground in one area guide me. Navigating the cavern, I'm surprised at how much better I can sense my surroundings than when I first was thrown in.

My bare foot steps down onto something sharp, and a sting worse than ten hornet bites pierces it. I yelp and lift my foot, feeling something slither from my toe to my hand and sting it again. A centipede! I fling it away, but another man yells in alarm. "Centipedes! Here!" I say. My foot throbs.

I follow my nose to the pee hole and add my own contribution to the stench. On my way back, I pass a man asking, "Dead? Dead?" It would be laughable if it weren't real. Then someone says, "Here." A man drags a body across the cavern and announces, "Lord, take this man to heaven. Amen."

That's not how it works. It must make them feel better believing you can ask God to take someone else to heaven.

While two men argue over sleeping quarters, I hear the body being thrown down with a thud. "Dead?" the undertaker continues his chant. "Dead?"

My nose still burns from the ammonia of the urine, but I'm becoming numb to the smell. Tracing my way to where they threw the body, I feel a cliff's edge with my toe. I toss a rock over the edge. It takes a second before I hear the thud at the bottom—or onto the pile of decomposing bodies. Will we all be thrown down into the carcass pile soon? Was my dream of rescuing POWs just an illogical hope, a pipe dream? I'm the logical one of my brothers. This is beyond logic. How could I have completely fooled myself? I, of all people, should have known better than to let myself get into this situation and then to drag Bumble into it too . . . and Mia. My hand covers my face. I let him believe that we could be rescuers, not victims. I should have seen what would lie ahead and told the Neverborn cadets to survive in the Kauaian jungles, with beaches, showers, bathrooms, clean water, and plenty of pig and fruits.

The music begins, its relentless sound ripping away my peace and tormenting me with its lies. I cover my ears but still hear the cacophony. It takes hours to trace the sound's source, but I need a distraction from the "feasting" in the center of the room. Two speakers blare, their location hidden. I walk around the room, trying to find where the speakers are.

Suddenly, the sun beams directly down the hole, turning the black and gray into creams and browns. My eyes burn. I glance up in short spurts, as long as I can tolerate the pain. The rock shines, reflecting the light from above—brown streaked with white limestone, an opal mine for sure. I see sores on the men, infected and filled with pus. Bats hang high on the walls. Will they suck blood from us as we sleep? Giant ten-inch centipedes dangle from the ceiling, ready to attack the bats. I didn't notice last night, but I was deep within an alcove. Maybe that's why men gravitate toward the edges.

There are speakers high around the perimeter of the great room, and bell-shaped lights with large bulbs in the middle turned off or not working. I think I see a cord connecting them, but I can't move quickly enough to trace where the wires enter the cavern.

The light fades.

A creaking sound draws every eye to the door. Light streams in like sunlight as the door opens. A man is thrown in, his head still covered. The door slams shut like a guillotine.

"What the devil?" he exclaims as people scramble to fight over the bag on his head.

I recognize the voice. "Bumble?"

"Kana?" Bumble turns, but his vision is obscured.

I make my way to him and push away the scavengers, trying to rip off his clothing. "Yes, Bro, I'm here. I'm here," I yell over the music until I touch his shoulder.

He embraces me in a Bumble bear hug, holding me for what feels like an eternity. "What is this place? The smell! It's like raw sewer meets garbage dump times a thousand."

"Wait until you can see it."

"You can see in this hellhole?"

"Come, put your hand on my back and follow me. Be careful not to fall. There are men all around on the ground, and centipedes!"

"Centipedes? Here? Like on Kauai?" Bumble's big hand rests on my thin shoulder.

"Yep, I just got stung—on my foot and my hand."

"Dang!"

I guide Bumble to a quieter section of the cave. The air here is thicker, somehow heavier, like the cave itself is closing in on us. Bumble gasps behind me.

"How do you breathe in here? It's like . . . we're buried alive," Bumble says.

I shake my head, trying to ignore the sour tang of rot on my tongue. "Well, none that doesn't stink. You get used to it. Eventually."

Bumble's tone is impatient. "What happened at Cheriya's? Why did she rat us out?"

"I think she thought I wouldn't leave to find her son. She forced the issue by calling to trade us for her son or sell us. What happened to you?"

The music pounds, but it's less oppressive in this shaft. "Wait, let me make us a place to sit first. We'll need our energy."

"Ouch! You can't sit down with all these rocks." Bumble hunches due to the low ceiling. I touch the area to find a rock. When I return, I pound it with a rock from the ground to break off protrusions and scrape it to make a flatter seat. My vision blurs, and my legs wobble as I pound. My hands shake as I feel the smoothed-out rock. Hunger gnaws at me, making my every action feel like it's draining what little energy I have left.

"A lot of work just to sit," Bumble says, swatting at flies. "Geez, we should eat the flies instead of them eating us."

We sit with our knees almost touching our faces.

"No cushions? These people have no manners," Bumble comments.

I laugh until my side hurts. Bumble catches on and his laughter joins mine, making the room echo with our sound. Death is as close as our own toenails, but laughing releases some of my tension.

When we regain our composure, Bumble says, "You walked toward the enemy, and I stood there wondering what in tarnation you were doing. When I finally realized you were sacrificing yourself so I could escape, I ran. But it was too late. A gorilla of a guy caught me, flipped me over faster than a mosquito could sneeze. He tied my hands and covered my head with a bag. I waited over an hour, lying face down. Cheriya talked to them, but in Thai. I couldn't understand. When a second truck came, I had to climb in and then sat tied for a whole day. Different guards took turns watching us. They only spoke Chinese. Then I got trucked over here."

He looks around. "My eyes are adjusting a bit. I can almost see the walls."

"Dark adaptation. It gets lighter at midday for about fifteen minutes when the sun shines through the daylight hole. The rest of the time, it's this dark."

"What about food?"

Leave it to Bumble to think of food. My stomach grumbles, almost in response. "I'm starving. You don't want to know about the food."

"No, I do," he insists. "I haven't eaten since Cheriya cooked our last meal together."

"I see some people eating things they find on the rocks. Probably dung beetles, earthworms, termites, larva from blowflies."

Bumble gags.

"How do we get out?" Bumble adjusts his position, feeling around the rock formations.

"Even if we could get the iron door open, the light would blind us, and we'd just get shot. Our only chance is up."

"That hole is way up there. Have you tried climbing?"

I sigh. "When the light shone directly down, I looked. It's nearly vertical. With crampons and a pickaxe, I might attempt it, but without them, it would be suicide—a fall to my death."

"What resources do we have here that could help? Any knives or forks?"

I chuckle. "Nope. All we have is bones." Then it hits me—a femur broken in half might have a sharp edge. If I drive it into the rock wall with a stone, it could make a foothold.

"That's it, Bumble. Bones!" I say.

"Bones." His tone is flat.

"We'd need to work together. One of us would have to descend into the pit of dead bodies and collect femur bones. Then we could break them to create points."

"Dip into the pit of dead bodies?" he says.

"If we don't, we'll end up in the pile."

"You can swim among the rotting flesh and bones. I'm staying on dry ground."

"Okay," I say, frowning at the thought. "But we need a rope for you to pull me out."

"Rope? You think there's rope in here?" He sounds amused. "We're not really getting out here, are we?"

"I don't know," I admit. Hope was almost real for a moment. Every moment we sit idle, we grow more drained, more tired, more hungry—closer to joining the pile of the dead.

CHAPTER THIRTY-NINE

Mia

I find a job waiting tables at a local spot named *Pitta's Nest*—the English translation of the name— after a bright teal bird in Thailand. It's small, cozy, and bustling, a place where tourists and locals mix. Learning the Thai menu and enough of the language to hold a conversation fills my days. After a couple of weeks, I feel confident enough to start investigating what happened to Kana and Bumble. Whenever Americans come in, I probe subtly, asking about their backgrounds. No one has heard of them.

A buff American walks in, sitting down at one of my tables with a couple of guys.

I offer them a menu, get them water, and ask where they're from.

"Max!" the American offers his hand. "From Orange County, California."

After juggling the water pitcher, I shake his hand. "Mia, from New Mexico."

"How did you get here? Or, rather, why did you come to war torn Thailand?" He doesn't even glance at the menu.

I take a deep breath. "It's a long story. I came with MANA cadets, but we were abandoned."

Max's eyebrows go up. "You were with Kana and Bumble?"

I almost drop the menus in surprise. "You know Kana and Bum?" The water pitcher tips in my hand and spills water on my feet.

The table of guys laughs.

Max pats the table. "When do you get a break? Can you come talk to me?" He hands me his card.

Like in a dream, I take their orders and fight to concentrate on my tables of people.

Finally, after the rush is over, two of the guys leave, but Max stays.

"Okay, I'm off as soon as I finish your payment," I say breathlessly, inputting his card information into my hand-held device. My pulse quickens. "Have you heard from either of them?"

"Yeah. I heard Kana's planning to infiltrate a POW camp . . . to rescue the prisoners."

My stomach drops. "Infiltrate? As in . . . work for them?"

"Exactly. He's walking into the lion's den, Mia," Max says, his voice low. The clatter of dishes and laughter around us seems to fade, replaced by the loud thudding of my pulse in my ears. Max leans in slightly, his eyes narrowing as if measuring my reaction. The air feels thick—hard to breathe. My fingers tighten around the pitcher, white-knuckled.

"Is there anything I can do to help? Anything at all? I'm in contact with Kana's brother, Canyon. I told the Navy that Canyon thinks Kana will go to the opal mines in Myanmar to get the POWs out."

Max hesitates. "Really, if you hear anything, call me, okay?"

"Thank you, Max. For everything."

"Stay safe, Mia."

He leaves, but I want to chase after him and keep him close. At least I have Max's phone number to bug him and see if he's heard from the guys. *Kana is walking into the lion's den. Lord, protect him!* I walk home in a daze.

That night, the silence feels deafening as I clutch my pillow, but my mind races. What if he doesn't make it? What if he's caught? The thought twists my stomach into knots. I stare at the ceiling, willing the fear away, but it won't go. My fingers grip the edges of my blanket as if I could anchor myself to something solid. But everything feels like it's slipping out of control. I can't lay here and wait while Kana walks into danger. Not after everything we've been through. I think of the way his eyes softened when he talked about his family, the way he risked everything to protect Bumble and me. There's no way I can abandon him now. Tomorrow, I need to contact Canyon again and go back to Navy headquarters to see what they're doing to monitor the opal mine.

CHAPTER FORTY

Kana

"**C**ome on, Bumble. It's torture with the music blasting, but if it's a sunny day, we need to see the cavern walls in the light. The sun's only up for a few minutes," I say, trying to steady my voice despite the oppressive noise.

On one hand, I'm relieved to have my friend with me; on the other, the thought of putting his life at risk weighs heavily on me. He keeps his hand on my shoulder, leaning on me for balance as we navigate through the crowd and rocky terrain.

The next day, Bumble and I stand in the cavern for what feels like hours. The speakers above assault us with relentless noise, making conversation impossible. Finally, the room brightens as light seeps in. I shut my eyes, covering my face with my hands against the painful glare. Bumble groans beside me. When I open my eyes again, I notice the wall is covered in calcium deposits—like a rough mosaic of small rocks rather than a solid sheet. The opening at the top seems too small for a person to fit through, but it's hard to judge from this distance. The cavern is swarming with thousands of flies.

"See where the speakers are?" I point to the end of the main room in the cavern, about fifteen feet up.

Bumble gasps. "Yeah." I turn to see him staring at the lifeless bodies scattered around the cavern. He curses under his breath. The sunlight fades, plunging us back into darkness.

"How many people are in here?" Bumble asks, his voice tense.

"I don't know. Maybe a hundred," I reply.

He swears again. "Almost none of them can climb that cliff, footholds or not."

"Yeah. We need a rope," I agree.

"Back to the rope idea," Bumble says. "Do you have anything we could use?"

I shake my head. "No grasses, no cloth. Even our rotting underwear tears apart easily."

"What else can we use?" he presses.

The soundtrack above falters briefly. "What if we pull out the speaker or lighting wire?" I suggest.

"That might work, but we'll need a long piece to reach the top of the cavern."

I wait for my eyes to adjust to the dark again. "Let's go." I lead the way, with Bumble keeping a hand on my shoulder. We search the area around the door, feeling for any wires. It's too high to reach the top of the door. "Bumble, let me stand on your shoulders."

"You're crazy. You know that, right?" he protests.

"Come on, bend your knee." I touch the leg I want bent. He complies, and I carefully step onto his thighs and then his shoulders. As I balance on him, I reach up, feeling around the top of the door. I find a package—duct tape over wires. "Can you step left?"

He shifts, and I nearly lose my balance but catch myself just in time. I feel the wire running straight up. Bending down, I tap his head, and he helps me down. We almost stumble in the dark, but I hold on to the door frame until Bumble regains his footing.

"What's up?" he asks, swatting at the persistent flies.

"I need a rock that can saw and one that can cut the duct tape," I say.

Excitement tinges his voice, giving it a bright, eager edge. "It might work? Really?"

"By the grace of God, it might," I respond with a weary smile.

For hours, we search for suitable rocks, examining every edge for sharpness. Bumble stays close, and together we collect ten cutting rocks and twenty sawing rocks. I find a bag—probably used to cover someone's head—and use it to hold the rocks. A centipede crawls up my chest while I'm carrying the bag, making me shudder. After flicking it away, I hear someone nearby eating it.

It reminds me of Canyon daring Kekoa to eat ants during one of our overnights in the jungle. We spent all afternoon scooping up ants, trying to keep them contained for Kekoa to cook. He made a slurry of mangoes and dumped the ants in, cooking the concoction over the fire in a gallon tin can. We all ate some. *I better not think about food now.*

I stand on Bumble's shoulders again and start working on the wire. The cutting rocks make progress with the tape, but sawing through it will take time. I have to be careful to avoid being electrocuted, too. After a while, Bumble says, "Hey, can we take a break? My shoulders are killing me."

I cling to the door frame while Bumble lowers me down. "What are you doing?" a man's voice grumbles.

"Pulling off the wire to help us all get out of here." My feet touch the ground.

"We're never getting out of here. Never," he replies, his voice filled with despair. "You think you can just climb out of here?" the man laughs, a hollow sound that bounces off the cavern walls. "You're dreaming, kid. You're as dead as the rest of us."

"I'm still breathing," I say, my voice tight. "And as long as I am, I'll keep trying."

"Trying for what? More suffering? You think you're a hero? There are no heroes here, just bodies waiting to drop."

I grip the wire tighter, my knuckles white. "Maybe. But I'll die on my own terms."

"Good luck with that," he mutters, bitterness dripping from his voice.

After more sawing, the cord finally severs. The sound of the music stops abruptly, and a collective gasp fills the cavern. I tug on the cord, but it barely moves. Using all my strength, I pull on the wires, and they come unstapled about ten feet. Now I can pull from the ground instead of on Bum's shoulders. I accidentally step on someone's foot.

"Hey!" he yells, cursing at me with unfamiliar insults.

"I'm sorry, I'm sorry. We're trying to find a way out for everyone," I apologize.

"Liar. You're all liars," he snaps, limping away.

"Bumble, help me," I say. Together, we pull down more wire. With a final, combined effort, we get another ten feet of wire down. The cavern is filled with an eerie silence, broken only by the buzzing of flies. I swat them away from my face and nose as they swarm.

A speaker crashes to the ground with the next pull. I yank someone out of the way just before it lands. The men around us start to get agitated, growling in frustration. There's a collective yelling and swearing.

"Men, friends, Neverborns, soldiers. We're one of you, captured, interrogated, and thrown in here to die. I'm Kana. This is Bumble, and we have a plan to get us all out."

A roar of discontent rises from the crowd, not a roar of hope, but one of anger and frustration. Their anger feels like a storm, ready to break.

"We want music!" someone shouts.

I start singing a song I wrote that seems to fit, "When the dark clouds hang over crying—when the tree bones silhouette the sky—icy gusts blow hope, send them flying, the dreams of your life pass you by. Choose not to fear, for God is with you. Do not be dismayed. He will strengthen, he will help you. Do not be afraid." To my surprise, the crowd quiets down. I continue singing softly, as Bumble and I continue to pull at the wire.

"The last speaker will come crashing down. Don't be frightened," I say to those around. "Please move if I'm close to you now." Some men shift to make room. I spot the remaining speaker overhead. As I pull at the wire, my hands trembling from exhaustion, I feel the weight of every man's impending death in this room pressing down on me. *What if this fails? What if we're all just walking toward death together, and I'm leading them into hope when there is no hope?* We put all our strength into pulling it down. Nothing. It doesn't move. "Again," I yell. We pull long and hard.

There's a cracking sound. "Again!" It crashes to the ground with the last of the wire.

"Sing!" someone commands.

The air in the cavern clings to my skin, thick with the scent of decay and rot. The flies are relentless, their tiny wings brushing against my face like living dust. Sweat slicks my skin, mingling with the grime from the rocks. I feel the darkness, an almost physical force, pressing against my chest.

I sing until I hear some men start to snore, as Bumble and I coil the wire and free it from the speakers. I let my voice soften, finishing my song gently.

Bumble detaches the speaker from the wire and sets it aside. We coil the wire and make our way in darkness to the pit of the dead. I fashion a makeshift diaper out of the wire and Bumble ties a part of it around a large anchor rock, lowering me into the pit. I feel around for the squishy bodies and manage to collect some leg bones. It's a grueling task, made harder by the stench and the difficulty of detaching the femurs from the hip socket and knee cartilage. The bodies are splayed across the pit, some twisted at unnatural angles, others lying with a quiet stillness that makes them blend into the rock. The flies buzz over them like vultures. I try not to look too closely, but the stench lingers in the back of my throat, making me retch. After what feels like forever, I have enough bones.

"Okay, Bum, pull me up," I say, and he hauls me up, supporting an armful of leg bones. I dream of cleanliness, of being free from the filth and stench. I'll never take being clean for granted again.

The next day, I can barely move. My leg spasms painfully, and I massage it, walking to shake off the stiffness. With no food and little water, exhaustion clouds my mind. Nutritional deficiencies are causing the spasms. What other symptoms will it produce? When the men wake up, I explain my theory about the Chinese using videos as propaganda to manipulate us. "They drugged us, learned our loved ones' names and locations, then used social media to fabricate torturous murders. Most either lost their will to live or were driven to anger against their own people. If they couldn't find pictures or we didn't react, we were left here to die."

Meanwhile, Bumble breaks the bones against a solid rock, arranging them as footholds against the cavern wall. He steps on each one to test its strength.

"We're going to try to get you out, if you want to go," I say.

"How on earth are you going to do that? We can't fly out of that tiny hole," someone scoffs.

"My plan—"

"Pssh, his plan," someone interrupts.

"My plan is to create footholds from the bones and drive them into the stone wall with rocks. Once I get out—"

"Once he gets out, he's never coming back," someone close to me says.

Bumble's voice rumbles in agreement. "No. Kana did a Jesus thing. He walked toward the Chinese to get captured because he wanted to set you free. He came here because he cares about you. I didn't. A guy tackled me to the ground and drug me here, but Kana chose this—for you." He puts his hand on my shoulder.

Because I can't see people's facial expressions, the touch means much to me.

"Benedict," Bumble says. "My mother named me Benedict. Like Benedict Arnold, who sold out to the British during the Revolutionary War."

I pat his arm. "Benedict is Latin for 'blessed.' You're a blessing to me. I'm grateful to be your friend. You're not Benedict Arnold. You're Benedict McFee."

He doesn't grumble but sits still thinking.

The room quiets, and I sing to the men for a while.

My hand feels along the rock wall. I try to climb different sections and get up ten feet before it's too steep. The cavern is limestone, crumbly and soft. Opals are found in limestone. The danger for me is driving a bone into the stone but having it come out with my weight on it. I pick up my stone and pull out a bone to hammer it in. Bumble breathes heavily below me, the sound of his labored breaths blending with the buzz of flies that never leave us. I hear the faint scrape of bones, brittle in my hands as I drive them into the stone. It takes a lot of hammering, but I can get it in. I stand on it and tumble down to the cavern floor.

CHAPTER FORTY-ONE

Kana

Pain stings across my body from cuts I barely notice anymore. I lie on the cold cavern floor, aching from the fall, weariness pressing down like a weight I can't shake. I've tried my best and failed. If I die here, at least the infected wounds will expedite my journey to whatever lies beyond. It's strange—I've never truly thought about dying until now. There's much I haven't done yet. Fall in love. Get married. Get a job in tech. But those are dreams for someone else, someone who isn't Neverborn. I lie where I fall, staring at the wall that curves around.

"Kana, you okay?" Bumble's voice, filled with concern, pierces through.

"As okay as I can be, considering," I reply, sitting, brushing off the pebbles that have embedded themselves into my skin. Lack of air, water, and food has made my brain fuzzy.

Bum extends a hand down to help me up. He hugs me. "Kana, you're amazing. Your God is amazing. Bro, you almost did it!"

His love gives me an ounce of energy and hope. As a boy, I built a climbing wall with my brothers, positioning pitons at an angle.

I drop my rock and bones into the torn bag, slip it over my shoulder, and start climbing again. With my rock, I drive a bone stake into the wall at a forty-five-degree angle, leaving only the greater trochanter, head, and neck of the bone exposed—just enough to bear my weight. It holds.

Bumble whoops from below. He knows I haven't fallen.

I smile down at him standing on my "stake" in the wall, my joy mingled, hoping others are listening too.

It takes the rest of the day to drive in the bone stakes. My hands slip against the slick rock as I try to pull myself higher. The bone I'm holding is slick. I glance down—the cavern floor seems to stretch further away, like it's hungry, waiting for me to fall. Every muscle in my body screams in protest, but I force myself to keep driving stakes in and climbing higher. The rock is soft, crumbling beneath my fingers, and I can feel it giving way when I finger the area for handholds. The bones snap as I hammer them in, their dry, brittle edges giving way under the force of the rock. I don't let myself think about who these bones belonged to, what their lives were before. They're just tools now. If I let myself think otherwise, I might not be able to do this.

I'm three-quarters of the way up when the door swings open, and the soldiers throw a man in. The door slams shut, and a soldier speaks in Chinese, likely noticing the sudden silence. I freeze, pressing myself against the cavern wall. If he notices the absence of sound or, worse, brings in a light, they'll shoot me. The door closes again. My heart pounds. I start to lose my balance. My fingers find a handhold. The world spins. This is no time to faint or lose my balance. *Lord, help me.*

After a minute, I stop feeling dizzy. Only six more bone halves remain in my bag. I hope it's enough. Vomiting amid rotting flesh has left me weaker and dizzier. My leg spasms. I stop to massage it and move it in circles in the air to restore circulation. Ferns are growing near the top of the wall. Adrenaline surges through me as I taste fresh air. I pinch off some fiddleheads from a nearby fern and pop them into my mouth. They taste like a mix of asparagus and green beans. Moss makes the wall slippery. I insert another piton, but it comes loose. After finding a larger rock, I wedge the stake beneath it, and it holds. A natural ledge provides a foothold. I pound in another stake.

The hole above me isn't large enough for my shoulders. I hammer in two more pitons and stand on them. Grass has grown into the hole, and as I pull it away, dirt falls on my face. *Steady. One wrong move could end it all.* After slamming another bone stake into the wall, I tear at the grass. Loose rocks tumble out, and I push a larger one aside. If the extra force combined with my weight causes my footholds to fail, I could plummet. The space is now big enough, if it the rocks at the opening don't fall to the ground with me still hanging onto them. I descend, nearly slipping as my feet, wet from the moss, struggle for grip. Down is harder than up. My excitement is almost unbearable. If no one discovers me, I could be free. We all could be free.

But reaching the top is just the beginning. We need to figure out how to carry scores of half-dead men to safety. There's a river nearby. If we can get a boat, we might save them. They need medical attention urgently. The Chinese will shoot us on sight. Hiding a hundred men too weak to walk seems impossible. Yet, I cling to hope. Death by gunfire seems preferable to the slow suffering of becoming centipede bait.

When I reach the bottom, a dozen men stand around me, their expressions unreadable. Bumble has found the new guy who was just thrown in. They wait for me.

Bumble hands me the rope. "You did it, you twit. You scaled our mountain."

I hug him, feeling a rush of relief and accomplishment.

Just then, the door opens, and the new man stumbles over. "Coming," he says.

"Bumble, did you . . . ?" I ask.

"Yes. He knows what to say."

The man turns and yells, "Wait for me."

I tense. Did he blow our cover? Will the Chinese figure out what we're up to? All they'd need to do was inject him with truth serum, and he'd reveal everything. We might be in trouble now. If he pretends to be fighting mad, they might release him to kill Americans. Then we wouldn't be coming back. I can't climb if I'm worried the door might open again at any moment.

"Climb, boy!" one man says, pointing to the pitons.

The room is silent, save for the occasional cough and the persistent buzz of flies. All eyes are on me, filled with hope and anticipation, like a mother's eyes as she watches her baby leave for chemo. Will it work?

"They need someone to tell them the truth," I say, though I'd rather not be the one to do it. "Bumble, give a speech. Tell them they're not Neverborns; they're Alreadyborns."

Joy fills me. "Live in the victory, son, not in the temptation," Dad used to say to me. I sing, "You heal my broken spirit. You understand my pain. I kneel before your mercy. Nothing is the same. Your eyes have only love now, when you look upon my shame. Sin's power now is broken when I praise your holy name." I've never sounded so good.

The door opens again, and the same man is thrown inside. The door shuts.

"Welcome home," I say.

He laughs, and the room erupts in laughter. Tears well up in my eyes. Hope. The men have hope. I climb the wall, trying to be cautious. My feet seem to possess an instinct about how to balance. At the top, I push the wire through and freeze, expecting the crack of gunfire any second. Do they know I'm here? My fingers fumble, looking for something solid, and I find a plant—a thick trunk— and haul myself. Once I'm out, I roll over and look up at the blue sky. My eyes burn despite covering them with my hands.

When my vision clears, I scan the area. Fifty soldiers are exercising outside and have guns. No soldiers are visible on the mountain top. Scanning for a stronghold to tie the wire to, I find nothing close. A faint thrum of a helicopter in the distance grows into a deafening roar. I throw myself into the grass, heart pounding, but it's useless—the pilot's eyes are already on me. The helicopter hovers above, and a machine gun fires on the Chinese below. Explosions make the ground shake. I hope it doesn't collapse the mountain and kill us all. Wait . . . the helicopters are on our side! I cheer, my relief palpable.

More helicopters arrive, attacking from the other side. One hovers directly overhead. A man climbs down from a ladder. I steady it as he descends, and a huge rope is dropped, still connected to the helicopter.

"Kana?" he yells into my ear.

I step back, and he grabs me, pointing to himself, and shouts, "Walter."

"How?"

"Talk later," he yells. "Entrance?"

"Yeah," I nod.

"How many men?"

"A hundred or so."

He wraps a separate rope around himself and ties it to the ladder, then looks into the hole. He turns and pukes from the stench.

"Wait till you smell it from the bottom," I shout, though the noise of grenades and gunfire makes it difficult to hear.

Walter throws the giant rope down. I remember the angle—it can't fall straight down. It must be brought from the side of the cliff to the bottom. I slide down the rope, wrapping my legs around it. The speed reminds me of our zipline at home. My hands burn as I squeeze to slow myself. My feet bang on the side, swinging me back out on the rope. I slam into the wall again and grab a piton for stability. Once centered, I throw the rope down the rest of the way.

The men fight over who goes first. Bumble raises the rope above his head, voice steady but firm. "Calm down! Everyone will get their turn. You just have to wait."

"Make a sling," I suggest. The men are too weak to hang on for long.

"Right," Bumble agrees. "The first man to bring me his cloth bag gets to go first."

I see people scramble and work my way to the bottom. Together, we take three bags, rip them open, and tie them to form a makeshift diaper. We fasten it to the rope and tie a knot three feet lower. Then, the men can stand on it. We put the first man in and shout up to Walter. I glimpse the helicopter as it lifts off, the rope tensing. The man is dragged across the slanted wall. I scramble up, pushing the rope away from the side to let it ascend smoothly. As the man nears me, his grin is a brief but comforting sight. The rope flies upward without obstruction, and he's inside the helicopter within a minute. The rope drops again, and we repeat the process.

Men are being brought in from the outer alcoves. Once the able-bodied men are evacuated, Bum creates a knot a couple of feet up from the diaper and uses the torn sacks to secure the chests of the invalids. After some experimentation, he gets it to work. We move the invalids up. Every man wants to go, some hugging Bumble, before stepping into the diaper. Many cry as they pass me, their hands reaching out to touch my arm.

Bumble disappears up the rope, and soon after, the sling drops down for me. My fingers ache as I grab hold, too weak to keep a firm grip. But I don't have time to think—I wrap myself in and let it pull me away from the collapsing cave.

Suddenly, there's an explosion behind the door. The cave shakes, rocks and stones tumbling down. I don't wait. "Go!" I shout hoarsely.

The rope pulls me up, rocks pelting my body. The rope swings more violently than before. As I reach the top, the ground is giving way on the top of the cavern. A soldier stands ten feet back, and the helicopter pulls me toward him as the ground crumbles. He grabs the rope, and we hang on as the helicopter swings down the mountain, its speed sweeping us nearly sideways. My eyes are still adjusting, gunfire popping sporadically. We land on a rocky bluff where the helicopter lowers and drops a ladder. The soldier hands me the ladder, and I climb up. I'm pulled into a seat in a ten-person helicopter.

Ahead, I see the soldier and a dozen other helicopters heading toward Bangkok. This is a high-stakes rescue operation, a swift entry into enemy territory. Fighter jets are taking out the enemy aircraft behind us.

A burly man in a crisp Air Force uniform leans in, yelling over the noise, "You're a hero, son. You've saved the lives of a hundred thirty-two men."

I let out a relieved sigh. My bones ache from days of sleeping on sharp rocks, and spasms of pain shoot up my legs. I massage them, hoping to restore circulation. Mom said leg cramps can be caused by magnesium deficiency. I'm starving. A soldier hands me a bottle of water, and my hand shakes as I gulp it, spilling it onto my mouth and chest. It's refreshingly clean. If we don't get shot down, I may be able to eat tonight.

As we land in U.S.-held territory in southern Thailand, we're hosed down before being allowed to shower and given hospital gowns instead of clothes. Some are taken to a hospital. Afterward, we're assigned a waiting area for a check-up. I'm last to be seen, but lying on a clean floor feels like a luxury. My weary body drifts off to sleep until a nurse wakes me for my turn.

"You'll be fine, son," the older doctor says. "You're dehydrated and malnourished, but you'll be better soon. Start with crackers and electrolyte-rich juice, then fruits and vegetables tomorrow. No meat for a week."

"Thank you, sir," I reply, eagerly anticipating food. Maybe there's mango juice.

As I leave, a soldier stops me. "Kana Munson, General Holden would like to speak with you, sir."

"Can I get some clothes first?"

He chuckles. "Follow me, sir."

I choose a camo T-shirt and standard-issue brown pants. The shoes feel like foot traps, and the socks are too warm, but I wear them anyway.

"Sir." I enter the General's office.

"Son, on behalf of the United States of America, thank you for your unusual courage and valor in rescuing these hundred thirty-two men."

My face flushes with pride. "You're welcome. But I had help. Bumble and I did it together, and my brother, Canyon, helped too." I miss Bumble and Canyon. "Sir, how did you know our predicament?"

"You don't know?"

I shake my head.

"Mia, your colleague in MANA contacted the Navy and your friend Max. From that information, we knew you'd try to rescue the POWs and pinpointed the approximate location. You pulled it off by getting out, and because of Mia, we were ready to support you."

"Mia's okay?" I sink into a chair.

The General laughs. "She looks pretty okay to me."

"But . . . how did they know . . . how did you know when I could get out?"

"Mia convinced the Navy you would succeed and provided information that allowed us to confirm the POW camp's location. We couldn't risk an all-out attack, but we monitored satellite surveillance continuously. As soon as we saw you emerge, we launched the rescue. You can thank Mia."

"That was a brilliant rescue, sir," I say, amazed at the quickness of the helicopters.

He smiles. "It was. We got every man out in an hour and a half. The news will love this."

"Sir, was Arun Wang one of the POWs we rescued?" I ask, my gut tightening with anticipation.

The General checks his computer. "Yes, Arun Wang."

I laugh, thinking of Cheriya seeing her grandson return home. "Yes!" I remember Max. "Might I make a request?" I can't stop smiling.

"What is it?"

"Can I call Max? He deserves to hear this story."

The General rises and shakes my hand. "He's already on it. Max insisted on being in the first helicopter to capture the footage. He's making you a hero, son." He hesitates, adding, "It's not just this POW camp that's been affected by your courage. It's reported that the Chinese can't use their tactics of making prisoners believe Americans killed their families anymore. Mia heard from your brother that you were working on sending videos. Did you put a virus in the videos you sent?"

"I did, sir." My smile broadens. "Oh, am I still in MANA? My chip was deactivated as soon as I landed in Bangkok."

"Well, that's our little secret. Max has made you a war hero. You'll have a couple of months at home, then college, and an officer training school as a decorated soldier. If you agree."

I step back, overwhelmed by the prospect of home, college, and a future in the military. I sit back down. "Wait. Bumble. He helped too."

The General chuckles. "Bumble will be given the same, and Mia. Son, I have work to do, and I understand you have someone waiting for you in the visitor's center." There's a twinkle in his eye.

Stumbling out, I steady myself with a hand on the wall. A visitor? I hope it's Mia. "Mia. Mia. Mia," I repeat, rushing to find the visitor's center. The complex is vast, and I'm unsure where to go.

A nerdy-looking man with rounded shoulders approaches, carrying a stack of books. "Excuse me, sir," I ask. "Which way to the Visitor's Center?" Without a uniform, he seems uncertain how to address me. "Just tell me," I snap, frustration in my voice.

"Let me draw you a map," he says, his tone like a teacher's.

I stand impatiently, my heart racing. Who is waiting for me? I'll be disappointed if it's just a journalist.

After the man finishes drawing the map, I make my way to the Visitor's Center. Ten minutes later, I push through the door and see a woman with medium-length dark hair, shiny and flowing around her face. She's wearing a flower-patterned dress, ruffled at the bottom, sleeveless. Mia? I touch her shoulder, my hand trembling. She turns around, her big brown eyes filled with deep affection.

"Mia!" I exclaim, holding my arms out. She wraps her arms around me, her cheek resting against my chest.

"Kana. Kana. I was terrified."

"But you didn't give up on me or forget me. You figured it out and got help."

Her face pulls back. "Yeah. How could I forget you?"

Her words fill every lonely crevice inside me. "How could I forget you?" I repeat to myself.

"Are you okay?" she asks.

"Are you kidding? I'm with you. I'm a firework of happiness."

We lock eyes, and the intensity makes me pull her into my arms again, holding her tightly.

"What now?" she asks. "Where will you go?"

"I've been given a couple of months at home, then college. You too! Where will you go?" I ask, torn between joy and the fear of leaving her.

"Whatever college you go to, that's where I want to go," she says, hugging me tighter.

"Then it's Kauai Community College for both of us for the first two years, anyway!" I choke on the words. I'm so happy.

"Really?" She looks at me, radiant. "I love Kauai!"

She tells me all about Nan. The girl wants to stay with her new friend Chai, and Chai's parents want to adopt her.

CHAPTER FORTY-TWO

The next morning, Max knocks on my door. "Get up, hero. I need an interview," he says through the door.

He sets up a camera at the small table in my room while I'm in the bathroom showering. When I come out, he's ready. "Kana, sit. Can I cash in on a debt and interview you?"

"Sure, like anyone's going to want to know what I think?" I get myself a glass of water.

He laughs. "You have no idea. Okay, here we go. Kana, tell me from the beginning what your experiences were with MANA and how did you ever manage to break yourself, and everyone else, out of the Chinese POW camp?"

I recount the story, glad it's just him and me.

"Why did you do it?" Sincerity shows in his voice. "Why did you risk your life to even try to save POWs instead of living life as a tourist in Thailand?"

I think back on what Bumble said to me last night, knowing this moment would come. "Dude, it's your speech to deliver,"

Bumble said. "Peel off that shell and stop thinking it's someone else's job. And don't say Kekoa always knew what to say. You do too. Say it."

I chuckle, and with a deep breath, I begin, "I'm a Neverborn by society's standards, but like you, God planned me when I was forming in my mother's womb. Others may have told you that you're worthless, but the God who created the heavens and the earth loved you enough to come to earth and die for you. I know what it's like to be in this hellhole. I can imagine what it was like for Jesus to come to earth, leaving heaven behind. Who among us would leave home to save others from this place? Jesus came to die to pay for your death sentence. Whoever receives his love can join his family. Man doesn't dictate your value; it's what God already predetermined. You are priceless. God died for you because he loves you. That's why. Only through God could I have done it. And I wasn't the only one. Mia contacted the Navy, who were ready. Without them, I'd just have been shot by the Chinese. And Bumble, who helped me get the bones to jam into the rocks. I couldn't have gathered them without him. I needed him. Mia and the other women saved my life in the Alakai Swamp. Arun's notes taught me about computer code and how to use it. It took a team."

Bumble, Mia, and I sit together at dinner in the mess hall, all talking at once before breaking into laughter and taking turns telling our stories. "Bum, you're going home for a couple of months?"

"Yeah," he says. "I called my old girlfriend from home. She'll be at the airport to meet me. I can't wait!"

Mia and I hoot and clap. "She won't know you," I say. "You're buff, slimmed down, and a hero."

"I'll introduce myself," he says, grinning with his eyes and his mouth.

Arun joins us, emaciated, but alive, and thanks us, but I explain that he taught me what I needed through his notebook and correspondence. One after another, former POWs come over to thank us.

"Am I dreaming? Or did this all really just happen?" I ask Bum and Mia.

***

As I step into the luggage claim area at the far side of Lihue Airport, the warm, gentle breeze carrying the scent of salt settles my anxiety. Outside, cameramen flash pictures of me, now a national hero. I turn and see Katrina's face—a reminder of past troubles. Will she tell the media about how I ruined her life? My duffle bag comes up on the carrier, mostly filled with Thai souvenirs for my family. Katrina stands outside, her smile almost worse than if she were angry.

I walk toward her.

"Kana, I wanted to thank you."

"Thank me? Because of me, you broke your leg." The camera flashes make me uncomfortable.

"Actually, you opened my eyes. I broke up with Oliver. You showed me the difference between talking about loving someone and loving them."

I put my weight on my other foot. "I have a girlfriend I love very much." A shock waves through me. Did I really just say that?

"Wonderful!" she says reluctantly and looks down. "You've come a long way."

"We all have our Goliaths. It sounds like you conquered yours when you realized what love is and what love isn't. Is your leg okay now?" I ask.

"Yes, and it wasn't your fault. Oliver talked to a lawyer because he thought he could get a lot of money if I sued. And that, of course, I would give him all the money." She laughed uncomfortably. "But the lawyer said it was the job of the employee to make sure I was buckled in, not the job of the volunteer just in training. He gave up on the idea of suing when I gave up on him."

"Thank you, God," I say, and the tension in my stomach disappears.

I see a familiar Navy-blue truck pull up, old, rusty, beat-up, and beautiful, pulling up to the curb. "Excuse me," I say to her. "Thank you for telling me. I'm glad you're doing well."

Kekoa and Canyon get out, and I run to them. We all hug in a threesome group hug and pat each other's backs. "Mia, come here," I say.

She rushes forward, beaming. "You're Kekoa." She reaches out to hug Kekoa. "And you're Canyon." He grabs her for a hug.

"I've always wanted a sister," Canyon says.

I'm home at last.

The NEVERKNOWN will be coming out in the fall of 2025. To be notified, please sign up on the authorbbbrighton.com website.

If you liked The Neverseen, please rate the book and leave a review on Amazon. It will make such a difference! Thank you!!

THE NEVERKNOWN

A Young Adult Dystopian Novel

B.B. BRIGHTON

CHAPTER ONE

Canyon

My hoverboard slices around a hale koa shrub, swiping away a branch that tries to pull me toward the plant—toward a crash. I cut away like I would on my surfboard. My hair rises with the danger, and I swoop up higher than I know is safe lifted by the updraft of offshore breezes. In my mind, I hear Dad's warnings—"You're reckless, son. You're going to get seriously hurt or die if you don't stop risking your life for every thrill around."

I'm twenty feet off the ground with rocks below—but what of it? I'm a Neverborn: a nobody with no future, no identity, no privilege, no life.

Ferns catch my attention out of the corner of my eye, and I remember my task. After slicing and bagging a couple dozen fiddleheads, I figure that should be enough for dinner. My board glides down the valley toward home.

Just past our zipline upper ramp, through the trees, I see glimpses of Dad lying down, Mom beside him. Wobbling on the board, my feet slide back, and I focus on balance. My breathing intensifies while my heart races like a horse's hooves pounding toward the finish line. The silence hits me. No hoeing sounds. No humming as he works. Just Mom's quiet sobs, carried off to the mountains by the breeze. What happened?

My toe taps the off button on the board. I stop, drop my backpack, then sprint down the hill toward them.

Dad isn't moving.

Mom turns toward me and pulls up from lying on his chest, her knees crushing red tomatoes on a low vine. "He . . . he wanted . . ." Her voice stutters, firing out panic in broken bursts.

I drop to my knees and press my ear to his heart. Nothing. No thump, no breathing. Just silence.

"Gone," she whimpers.

"He . . . he asked me to cut out his chip . . . to give you." She sits back, staring out into space.

"What?" I jerk up. "Give it to me?" My gut twists.

Mom's hands tremble as she sets his hand on his stomach, pats it, and stumbles to her feet. She takes a couple of steps toward the house, then stops. "You get it. Run. Fast. Get the silver paring knife."

"Why?" I blink and glare at her. Will she cut his identity chip out? Isn't that illegal? The chip contains information about his Social Security number and banking. How is that going to work? If I go to college, teachers will know I'm not sixty-eight. No, I'm not going to become my dad.

"Go!" she snaps.

I scamper back to the house to grab it, then return, and hand her the knife.

She pauses, staring at Dad's wrist like she can't quite believe what she's going to do. Then, with trembling fingers, she leans forward and starts cutting his flesh. The knife glints in the morning sun, darkened with his blood.

"I don't need Dad's chip," I say. "I can do just fine without it. Great, in fact. You'll see."

"Son," she shakes her head, her brows furrowed. "You always have to win—and it just makes you lose." Sadness coats her voice as she grabs my wrist.

"I don't need Dad!" I pull at my wrist, smelling the blood. It would make me less . . . me? I can never be him.

Her grip is iron. She cuts into me. I groan, turning my face. Flies buzz in eager circles. "You are clueless!" She barks, her eyes blazing. "You're a Neverborn. Without this, you can't survive. You can't charm your way through the real world. Without it, you're not even a U.S. citizen. Dad asked me to give you his chip so you can have a chance. It's a gift." She jerks my hand back into place, slicing deeper.

"Ow!" I jerk my hand back and then offer it to her. My head pounds, and I rub my temple with my free hand. My gut sinks to my toes and aches. At breakfast, he asked me to hoe with him, but I wanted to go hoverboarding. I said I'd get some fiddleheads for dinner. If only I'd gardened with him instead of hoverboarding. Why did I fight him in life—only to need him now?

The earth spins. I press my shirt bottom against the wound.

Dad's bleeding hand rests on his stomach where Mom put it.

Mom murmurs something, lost in the breeze. Dad's hand lies curled, calloused, and colorless--except for his dirty fingernails.

I suck a ragged breath, but it's too much. My head falls to his shoulder, brushing against Mom's hand. She lies over on his chest, flowing in tears, talking to him.

Mom—I sit up and see as if I'm seeing her for the first time. I drink in her broken frame glued to his chest, needing him, wanting him. And I've taken it all away from her. My stomach lurches in chaos.

Only now do I realize the resentment I've held against him for not being my real dad—but the man who raised someone else's fatherless son.

His face shrinks, wrinkles tightening around his vacant eyes, cheekbones jutting like something from a horror film—white and cold.

Dad. My world. My polar opposite. The man who never raised his voice.

Now I want him. If only I could say "I'm sorry." It wasn't his fault my birthmother wanted to abort me.

I move my head to his bony shoulder, drained of all energy, and curl up next to him in my cloud of confusion.

How can God let Dad die? How can I let Dad die? It's my fault.

I sit up and take in his face. The face that was once alive with love is now empty. Gone.

How long have I been staring at Dad's closed eyes, waiting for them to open? How long has Mom been rocking back and forth, singing love songs to Dad?

My spell breaks when my brother, Kekoa, puts his hand on my shoulder, kneels, and pulls me into a hug.

Kana, our forever brilliant brother, stands at Dad's feet, and says something about heaven, but his voice is distant—like it's coming through water.

Kekoa releases me, and I put my weight on my hands and knees watching Dad, waiting for him to move. Mom sobs into someone's arms.

I smell the eucalyptus trees in the breeze as it tousles my hair. Everything keeps moving—everything but Dad.

A fly lands on Dad's half-closed eye. I try to clap my hands to kill the beast, knocking my blue Seahawks cap off Dad's head.

Kana gasps. His eyes lock on something.

My breath catches as I follow his stare. Dad's shiny white hair is matted and motionless.

There's a spot of red in his hair. Blood?

Kana looks pale, staring at the red.

I lean in and spread his hair, revealing the small spot. There's something stuck in my cap—like a wire.

Kana plucks out a tiny dart from the fabric. We both examine its black, serrated, knife-life edges.

The dart's placement on the cap matches the blood spot.

"This killed him—not his heart." Kana says. He holds the sharp point and empty vial like it's made of dynamite.

Kekoa takes it. "Oh my gosh! Poison?"

"Curare, maybe," Kana whispers. "Paralyzes the lungs. He suffocated. A scent-guided drone must have detected Canyon's scent from the cap and shot it through the fabric."

My cap. My scent. His death.

I sink forward, breath hitching. My stomach clenches so hard I want to vomit.

The dart of truth—sharp, serrated, irreversible—lodges itself in my ribs, pressing until I can't breathe.

I lay my hand on Dad's stomach, willing him to breathe, but his chest doesn't rise.

My fingers grip his shirt, curling in the fabric as if I can hold him here. As if I can keep him from slipping away forever.

I'm so sorry Dad. I never meant to hurt you. How can you ever forgive me?

The quiet of the breeze and the distant funeral conversations seal the truth.

I feel my brother's hand on my back.

"It was . . ." I can't even say it. "Me."

If I hadn't left my cap lying around. If I'd gardened with him. If I'd seen the dart and yanked the cap off his head—Dad would be here. Laughing at me. Ruffling my hair. He'd tell me to knock off the drama. But he isn't. And won't be.

Who would do this? Why?

"General Shipley's been released—pardoned by the President yesterday," Kana says, as if he's reading my mind. "I read it on Newsweek's Daily Download this morning."

His voice sounds graver than I've ever heard.

"He didn't lose any time finding us," Kekoa says, rubbing my shoulder. Kekoa loved Dad as much as I did.

"He's going after all three of us," Kana says. "I found bones in the Alakai Swamp, proving Shipley killed Neverborns in the swamp. Kekoa, you gave the lawyers what they needed. And Canyon, you're making videos that show Neverborns are actually people. We're all on his hit list."

Kana bites his lower lip. "But it was your scent on the cap that made the dart release its poison. We're in imminent danger and need to get inside—somewhere drones can't reach us. Then we need to all disappear."

I bolt up the hill, reach the zipline launch, and shove it over. Plucking rocks, I throw them into the canyon and scream. I slam my shoulder into the tree that anchors the zipline, pounding it. Once. Twice. A third time—until my knuckles split. The pain is sharp and immediately grounds me in a way nothing else does.

I need to hurt. Need to bleed. Need to feel something that isn't this crushing weight pressing my ribs together.

But the tree doesn't flinch.

Doesn't crack.

Doesn't feel a thing.

Just like Dad.